"IF IT IS ST⟨ ⟩ AND KISSES YOU DESIRE, SARAH, WHY NOT MINE?"

Before Sarah could say a word, Lord Eustace had pulled her into his arms. He crushed her to him and proceeded to kiss her thoroughly.

Sarah's senses swam. She did not know how long it was that he kissed her before he raised his head. She heard him murmur something, before he took her mouth again.

She clung to his lapel, swaying against him. She had dreamed for a very long time of this very moment. Time seemed to stand still.

When he forcibly set her aside, Sarah nearly stumbled. Her eyes wide and dazed, Sarah slowly raised her fingers to her lips.

Lord Eustace was breathing heavily. There was a tight, white look about his eyes and mouth. He said hoarsely, "Very satisfactory, Miss Sommers. I congratulate you on your natural talents."

Sarah's world reeled and crashed. "Dastard!" she breathed.

Tempting Sarah

·⊰❖⊱·

Gayle Buck

A SIGNET BOOK

SIGNET
Published by the Penguin Group
Penguin Putnam Inc., 375 Hudson Street,
New York, New York 10014, U.S.A.
Penguin Books Ltd, 27 Wrights Lane,
London W8 5TZ, England
Penguin Books Australia Ltd,
Ringwood, Victoria, Australia
Penguin Books Canada Ltd, 10 Alcorn Avenue,
Toronto, Ontario, Canada M4V 3B2
Penguin Books (N.Z.) Ltd, 182-190 Wairau Road,
Auckland 10, New Zealand

Penguin Books Ltd, Registered Offices:
Harmondsworth, Middlesex, England

First published by Signet, an imprint of Dutton Signet,
a member of Penguin Putnam Inc.

First Printing, March, 1998
10 9 8 7 6 5 4 3 2 1

Chapter One

An unusually heavy snow two days earlier had cast drifts to each side of the narrow road. Ice frosted the fields and hedgerows. The horses' breath trailed smoky streams as the antiquated coach rumbled heavily over the rutted road.

The occupants of the coach were fairly warm. The Misses Sommers had hot bricks to their feet and numerous rugs tucked around them. They were attired in warm woolen pelisses over their traveling dresses and had tucked their hands into large fur muffs. Their maid, sitting opposite them with her back to the horses, appeared to be asleep.

"Surely we are almost there? Can you see anything out of your window, dear Sarah?"

Miss Sarah Sommers was short of stature, her figure trim. Beneath her velvet bonnet, a riot of dark curls framed her face and accentuated the piquancy of a pair of laughing hazel eyes set under winged brows, a short nose, and well-formed mouth. Sarah smiled at the eager note in her younger sister's voice. Their first journey out of their own county was exciting for them both, but for Margaret, it was embued with all the trappings of a fantastical adventure. Sarah was the eldest by only two years, but sometimes she felt much older.

"No, I cannot see a thing. The window is too glazed over," said Sarah. "We went through the last village only a bit ago. Even if we could look out, there would be nothing but hedgerows and fields to see, I daresay."

Miss Margaret Sommers had been emancipated from the schoolroom scarcely a year past. She was just turned seventeen and was taller than her sister and more beautiful. She peered unsuccessfully through the whimsically frosted window. With her gloved palm she vigorously rubbed a spot on the glass until it was clear and then pressed her face to it. "Surely we are near London!"

Sarah laughed. "Come, Margaret, that is what you have been saying since we left home two days ago."

"Then most assuredly we must be close by now!" exclaimed Margaret, turning an animated countenance toward her sister. Her vivid blue eyes sparkled. "Oh, I know that you think me foolish, Sarah, but truly, truly, it is a grand adventure and I do not wish to miss a single moment of it."

"You shan't, goose. Grandmama promised in her letters to treat us to the Season, which hasn't yet begun. So rest easy, Margaret," said Sarah.

"Aye, miss, give over, do," said the maid, suddenly opening her eyes. "You'll have fretted Miss Sarah to flinders with your excitement and questions before we ever arrive if you keep on so."

"Oh, you're awake, Holby!" said Margaret, delighted.

"No, miss, I am not," said the maid with finality, closing her eyes again.

Sarah chuckled again. "There, Margaret! You have exhausted poor Holby."

"I am sorry. But, truly, I can't help it, Sarah. It is all so prodigiously exciting. I never thought Papa could actually be brought to consent to our going up to London to stay with Grandmama," said Margaret. She made haste to clarify herself. "Not that Papa isn't every bit of a saint. But he will put his head in his books and not come out for days. I sometimes think that he doesn't even recall our names when he does see us."

"Yes, Papa can be rather absentminded," agreed Sarah. She chuckled. "But I think even Papa must have begun to realize that he had to do something with us. It did not matter so much when I emerged from the schoolroom, for I was able to keep busy managing the house. But then you outgrew your lessons, too."

"Even Papa could not expect us to spend the rest of our days living in virtual seclusion," said Margaret, nodding. "I made certain that he knew my thoughts on that!"

"Yes, poor Papa scarcely had any peace at all once you

found out from Lucretia that she was going to the assemblies," said Sarah, shaking her head.

"Well, if Papa had let Mrs. Bagnold take us more often, I might not have teased him about it," said Margaret reasonably.

"You know very well that the Bagnolds are considered very good-natured, but can be rather vulgar in their manners on occasion. That is why Papa was reluctant to allow us to spend more time in their company," said Sarah.

"I didn't see any harm in Lucretia and Theo and Tiffany," said Margaret, tossing her head. "But Miss Spoonsby agreed with Papa, so I suppose that it must have been true."

"Poor Papa! He explained it so patiently. He did not wish us to pick up any mannerisms that would stigmatize us as dowdies in more exalted company," said Sarah. She sighed suddenly. "As though we ever had the opportunity to run in any other circles. Other than our friends such as the Prices and the Bagnolds, there were hardly any other families with whom we could associate that had the least claim to gentility."

"That is why Grandmama's invitation was such a godsend for us. Why, we know scarcely anyone and now we shall be introduced to all of the *ton*!" exclaimed Margaret.

"I'm certain Papa thought that Lady Alverley's invitation was a godsend, as well, Margaret. I have suspected for some months now that the question of our future had begun to weigh upon him, especially after Miss Spoonsby informed him that she had taught you all that she could and that it was time for her to find another post," said Sarah. "But Papa has become such a recluse of late years that he didn't have the least notion about how he was to provide for us."

"I have often wondered how Mama ever came to marry him," said Margaret reflectively.

"Margaret! What a thing to say," said Sarah, laughing again.

"No, no, I mean it, Sarah. You will admit that there is nothing at all dashing or—or extraordinary about Papa. Sometimes I suspect that he cares more about his scholarly endeavors than about living, breathing people," said Margaret.

Sarah couldn't deny that there was some truth in her sister's observation. She had thought much the same thing, though a little guiltily. She held her father in true affection, but she was not blind to his most glaring fault. The world practically had to force itself upon him before he could be brought to notice anything beyond his library. That was what Margaret had meant when she had said that she had to badger him about going up to the assemblies. Sarah knew that must have been when Sir Francis had begun to think about his daughters' futures.

Far more than Margaret, Sarah could recall a time when their father had not been more interested in writing his books than in life outside the walls of his library. Margaret had scarcely passed out of leading-strings when their mother had died of a fever. "It is a pity. I think Papa might have been different if Mama had not died," said Sarah regretfully.

"Yes, well, that is as may be, Sarah. But it is of no use thinking about what might have been," said Margaret with unexpected pragmatism. "At this moment we are on our way to a perfectly splendid adventure! I wonder what Grandmama is like? Do you recall anything about her, Sarah?"

Sarah shook her head. "Very little, except that she seemed to me to be a very grand lady. I recall that I was a little frightened of her."

"Well, I shan't be frightened of her, no matter how grand she may be. She has invited us to stay with her and that must surely mean that she is kindly disposed toward us, don't you think?" asked Margaret.

"Yes, I do," said Sarah, smiling at her eager sister.

Margaret rubbed the glass with her gloved hand again and looked out. "Oh, why doesn't John Coachman whip up the horses? It can't be far now!"

"John Coachman knows his duty, miss, and it is not driving neck-or-nothing down an icy road," said the maid without opening her eyes.

"Holby, you cannot possibly be asleep! You are shamming it," said Margaret accusingly. "It's my belief that you don't wish me to address anything to you and so you have been pretending all along."

The maid gave a loud snore.

Sarah broke out laughing. "Never mind, Margaret. I am listening to you and—"

There was the sound of a sharp crack. The coach lurched violently, then began to tilt over on its side. Sarah and her companions were tossed from their seats in a welter of furs and arms and legs. Sarah cried out in surprise and in the same instant heard her sister's frightened squeak.

Once the carriage stopped moving, the door was forcibly yanked open above them. John Coachman's anxious face appeared in the opening. "Miss Sarah! Miss Margaret! Be ye all right?"

The women untangled themselves. Sarah called out in reassurance. "Yes, John, of course we are. At least—Margaret?"

"Oh, yes. But I fear that I fell on poor Holby," said Margaret, helping the maid right herself.

The maid wheezed for air. "The wind was knocked out of me, is all. I'm fine, miss."

"Thank God. Here, John, help us out," said Sarah, helping both her sister and the maid to the canted door of the coach. When she had also been helped up through the door and had scrambled over the side onto the road, she looked at the coach in dismay. "What happened, John?"

"An axle broke, miss," said the coachman grimly.

"Oh, dear." Sarah looked at the coach tilted on its side. The trembling horses were standing in the twisted traces, rolling their eyes so that the whites showed. In the excitement Sarah had forgotten her muff and she wrapped her arms around herself to conserve warmth. Cold was beginning to seep into her boots from the iron-hard frozen ground.

A flake touched her cheek and Sarah looked up, startled. The clouds were high and thin and slate colored, becoming indistinct even as she watched. Sarah realized that it was beginning to snow again. The gray twilight was turning swiftly into the black of night. Sarah knew that their plight was grave.

"What are we going to do, Sarah?" asked Margaret, a breathless quality in her voice. Her eyes were round as she stared at the coach.

"I don't know yet, Margaret. But we will be fine, I know we will," said Sarah with a reassuring smile. She turned to the coachman, who had bent over to assess the damage again. She heard him muttering under his breath. "What do you think we should do, John? How far are we from the next village?"

The coachman straightened. His wrinkled face was worried. "I don't know for certain what lies ahead, miss, not having been up to Lunnontown before this. We'll need to have a wheelwright put on a new axle and that can be had only in a village."

"Yes, of course. And it is late, too, so it is unlikely that it can be done this evening," said Sarah.

The coachman nodded. "Aye, that's it in a nutshell, Miss Sarah. I'm thinking that you and Miss Margaret will want to bespeak a room this night and so it seems best to me that we go back to the last village that we passed through. There was a respectable inn. I noted it particular on account of its sign— The Rook and Crane."

"Oh, no, no! I could not bear to go back when we have already come this far," exclaimed Margaret. "Can we not hire another coach and go on, Sarah?"

Sarah inwardly agreed with her sister. Her heart had plunged to hear John Coachman's verdict. She also was anxious to make their destination. However, Sarah felt herself to be too unworldly to judge exactly what they could afford to do or not do. The expenses of the trip had been entrusted by their father to John Coachman. "John?"

The coachman frowned as he thought things through. "It's not what I like, Miss Sarah, hiring job cattle and all. Then there still be the possibility of the added expense of putting up another night at an inn if the cattle are real slugs and can't make it to Lunnontown tonight as we'd set out to do."

"But we can afford a chaise?" asked Sarah.

"Oh, do say yes, John Coachman," said Margaret pleadingly. "I do so want to continue on our way."

The coachman was not impervious to her coaxing. "Aye, Miss Margaret. There be adequate for a chaise. Now mind"— he held up a thick gloved forefinger in warning—"it won't be what ye're used to, with a nice brick and all."

"I don't care a fig for that, as long as we are still going toward London," said Margaret.

"Then it's settled. We'll walk back to the inn and hire a chaise," said Sarah.

"Begging your pardon, miss, but that is all of five miles. It is coming on for dark now. Ye'll not want to be stumbling about on the ice. It'd be better if I ride back and send the chaise to fetch you," said John Coachman.

"There is the baggage to consider, too, Miss Sarah," said the maid. "You'll not want to leave it all unguarded on the public road."

"No, I suppose not. Very well, John, you ride back and send a chaise for us, while we wait," said Sarah. She shivered and glanced up at the darkening sky. "I do hope that you are not delayed. We shall have to wrap up in the rugs to keep off the chill."

"We can build a fire to keep warm," suggested Margaret. At her sister's expression, she said, "Why, it is all part of the adventure, Sarah! We can pretend to be tinkers or gypsies. I daresay it will be quite exciting."

"I hope so, Margaret," said Sarah.

John Coachman cut the team loose from the traces. Sarah held the bridles of the horses, speaking calmly to them as she led them forward through the slippery snow, freeing them of the entangling leathers.

The coachman shook his head. "That one be lamed, Miss Sarah," he said heavily. "I'll go faster if I leave the poor beast with you."

"We shall manage, John," said Sarah quietly, her hand still on the bridle of the lame horse.

Preparing to mount, the coachman chuckled suddenly. "I know that, Miss Sarah." He heaved himself onto the bare back of the horse.

Suddenly a postchaise swept round the corner, pulled by a matched team of bays. Twin lanterns hung from its sides and burned yellow. It veered to one side of the scene of the accident. The chaise stopped, the high-strung team stamping nervously. A window was let down and a pleasant male voice said, "Is everything quite all right? May I be of assistance?"

"Thank you, sir, but there is really nothing that anyone can do," said Sarah. She gestured toward the coach lying on its side. "We have broken an axle."

At once the postchaise door was flung open. A gentleman alighted. He came forward, his boots crunching on the icy ground. He was attired in a voluminous greatcoat and a beaver was pulled well over his brow. He appeared to be of medium height and carried himself gracefully, with the lithe movements of an athlete.

"I am Lord Gilbert Eustace. Pray allow me to express my regrets over your misfortune. I will render whatever assistance that is within my power, of course," said Lord Eustace. He bowed politely.

"I am Miss Sarah Sommers. This is my sister, Margaret. Thank you for your concern, my lord. We are on the point of sending our coachman back to the last inn we passed, in hopes of hiring a chaise," said Sarah.

Lord Eustace bowed to Miss Sommers's sister, who dipped a schoolgirl's curtsy. He surveyed the maid and the coachman and the direction that the coach was pointed, coming at once to a conclusion. "I apprehend that you are journeying up to London, no doubt to enjoy the beginning of the Season. You are expected, of course?"

"Yes. Lady Alverley is our grandmother," said Sarah.

"Ah! I am vaguely acquainted with her ladyship. Does Lady Alverley expect you yet today?" asked Lord Eustace. He frowned slightly. "Her ladyship will be unhappy that you have been delayed."

"I fear that our journey will be delayed slightly," said Sarah. Her finely drawn brows drew together over her hazel eyes as she steadily regarded Lord Eustace. She wondered at his lordship's passing observation regarding their grandmother. It was almost as though he implied that Lady Alverley was ill-tempered, she thought.

"Do you mean that our grandmother will be angry with us for coming to her late?" asked Margaret forthrightly.

Lord Eustace shook his head. Gently, he corrected her. "I did not say so, Miss Margaret. It is my observation that while you are waiting for your coachman to return with a chaise, you will be left standing about in this chill wind. I have a better notion. Let me offer a seat to you both in my chaise. And also to your maid, naturally. I can easily convey you to the next town, which is not above half an hour away. There is a respectable inn, I believe, where you may bespeak a room or hire a chaise."

"Thank you, my lord," said Sarah. She was surprised and hesitant. "I scarce know what to say." She was naturally grateful for the invitation, but she was not certain that it would be wise to entrust themselves into a complete stranger's hands.

Of course, Lord Eustace did appear to be respectable and he had offered a seat to their maid. He was at least fully aware of the conventions. But still, the gentleman was unknown to her and Sarah was unsure of what she should do.

Apparently her sister felt no similar constraint. "Thank you, Lord Eustace, for your most obliging offer. We are indeed most anxious to resume our journey," said Margaret. She looked at her sister. "Are we not, Sarah?"

Lord Eustace threw a glance in the elder sister's direction. "I would consider it an honor to be of assistance, Miss Sommers," he repeated.

Despite her reservations, Sarah consented to accept Lord Eustace's offer. In short order she and Margaret, with their maid and some of their baggage, were settled into Lord Eustace's chaise.

Before they left, Sarah talked with John Coachman again. It was arranged that he would bring the carriage horses, together with the rest of their baggage, to the inn that Lord Eustace had told them about. There, John Coachman hoped to engage the services of a wheelwright to repair the coach. The coachman would leave instructions for the wheelwright and the care of the team while he engaged a chaise to convey his charges the remainder of the way to London.

"Then I'll drive the hired chaise back to the inn. The wheelwright will be done with the repairs, no doubt, and if I can manage with the lamed one, I can drive the coach back home," he had said. Sarah agreed that would be best.

Chapter Two

A s Lord Eustace's postchaise bowled down the road, Sarah relaxed against the silken squabs. She was very comfortable. Unlike their old coach, the chaise was very well-sprung. She thought that she had never ridden in such style before. In addition, Lord Eustace had insisted that their rugs be transferred to the chaise so that the women could snuggle into the warmth.

Lord Eustace politely initiated conversation with his unexpected passengers. Sarah participated little in the resulting exchange. She was content to let her sister have full rein. Margaret was at her chattering best, entertaining and droll by turns. Sarah smiled affectionately as she listened to her sister's nonsense.

Lord Eustace addressed them both equally at first, but his remarks became more and more directed to Margaret. He frequently laughed at some inconsequential observation that she made. He had already learned much of their history from Margaret and the reason for their trip to London.

"I predict that you will be a marked success in your come-out, Miss Margaret," he said. As though recalling himself, he at once turned toward Sarah and politely added, "And you as well, Miss Sommers."

"Thank you, my lord," said Sarah quietly, smiling. It was obvious to her that she was compared unfavorably with her sister. Beside Margaret's vivacity she must appear to be rather dull in his lordship's eyes. It was obvious that her sister had succeeded in captivating his lordship, but Sarah was not made uneasy. She knew that Margaret had not deliberately set herself to do any such thing. Margaret was simply a child-woman. Her enthusiasms, wise and childish by turns, had a way of sparking the interest of others. Margaret had always had a gift for swiftly and easily making friends. Apparently she also had a natural charm of manner that would intrigue the gentlemen.

"I have seldom fallen into more delightful company," said Lord Eustace. His tone was warm as he smiled across at Margaret.

The short miles were soon put behind them and the postchaise turned into the yard of an inn. Lord Eustace helped the ladies down out of the carriage. Sarah thanked him and accepted his arm as he escorted them inside. She was aware of the muscular strength of his forearm under her kid-gloved fingers and she stole a glance up at his handsome profile. It was seldom that she had ever been in such close proximity with a gentleman, especially one of such obvious quality.

His lordship's driver and the maid brought in the baggage. Lord Eustace was recognized by the innkeeper, who greeted the gentleman by name and a low bow. Sarah at once felt that she had made a wise decision when she accepted a ride for them in Lord Eustace's chaise. He was obviously well-known and respectable, not at all the sort to take advantage of two naive country misses. In fact, Sarah was rather ashamed now that such a thought had even crossed her mind, no matter how fleetingly.

Lord Eustace explained the circumstances that had brought him to the inn. He bespoke a private parlor and refreshment for the ladies. "I imagine that you are both rather chilled," he commented, smiling at them.

"Oh, no! We were perfectly comfortable, truly," said Margaret.

"Indeed, I do not know when we have enjoyed traveling more," said Sarah, anxious to add her own expression of gratitude.

Lord Eustace bowed. Then he inquired of the innkeeper about the hiring of a chaise and the availability of a wheelwright. The innkeeper's face lengthened and he shook his head. He expressed his regret that there would not be a chaise available until the following day.

Sarah and Margaret glanced at one another in dismay. "Oh, dear," murmured Sarah.

"But that means we shall not be able to go on to London until tomorrow," said Margaret, stating the obvious.

"I fear not, miss," said the innkeeper regretfully. "But I have clean rooms if ye be wishful to stay the night."

"I suppose that we have no choice but to do so," said Sarah. She had already decided to make the best of things. She smiled at the innkeeper. "My sister and I will share a room, sir. Please instruct our maid where we are to be. We should like some dinner as well."

"Certainly, miss," said the innkeeper, rubbing his hands. He bowed and went away.

Lord Eustace saw that things were well in hand and he prepared to depart. "I am glad that I was able to assist you, Miss Sommers, Miss Margaret. I shall leave you now, but I trust that I shall see you again in the future."

"Can you not stay and join us for dinner," asked Margaret, her smile one of open friendliness.

Lord Eustace shot a surprised glance at the young lady. "I do not think—"

Sarah caught her sister's eye and frowned at her. She shook her head very slightly. "I imagine that Lord Eustace is expected elsewhere, Margaret."

Lord Eustace glanced then in her direction. Sarah felt herself coloring under his thoughtful gaze. He smiled slightly and turned again to her sister. "It is quite true. I have an engagement already in the neighborhood that I must not neglect. But with your permission, I shall call upon you at Lady Alverley's house."

"We would like that, my lord," said Margaret, giving her hand to him. She was almost of a height with him and smiled directly into his eyes.

Lord Eustace bowed over her fingers, then turned back to Sarah. He smiled down at her. "And I look forward to calling on you also, Miss Sommers."

"You will be welcome, my lord. Thank you for your kindness," said Sarah.

His lordship bowed. Then just as quickly as he had entered their lives, Lord Eustace was gone.

The innkeeper returned to show the two young ladies upstairs to their parlor. A roaring fire had been built in the low-hung fireplace and the covers had already been laid on the table for dinner. A connecting door led into a bedroom, where

Holby was making down the bed. Sarah and Margaret went into the bedroom to lay aside their pelisses and bonnets and gloves, then returned to the warmth of the parlor.

Holding her chilled hands out to the cheery flames, Sarah said, "We were indeed fortunate this night, Margaret. If it was not for Lord Eustace coming along just as he did, we might still be standing about in the cold, stamping our feet to stay warm." She cast a glance toward the window, where heavy wet flakes slapped against the glass. With nightfall the wind had come up so that it rattled the sign outside on the front of the inn and whistled through the trees. "I only hope that John Coachman arrives soon so that he can get out of this weather, too. It is snowing more heavily now."

"I know John Coachman will be fine. We did not leave him far behind," said Margaret complacently, curling up in a chair close beside the fire and tucking her shod feet under her. "Tell me, Sarah, what did you think of Lord Eustace?"

Sarah sat back on her heels, glancing curiously at her sister. Margaret had propped her pointed chin in the palm of her hand and was gazing into the fire, blinking like a blue-eyed cat. "Why do you ask, Margaret? It is so unlike you to pay heed to any gentleman."

"I have not met many gentlemen before, so of course I have not heeded them," said Margaret reasonably. "But Lord Eustace is the first London gentleman that we have ever seen. I was only wondering if all the rest would be like him. He was so obliging and polite and easy to talk to that I quite forgot to be shy in his company."

"His lordship's manners were very pleasing and his kindness exceeded everything, certainly," said Sarah.

"Sarah, do you think that the other gentlemen we meet will be like Lord Eustace?" asked Margaret.

"I don't know if all of them will be like Lord Eustace," said Sarah. "But I certainly hope so, for I thought Lord Eustace to be very well favored." She smiled at her sister. "Did you like him?"

Margaret nodded. "Very much! Sarah, do you think that we shall wed this Season?"

Sarah was startled. She had never heard her sister voice such a question before. Lord Eustace must have made a greater impression on Margaret than she had realized, she thought, almost dismayed. Her sister was so very young and perhaps could be expected to be impressionable. Obviously Margaret had not the least notion how to relate to any gentlemen outside their own narrow circle of acquaintances. Only see how she had invited Lord Eustace to join them in their private parlor for dinner! Sarah knew herself to be almost entirely unworldly, but she did know enough not to dine alone with an unrelated gentleman.

Sarah saw that because she was the eldest and perhaps steadier in temperament, it was her duty to look after Margaret. It would not do for Margaret to tumble head-over-heels for some unrespectable, charming rogue who would break her heart.

"Why, I don't know, Margaret. I suppose that we might. It all depends upon how we take in society," said Sarah slowly. She wrinkled her nose a little. "It seems rather vulgar in a way, does it not? We are going up to London to see and to be seen, all in hopes of capturing the hearts of some as yet unknown gentlemen."

"If they are anything like Lord Eustace, I shall be content," said Margaret, shrugging.

"But what of love, Margaret? Don't you wish to be swept off your feet by some dashing blade?" Sarah asked teasingly.

"Well, of course," said Margaret, blinking in surprise. "That goes without saying. But I am in no hurry to be wed just yet, Sarah. I only meant that I hope that our dearest admirers will be like Lord Eustace."

"You relieve my mind. I quite thought for a moment that you had made marriage your only ambition," said Sarah lightly. Inwardly she was glad to hear that her sister's aspirations were not firmly set on making a hasty connection.

Margaret shook her head. "No, indeed. I wish only to enjoy myself this Season. I am far more anxious to spread my wings and see something of the world than I am to acquire a husband. If I do not receive an offer this Season, I shan't repine. I shall simply ask Grandmama to have me to stay again next Season."

"I am very happy to hear it, Margaret. You deserve to enjoy yourself a little before you begin turning your thoughts to such a momentous event," said Sarah, rising to her feet and going over to a wingback chair. She sank down into its faded cushions with a sigh. "Isn't it odd! I have been sitting all day long and yet I am too wearied to stand."

Margaret disregarded her transition. "But what about you, Sarah? You are already nineteen. Do you not wish to wed this Season?" she asked, regarding her sister with a measure of curiosity.

"Sometimes I think that I do, but at other times I don't know," said Sarah. She smiled at her sister. "Does that sound terribly idiotic of me?"

"Of course not. I think it just means that you don't know your own mind yet," said Margaret with an unconscious wisdom. "But if you do meet a gentleman who suits you, dear Sarah, it will be a different matter altogether, will it not?"

Sarah laughed and nodded. "Yes, I expect that it will," she agreed.

The innkeeper entered the parlor, a waiter coming behind him. Both carried trays with several covered dishes. The ladies rose and went to the table, only too glad to sit down to dinner. The innkeeper had news of their coachman, saying that the man had arrived safely and was at that moment bedding the horses and himself down in the snug stables.

The dinner consisted of a good soup, a roast fowl, and bread and cheese. After taking their fill, Sarah and Margaret went into the bedroom to make ready for bed. It had been a long day of being jostled about in the coach and they both pronounced themselves too tired to sit up any longer. Their maid attended to them, seeing them both safely in bed, before going over to lie down on her own warm pallet that had been made up against the wall.

Tired as she was, Sarah did not go immediately to sleep. She kept thinking back to what Margaret had said about finding a gentleman who suited her. Someone like Lord Eustace . . . yes, that would be nice. The image of his lordship's handsome countenance lingered in her mind. At length she fell asleep, a faint smile on her face.

Breakfast was slices of bread and butter washed down with tepid tea in the public coffee room. Sarah and Margaret then had nothing to do but return upstairs to their room. They amused themselves by looking out their window, which over-looked the innyard, and watch the arrivals and departures of the inn's custom.

It was already late in the morning when a chaise was finally available for hire. John Coachman rejected the services of hired postboys and climbed up on the box, pronouncing him-self determined to drive so that he could be certain that his charges arrived safely at their destination.

They were still a few hours away from London, but Sarah and Margaret found that the time passed swiftly enough as they recognized from increasing traffic and the more closely clustered towns and villages that they must be nearing the me-tropolis at last.

It was afternoon when they arrived at Alverley House in Upper Claridge Street. The door was opened by a porter attired in green and russet livery. When the porter was told their names, he bowed Sarah and Margaret inside into the wide hall and instructed footmen to bring in their baggage. Their maid was conducted upstairs to their rooms to unpack.

The butler came out of the nether regions. He was an im-pressive figure, holding himself with stiff pride, and gazing down his long nose. He ushered the two young ladies into a sitting room off the main hall. "I shall announce your arrival to her ladyship," he intoned, closing the door behind him.

Sarah and Margaret looked around at their surroundings with curiosity. They were immediately impressed. Sarah thought that she had never seen a more elegantly furnished room. The richness of the brocaded drapes, the silk-covered settees, the gleam of fine polished wood, the huge gilded mir-ror above the mantel, all spoke of comfortable wealth. "Good-ness, this room looks like something out of a furniture maker's or haberdasher's catalogue," she commented.

"Grandmama must be frightfully rich," exclaimed Margaret in awe.

"Indeed I am, granddaughter," said an amused voice behind them.

The sisters whirled. Swift color rose in both their faces, for they had not heard the door open again on its well-oiled hinges, nor been aware of Lady Alverley's soft-footed entrance.

Embarrassed, Sarah and Margaret could only stand and stare at the tall, fashionably dressed lady standing on the threshold. Though obviously well past her prime, her ladyship did not appear in the least decrepit. Lady Alverley's carriage was erect and stately, her gaze sharp and clear.

Sarah noticed at once that her grandmother was taller than she herself was. She glanced at her sister, reflecting that here was where Margaret had inherited her height.

Lady Alverley came forward with outstretched hands. There were several glittering rings on her gnarled fingers and bracelets encircled her thin blue-veined wrists. A costly Cashmere shawl with deep fringes was looped over her sleeved elbows. "Well, my dears, you have arrived at last. I expected you yesterday, but never mind. I am happy to have you here. You may kiss me."

Sarah reached up to obediently kiss her grandmother's powdered cheek. A faint hint of rose scent clung to Lady Alverley's person. Her ladyship had appeared very grand, very elegant, at a distance. Sarah realized now that much of her impression of youthful preservation was due to an artful application of cosmetics on Lady Alverley's part. Lady Alverley not only wore rouge and powder, but also darkened her lashes. Her ladyship's hair was a suspicious yellow tint. Sarah's vision of what she thought a grandmother should look like faded away forever. "I am glad to see you. How are you, Grandmama?"

"Very well, my dear . . . Sarah, is it? Yes, of course. I recall now that you were always a little dab of a thing. You take after your mother."

"Thank you, ma'am. You could not have complimented me more highly," said Sarah, smiling. She drew back a little to allow her sister to greet their grandmother.

"And so this must be Margaret! What a lovely girl you are! My dear Margaret, welcome," said Lady Alverley, also accepting Margaret's kiss. She held on to the younger girl's gloved hand and looked her up and down. "Yes, I can see your mother in you, too. But you take after me in inches."

"You are beautiful, Grandmama," blurted Margaret, gazing at Lady Alverley with an awestruck expression.

"We shall get along splendidly, I see," said Lady Alverley, bestowing a gracious smile on her younger granddaughter. She drew Margaret's arm through her own and patted it. "Now, come sit down. I have instructed Herbert to bring in tea and you shall tell me all about yourselves." Lady Alverley and Margaret sat down on a settee together and her ladyship nodded for Sarah, who had followed them across the room, to sit opposite in a wingback chair.

"We do appreciate your kind invitation to stay with you during the Season," said Sarah, setting aside her muff and beginning to pull off her kid gloves.

"Oh, yes! It was so vastly exciting when Papa informed us of it. I could scarcely wait to come," said Margaret enthusiastically, also divesting herself of her gloves. "I am so looking forward to the Season. I hope that there will be a great many parties to attend."

"I can promise you that there will be," said Lady Alverley. She looked around as the door opened and the butler entered, bearing a tray. "Ah, here is Herbert with our tea! You may set it on the table here, Herbert. I shall ring if I require anything else."

"Of course, my lady," said the butler, setting out plates of biscuits and tiny cress sandwiches and plum cake, a teapot and cups, the cream and sugar. He bowed as he left again.

Lady Alverley asked Sarah to pour the tea and she watched Sarah with an eagle eye while she did so. Lady Alverley nodded her approval. "You do that very well, Sarah. I commend whoever taught you the finer points of etiquette. I know that it was not your mother, for she died before you were of an age to be instructed in such things."

"That would be our governess, Miss Spoonsby," said Sarah quietly, handing tea to Lady Alverley and to her sister before she picked up her own.

"Then you have had the same advantageous training, Margaret? Very good!" Lady Alverley sipped her tea for a moment, before saying, "As I mentioned earlier, I had expected you yesterday. It is unfortunate that you are late, for I am unable to cancel all of my engagements for today."

"We had a broken axle to the coach late yesterday afternoon, ma'am, and were forced to seek out an inn for the night.

We were unable to hire a chaise until this morning," said Sarah quickly. "I hope that we have not put you out too much."

"Oh, no, no, nothing of the sort. It is a minor annoyance only," said Lady Alverley, waving her hand dismissively. "Now tell me about yourselves. I recall seeing you as a small girl, of course, Sarah. But I do not think that I saw Margaret more than a time or two when she was still in leading-strings."

At once Margaret began to relate all sorts of details about their lives. Sarah added a few words here and there, but she allowed her sister to do most of the talking. Margaret's artless, confiding ways seemed to amuse Lady Alverley and it gave Sarah the opportunity to observe their grandmother's expressions. She had been mindful of Lord Eustace's casual observation about Lady Alverley when they had first met and now she rather thought that she understood what he had meant. She could see the pride and even a certain arrogance in Lady Alverley, in her mannerisms and in the way that her ladyship posed certain questions. However, Sarah did not think that Lady Alverley was overbearing or ill-natured. Merely, her ladyship was a proud elderly lady who had become very much set in her ways.

Inevitably Margaret mentioned the accident to their coach and Lord Eustace's timely appearance. Lady Alverley interrupted her granddaughter. "Did you say that Lord Eustace took you up in his own postchaise?"

"Yes, and he was so very polite and obliging about it," said Margaret. "I liked his lordship very much."

Lady Alverley turned a curious gaze on her eldest granddaughter. "And what of you, Sarah? Did you also like Lord Eustace?"

Chapter Three

"**O**f course I did. I thought that his lordship was everything one could wish for in a gentleman under such circumstances," said Sarah, a little surprised to be asked such a question.

"You are not so ready as Margaret to sing his lordship's praises," observed Lady Alverley.

Sarah smiled and shook her head. "I am more reserved in my enthusiasms, ma'am. However, what I know of Lord Eustace I do like."

"You are discreet, Sarah. It is a trait which I prize," said Lady Alverley approvingly. "I shall reassure you about his lordship. Lord Eustace is well spoken of in my circles. He is personable, of good birth, and possesses a fine fortune. Three years ago he was contracted to wed a Miss Leander. I never quite understood Lord Eustace's lapse in good judgment, for the young woman was wild to a fault. Vivian Leander was very popular with most of the gentlemen. In any event, she was killed in an unfortunate carriage accident before they could be wed."

"How awful!" exclaimed Sarah, her ready sympathy instantly aroused. Opposite her, Margaret was listening with widened eyes.

"It was a tragedy, certainly. But my understanding is that Lord Eustace has not lacked for companionship since," said Lady Alverley. "I tell you all of this so that you will understand what sort of man Lord Eustace has become."

"Do you mean that his lordship is a-a libertine?" asked Sarah hesitantly, with only a hazy notion of what she was asking.

"Nothing of the sort! You misunderstand me completely. And I will thank you not to use such vocabulary again, Sarah," said Lady Alverley reprovingly. "I meant only that Lord Eustace is in a singular position. He is a bachelor, very eligible, but few choose to pit themselves against the memory of a dead love. In short, he has become something of a fixture in London society. He is known everywhere and is seen everywhere. It is thought to be quite a cachet to be noticed by him. You could do worse that to attach him as an admirer, Sarah. It would do your social standing good."

A gleam of amusement entered Sarah's hazel eyes. It sounded perfectly ridiculous to her that any one gentleman's notice could be thought to be so important to her own eligibility. However, she would not voice her thoughts to her grandmother. Somehow she did not think Lady Alverley would appreciate the humor. "I shall keep that in mind, Grandmama."

"Pray do so, Sarah." Lady Alverley touched her forefinger to her chin. Her voice became reflective. "I must be certain to send Lord Eustace an invitation to your come-out. It will not hurt to throw out a bit of encouragement in that direction."

Sarah blinked at her grandmother. Surely Lady Alverley was taking what was a chance encounter in too serious a vein. "Of course I will be delighted to renew my acquaintance with Lord Eustace, my lady. But I do not think that his lordship took any particular note of me."

"That remains to be seen, Sarah," said Lady Alverley. "One must be optimistic, after all."

"Lord Eustace promised to call on us here while we are visiting with you, Grandmama," said Margaret helpfully. "Is that all right?"

Lady Alverley smiled. "Of course, my dear. I can have no possible objection," she said graciously. She set down her teacup. "Now, I shall reveal to you both a little of what I have planned for the Season, which I trust will meet with your approval. I intend to launch you into polite society with much fanfare and before the Season is out, I hope to receive several respectable offers for your hands."

"Do you truly think so, Grandmama?" asked Margaret, her eyes rounding again. "Sarah and I are not known at all in London. Why should anyone offer for us?"

"You are dowered with respectable portions, fortunately, so I do not anticipate any difficulties," said Lady Alverley. Her tone changed slightly. "I was very pleased to discover that your father has been too prudent, especially since attaining to the title, to have squandered his fortune away like so many of his set. That is one trait of your father's to which I never took exception."

Sarah glanced swiftly at her grandmother. There was a faintly critical note in Lady Alverley's voice that she did not like, since it was directed at her father. She rather thought that she knew what was at the root of Lady Alverley's obvious dislike for her parent, however.

Apparently Margaret was also aware of Lady Alverley's aversion. Wide-eyed, she asked, "Did you and Papa quarrel often, Grandmama?"

"We were not in one another's company enough to quarrel," said Lady Alverley shortly.

"Recall that Papa eloped with Mama, Margaret. Certainly our grandmother could not have been happy with either of them," said Sarah quietly.

Lady Alverley threw her eldest granddaughter an appraising glance. "You've wit, I see. That is quite true, Sarah. I was not made happy by their runaway marriage. At the time your father was a younger son with scant hope of attaining to the title. I did not wish my daughter to throw herself away on one whom I considered to be beneath her in advantages, birth, and connections."

"And so you refused your permission for their engagement and denied the house to our father," murmured Sarah.

Margaret stared at Sarah in dismay, then glanced at Lady Alverley. "I did not know this."

"It is old history, my dear. Perhaps it does hold a valuable lesson, however," said Lady Alverley. "I shall explain, and then we shall speak no more of it. A pecuniary life in obscure circumstances was not what I wished for my daughter. It was completely unacceptable to me. I was both shocked and angered by their subsequent scandalous behavior. Such marriages are frequently crippled from the outset, hurling the participants at once into hideous exile and abject poverty."

Sarah could not allow her grandmother's statements to stand unchallenged. She knew that however true the general circumstances as told by Lady Alverley, there were facts that had not been voiced by her ladyship. "Yet my mother and father were very happy," she said quietly. "Nor did we ever want for anything."

Lady Alverley's eyes narrowed and her mouth thinned. Sarah saw immediately that her grandmother did not like to be corrected. It even appeared that Lady Alverley possessed something of a temper.

Lady Alverley seemed on the point of uttering some remark when Margaret hurried into the breach. "Yes, that is very true! I do recall that Mama and Papa were always holding hands and laughing together. It is one of my earliest memories. And Papa is very well known for his books. I daresay he is almost as rich as you are now, Grandmama."

The tight look about Lady Alverley's mouth vanished as she allowed a laugh to escape her. She patted Margaret's hand. "He is not quite as rich as I am, I assure you. Now we shall not talk any more about what is past, if you please. I wish instead to talk about you. Though I shall admit that my daughter did well for herself in the end—your father did attain to the title, after all—she made a grave error that I am determined that neither of you shall repeat."

"What precisely do you mean, ma'am?" asked Sarah warily.

Lady Alverley threw a stern look at her. "That is the lesson of which I spoke. There will be none of this romantic nonsense that I so deplore in the younger set. Marrying solely for love, indeed! As though neither family nor position are in the least important." She lifted a long beringed finger and shook it at her granddaughters. "You will be guided completely by me, Sarah, Margaret. I will introduce you into very good *ton*, opening to you the doors that all young ladies of birth are privileged to enter. You will meet and be courted by gentlemen of birth and standing. And you will receive several fine offers, which you will naturally wish to consider. I will be quite content to see you both well established this Season."

"I assume that we shall be able to choose a gentleman who is also to our liking?" asked Sarah quietly.

"Pray do not be impertinent, Sarah! By no means have I implied that I shall in any way influence you to accept an offer which you find repugnant," said Lady Alverley sharply.

"Of course not. Forgive me, ma'am," said Sarah.

Margaret looked from her sister to her grandmother and back again. Her expression was troubled. "I am persuaded that someone very dashing and handsome shall offer for you, Sarah. You are so clever and pretty and kind."

Sarah smiled warmly at her sister. The affection between them was real and now it proved to be a buffer against the unpleasant tension that had risen between herself and Lady Alverley. "You are sweet, Margaret. And what of you, pray? Any gentleman would be fortunate to have you to wife."

Margaret gave a careless shrug and said cheerfully, "Oh, if you say so. But I am happy enough to be here in London with Grandmama. I hope to attend as many parties as I possibly can."

Lady Alverley had been listening to their exchange with an amused smile. She seemed to have regained her good humor, and she nodded. "I intend for you to be highly entertained, my dears. We shall scarcely dine at all at home, I daresay. First things must come first, however. We must do something about your wardrobes at once."

Sarah looked down at her well-made olive green pelisse, then exchanged an astonished glance with her sister.

"Why, don't we appear to advantage, Grandmama?" asked Margaret.

"Of course you do, Margaret dear," said Lady Alverley with a smile. "But fashions in London are just a bit different than what you are used to and so we must make a few adjustments. I wrote to your father that I would bear the cost of whatever you needed, including the expense of your Court dresses. I shall hand you over into the care of my own modiste, I think. The woman is a veritable genius. She shall have you done over in a trice."

Sarah and Margaret looked at each other again. Sarah saw the same dismay on Margaret's face that she herself felt. She voiced their concern. "Grandmama, we do appreciate what you wish to do for us. Truly we do. But Papa charged us not to be a great expense to you and he provided us with very generous pin money each month. Surely we may purchase whatever we might require."

"Of course, Sarah. Naturally you shall wish to purchase for yourselves such little things as might catch your eye. However, I have made myself responsible for the dressing of you and of Margaret," said Lady Alverley.

"But—"

"Pray do not voice any further objections, for it will cause me to be very irritable with you," said Lady Alverley with a warning frown. She rose to her feet and crossed to the bell-pull. "Now I shall send you upstairs to get out of your traveling clothes. You will naturally be fatigued by your journey, so I suggest that you lie down for an hour before supper. Due to your arrival, I am dining at home this evening. I shall see you again then. Ah, here is Herbert. He will see that you are conducted to your rooms and put into the capable hands of your maid. Herbert, pray send my cousin to me."

"At once, my lady."

Sarah and Margaret glanced at each other again as they rose to their feet. They curtsied to Lady Alverley and then followed the butler out of the sitting room. He directed a liveried footman to show them upstairs. "Supper will be served at eight o'clock," said the butler, stepping back.

"Eight o'clock?" repeated Margaret, her eyes rounding as she stared at the butler.

"Yes, miss. It is early, I know. Her ladyship felt that coming up from the country as you have that you would feel more comfortable with the earlier hours," said the butler.

"That was considerate of her ladyship," said Sarah, taking hold of her sister's elbow and propelling her toward the stairs.

"But Sarah—"

"Shh, Margaret." As they followed the footman up the stairs, Sarah said in a low voice, "I know. It is frightfully late by our standards. I wonder what time our grandmother does consider to be the proper hour for supper."

"Sarah, I am positive that I shall be utterly famished long before eight o'clock," whispered Margaret. "If I had known, I would have eaten more of the plum cake."

"We must rely on Holby to find us some dry toast and tea," said Sarah.

"Ugh, how horrid! But I shall not complain," said Margaret on a sigh.

At supper, Lady Alverley expounded further on what she had planned for her granddaughters. "Tomorrow morning I shall have my cousin accompany you to the modiste. Marie, I expect Sarah and Margaret to do me credit."

"Yes, my lady," said Miss Hanson quietly.

Sarah and Margaret had met Miss Hanson when they had returned downstairs to the sitting room where they were to join Lady Alverley before going in to supper. Miss Hanson was a maiden relative of Lady Alverley's, who had come to live with her ladyship years before. Dressed neatly and keeping herself discreetly in the background, she served as Lady Alverley's companion, handled her ladyship's correspondence, and generally took upon herself whatever tasks that Lady Alverley disliked or did not want to expend her own time on.

"The Season has not truly begun, so there will be time to have a satisfactory wardrobe readied. I will hold a small gathering a fortnight hence to introduce you quietly, my dears. I anticipate no more than a hundred guests, but that will garner several invitations for you," said Lady Alverley. "It will also give me an opportunity to see how you go on in society before your actual come-outs. Naturally you will have lessons in deportment and dancing if I see that you are in the least backward. However, you both carry yourselves so well that I scarcely think that will be necessary. Was there anything else that I am forgetting, Marie?"

"Horses, my lady," said Miss Hanson, consulting a list that she had taken out of her pocket.

"Oh, yes. Do you ride?" asked Lady Alverley, looking at each of her granddaughters.

"Yes, of course," said Sarah. She was still recovering from hearing Lady Alverley's definition of what constituted a small gathering. She had much to learn, it seemed. "We are used to such exercise every day."

"It was very hard to leave our dear mares," said Margaret on a sigh.

"I shall make available proper mounts for you. You will wish to take the air in the park. I do not ride any longer, but I shall ask an acquaintance of mine who happens to be an exceptional horsewoman to accompany you whenever necessary. No doubt Mrs. Jeffries will be happy to oblige me. She is a widow and was not left well situated," said Lady Alverley.

She turned to her companion. "Marie, they will need decent habits."

"Of course, my lady. I shall see to it," said Miss Hanson, nodding. She made a note on her tightly written list.

"But we have brought our own habits with us, Grandmama," said Margaret.

"My dear, I assure you that what you are used to wearing in the country will not do for you here," said Lady Alverley with a smile.

After supper, Lady Alverley dismissed her granddaughters by the simple expedient of sending them away. "You will wish to go up to bed presently. I shall not see you again until luncheon tomorrow, for I am engaged for the remainder of the evening and I never rise before noon." She required a kiss from them and then glanced at her companion. "I shall leave Marie with you to make such arrangements as she deems necessary." Lady Alverley nodded regally and left the dining room, her silk skirts swishing.

Sarah looked at Margaret and saw her own uncertainty reflected in her sister's eyes. They did not know what to make of their grandmother's cool dismissal. Lady Alverley had basically passed all responsibility for them into Miss Hanson's hands.

Miss Hanson rose from the table. "Let us go into the sitting room to await coffee." She nodded to the footman, who opened the door for her.

Obediently Sarah and Margaret followed their new mentor out of the dining room. When they had entered the sitting room, Miss Hanson requested that the door be closed behind them. She invited the two younger ladies to sit down and when they had done so, she said, smiling, "I know that all this must seem very confusing to you. I shall do my best to enlighten you as we go and answer any questions that you may have."

"I suppose the first question I must ask is why did Lady Alverley invite us to stay with her?" said Sarah with a direct look. "It seems to me that we are something of a nuisance to our grandmother."

"Yes, I particularly noticed Grandmama's coolness this evening," said Margaret, a shade of trouble still in her eyes. "I quite thought that she would like to have us staying with her. At least, it seemed that way when we arrived!"

"Perhaps on the surface it does appear that Lady Alverley is somewhat indifferent," said Miss Hanson. "However, I do assure you that her ladyship has genuinely taken your interests very much to heart. Lady Alverley is most anxious to establish you credibly in society this Season. Naturally I am privy to all of her thoughts and reasonings, since it was I who penned her ladyship's correspondence to your parent."

"Our father did not relate all of the contents of her ladyship's letters to us, only that she had extended an invitation to bring us out this Season," said Sarah slowly. "Miss Hanson, am I correct in assuming that Lady Alverley has grand aspirations for us?"

Miss Hanson hesitated, seeming to choose her words with care. "I believe that to be a fairly accurate statement."

At that moment the footman entered with the coffee urn. He set it on the occasional table, along with a bowl of nuts and fruit. Sarah declined coffee. Her thoughts were both sobering and troubled while Miss Hanson and Margaret were served refreshments.

When the liveried footman left, Sarah turned to Miss Hanson. "Miss Hanson, I shall be frank with you, just as I feel that I must be with our grandmother. I shall not wed where I have no affection," said Sarah quietly. "Position and wealth do not mean as much to me as a basis of mutual respect and affection. I saw the happiness in my parents' lives and it is what I wish for myself as well."

"I see." Miss Hanson regarded Sarah for a long moment, her expression unreadable. She turned her gaze on Margaret. "And what of you, Margaret? Do you also wed only for love?"

Margaret appeared surprised to be addressed. She paused in cracking a nut. "Why, I have scarcely thought about it." She gave a lighthearted laugh. "I think it is too soon to be pondering such serious matters. I, for one, intend to enjoy myself most prodigiously."

"That is a very sensible attitude, Margaret," said Miss Hanson approvingly. She glanced at Sarah and her expression lost some of its friendliness. "Miss Sommers, pray do not judge Lady Alverley prematurely, nor so harshly. She wishes only the best for you and your sister. If you could bring yourself to be more conciliatory toward her ladyship, I think you would discover that she can be most generous. I have been with Lady Alverley for several years and I have never found cause for complaint."

"I wonder, did you know our mother?" asked Sarah.

Miss Hanson looked startled, then a little vague. "Your mother? As I recall, Miss Annabelle had just turned seventeen when I became part of the household."

"Why, that is just my age!" exclaimed Margaret, pleased. "What was Mama like then, Miss Hanson? Was she very pretty? Did she like parties? Did she have many admirers?"

Miss Hanson smiled. "Yes, to all of your questions, Margaret. Miss Annabelle was all the rage when she came out, I believe."

"Then she eloped with Papa and there was a great scandal," said Margaret, nodding. "And afterward they lived happily ever after."

"I am certain that they did," said Miss Hanson repressively.

"Did I say something wrong, Miss Hanson?" asked Margaret.

"Pray accept a small piece of advice, Margaret. And you also, Sarah. The history to which you have referred is still very painful to certain parties. It would be best if you confined your recollections to private moments between yourselves," said Miss Hanson.

Margaret was bewildered. "I do not perfectly understand."

"Miss Hanson means that we are not to mention Mama, or Papa either, while we are here," said Sarah. She looked at the older woman. "Isn't that what you meant, Miss Hanson?"

The older lady regarded her with a frown. "I have not put it so bluntly, Sarah. But since you have asked, yes, that is precisely what I meant."

"And it is Lady Alverley who prefers that no one talk about our parents, isn't it?" asked Sarah.

Miss Hanson pulled her mouth into a prim line. She nodded as though she was being forced to acknowledge something distasteful.

"But why?" asked Margaret. She was frowning as she looked from her sister to Miss Hanson.

"I suspect that Grandmama's pride is involved, Margaret," said Sarah shrewdly. "Have I guessed correctly, Miss Hanson?"

Miss Hanson looked at Sarah almost with dislike. "You are by far too forward, Sarah. Might I suggest in future that you keep such reflections to yourself."

"But that is silly! As though Papa and Mama were murderers or——or something equally horrible," said Margaret, her lovely eyes welling with unshed tears.

Sarah reached out to hug her. "It is quite perfectly Gothic, of course. But we shan't let others spoil our memories, shall we?"

"No, indeed!" said Margaret, dashing a hand across her eyes.

Sarah addressed Miss Hanson. "We shall go on just as we ever have, Miss Hanson. I am sorry that Lady Alverley still harbors such distress. But Margaret and I shan't allow personal bias to taint our own fond memories."

Miss Hanson's mouth folded into a prim line again. "You must understand. Your parents' youthful folly remains quite a painful thing for her ladyship."

"I think that one's youthful follies should be forgiven, especially by those with whom they have the greatest bond. If her ladyship could bring herself to do that, then the pain that she still feels will lose its power," said Sarah.

"You do not know what you are talking about!" exclaimed Miss Hanson. "Her ladyship was betrayed, her wishes totally disregarded. Disgrace was brought upon her name. How can she forgive that?"

"I am persuaded that love must overcome the greatest difficulties imaginable," said Sarah staunchly.

Miss Hanson smiled again, but with a touch of pitying superiority. "You will no doubt one day find your idealism tempered by some rather harsh realities, Sarah. We all come to it sooner or later."

"I hope that I shall never become so hardened or cynical," said Sarah quietly.

Miss Hanson's sallow cheeks reddened. She rose abruptly. "You must both be fatigued. I shall allow you to go up to bed.

We shall be leaving the house quite early in the morning, so do get an adequate night's rest."

With that, Miss Hanson ushered them out of the sitting room and up the stairs to their bedrooms. She said good night in the hallway and left them to continue on to her own apartment.

"We've been shuffled off again," said Margaret with a shake of her head.

Sarah hugged her sister. "Never mind, Margaret. Everything will be fine. We've embarked on a perfectly splendid adventure, remember!"

Margaret's eyes brightened. "Why, so we have! Oh, I wonder what is in store for us tomorrow, Sarah? Do you think that we shall be given a great many new gowns?"

"I daresay," said Sarah, laughing. "Now do be good and go in to bed. I shall see you in the morning."

"Good night, dear Sarah," said Margaret, opening the bedroom door.

"Good night, Margaret."

Sarah waited until Margaret had entered her room before she went into her own bedroom. The charming apartment was decorated all in white and pink and gilt. The bedroom was sumptuously carpeted and the window drapes were heavy pink brocade. The wardrobe door stood open and she glimpsed her dresses and gowns hanging neatly inside. The cheval glass was nearby, along with a vanity. A pair of elegantly covered wing-back chairs were situated to one side of the tall fireplace. On the other side of the fire stood a steaming hipbath, partially screened from the rest of the room for warmth. On the bedside table was a large vase with a profusion of fresh flowers. Her bed was turned down and a fresh nightgown was laid out on the coverlet.

Sarah thought she had never been treated so royally before. She was startled by a reflection of movement in the large standing looking-glass and she turned. "Holby! I did not hear you come in."

"I did not come from the hall, miss. There is a small panel door set into the corner of the wall," said the maid, gesturing. "I have my quarters between you and Miss Margaret. You may call for me whenever you need me." She began picking up the bonnet and other articles that Sarah had discarded earlier and carried them to the wardrobe.

"I expect that Margaret will need you more than I do tonight," said Sarah.

The maid chuckled. "That is true, Miss Sarah. I left her rattling on at a good pace with the chambermaid. She'll need calming down before she will be able to sleep."

"Then just help me out of this gown, Holby, and I'll manage the rest for myself," said Sarah, turning her back toward the maid.

"I thought that would be so, miss." Holby's expert fingers made quick work of the row of tiny hooks and eyes down the back of the gown. "What think you of this place, miss?"

Sarah met the maid's speculative gaze in the mirror. As she got out of the gown, she said slowly, "I don't know yet, Holby. Lady Alverley seems to want us here one minute and the next instant I can't but feel that we impose on her good nature."

Holby nodded. She placed the gown over the top of a chair. She motioned her mistress to a seat in front of the vanity and picked up a hairbrush. "Since we arrived, I have been listening to what others say, miss. Her ladyship is determined to bring you and Miss Margaret into fashion. But her ladyship is known to be an impatient, proud woman and easily irritated. There is speculation that you were brought here on one of her ladyship's whims and that her favor may dissolve as quickly as it rose. I'm thinking it makes for an uneasy few months, miss."

Sarah sighed, frowning at the reflection of her own slim figure. Absently she played with the narrow satin ribbons that tied the front of her camisole. "I have already seen it, Holby, and I fear that you may be quite right. But Margaret and I must simply make the best of it. Papa desired us to heed our grandmother's advice and to make the most of our opportunities while we are here."

"No doubt you will do just that, Miss Sarah," said Holby comfortably as she brushed her mistress's hair. "I have known you and Miss Margaret from your cradles and I have never known either of you to settle for less than the best."

Sarah gave a wry chuckle. "Yes, Margaret and I can become

perfectly obstinate on occasion. Perhaps you are right. I need not be anxious at all over what Lady Alverley might say or do. We were brought up to know our own minds. Our heads won't be easily turned. Margaret and I shall make the choices that are best for us, even if it means returning home in disgrace with her ladyship. Thank you, Holby."

The maid nodded and picked up the discarded gown. "I'll leave you now, Miss Sarah, and go see to Miss Margaret."

"Good night, Holby," said Sarah, rising from the bench. She yawned behind her hand. "I think that I shall just take a quick bath and then get into bed."

"Good night, miss. I shall return later to see how you are faring," said the maid. She went out of the bedroom, closing the panel door behind her.

Chapter Four

After breakfasting the following morning, Miss Hanson took Sarah and Margaret out in one of Lady Alverley's elegant town carriages. Margaret ran her fingers over the fine velvet seat cushion and lifted her brows as she glanced at Sarah. Sarah smiled and nodded. It was still a novelty to them to be surrounded with such opulence.

The day was frosty and cloudy, but the snow had let up in the night. The cobbled streets were already being cleared, the snow turning to dirty slush under carriage and wagon and cart wheels. As they went, Miss Hanson kindly pointed out several points of interest and even the carriages of a few notable personages, which were also out at that early hour. In the bustling merchants' district, hawkers called out their wares, hagridden beggars darted between the horses' hooves, and equestrians all mingled. It was a veritable cacophony of sound and sight that was fascinating to two young ladies who had spent their whole lives in the quiet country.

"It is so very busy and bewildering," said Margaret, her eyes wide and happy as she stared out of the window. "I am already turned around with all of the streets that we have driven through."

"And I, also," agreed Sarah. She was leaning toward the window on her side of the carriage. "I don't think I have ever seen so many carriages and horses and carts before!"

"You will quickly become accustomed to it. Of course, it is early in the year still, so it is not near as crowded as it will be later. Most personages have not yet returned to town for the Season," said Miss Hanson with the tolerant pride of one immune to her surroundings.

Sarah and Margaret exchanged glances over what their

companion had said. Sarah suspected that Miss Hanson had to
be exaggerating just a trifle. Surely the streets could not ever
be more crowded than what they had already observed. The
carriage slowed and stopped outside a certain shop. Their first
stop was to the exclusive modiste patronized by Lady Alverley.

. When the modiste learned that she was to have the dressing
of both of Lady Alverley's granddaughters, she expressed herself to be ecstatic. "They are lovely girls! It shall be a pleasure,
Mademoiselle Hanson," exclaimed the modiste. "This one, so
dark and elegant. The sister, so tall and beautiful. Oh, *oui, oui!*
It shall be done just as her ladyship wishes!"

The modiste clapped her hands, giving a stream of orders,
and her assistants came running with measures and several
bolts of cloth. The array of silks and velvets and brocades and
muslins and laces tossed free of the bolts was dazzling.

Sarah let out her breath in a soft sound of awe, which was
completely lost as Margaret squealed in delight. Fingering a
delicate satin, Margaret exclaimed, "Oh, I do like this one!"

"We will measure. Then we will talk," pronounced the
modiste.

After Sarah submitted to having her measurements taken,
the modiste nodded approval. "You are of a neat, attractive
figure, Mademoiselle Sommers. For you, the most fashionable
of fabrics and an elegant style. You are of a petite stature,
non? Thus we must not overpower you with the quantity of
bows and trims and flounces. As for mademoiselle's sister—
ah, you are tall like Lady Alverley! We shall let our genius
flow for you, mademoiselle, for you shall be able to carry off
the frivolous, even the absurd."

After much discussion and consultation between Miss Hanson and the modiste, it was agreed that several walking
dresses, pelisses, daygowns, ballgowns, and a couple of riding
habits were the first essential items.

The modiste promised to have a number of garments ready
for fittings late in the week. "Be assured! I shall have my very
best seamstresses at work round the clock," she said as they
parted from her and left the shop.

Miss Hanson then conducted her charges to several other es-
tablishments. A mountain of awkwardly sized packages

wrapped in paper and string and at least three hatboxes threatened to take up all available space in the carriage. The packages contained only a portion of what Miss Hanson deemed necessary for Sarah and Margaret to be turned out in style. Gloves, both long and short, two Cashmere shawls apiece, straw hats trimmed with feathers, ribbons and flowers, daintily laced underthings, a half dozen pairs of pale pink silk stockings for evenings and as many cotton pairs for daywear, bunches of satin ribbons for trim, lengths of lace for refurbishing of gowns, gold and silver string for knotting reticules, and perfume were only a sampling of the treasures.

More than once, Sarah or Margaret voiced uncertainty about some of the purchases, objecting that they were too expensive or frivolous. But Miss Hanson was adamant. She brushed aside all of their protestations of not wanting to trespass too greatly upon their grandmother's good nature. Miss Hanson patiently explained over and over that Lady Alverley denied them nothing and that to refuse her ladyship's largesse was tantamount to insult.

"It is like a wonderful dream," said Margaret in a dazed voice.

"Yes, but one wonders where it will all end, too," said Sarah, shaking her head. It seemed outrageous to her that so much was being invested in their appearance. She and Margaret had never spent even a portion of this amount over an entire year and they had been very adequately dressed.

They were standing in a silk shop, waiting while Miss Hanson negotiated with the proprietor over the price of two dominos.

"They are too shockingly dear," remarked Sarah to her sister, fingering the lovely shimmering silk. "We shan't wear them above once or twice, I am persuaded."

The proprietor overheard her and immediately dropped the purchase price. Miss Hanson at once agreed. When the two dominos had been carefully wrapped in sheets of tissue paper and placed in boxes, she requested the driver to carry them out to the carriage.

After the ladies were once more seated in the crowded carriage, Miss Hanson gave instructions that they were to be driven back to the town house. She settled back against the velvet squabs with a tired sigh. After a moment, she looked over at Sarah. "Miss Sommers, I appreciate your concerns, but do try to understand. Her ladyship has commissioned me to do all in my power to turn you out as a young lady of high fashion. If I fail in the slightest degree to carry out her ladyship's wishes, then I shall fall under her displeasure. And rightly so! Do stop obstructing me in my duties in future, I pray. And you also, Margaret. It is most wearisome to be obliged to set aside protests at every turn."

"It just seems so very extravagant to be buying all of these beautiful things," said Sarah. "Why, Margaret and I could easily exist on a third of all that we have purchased today."

Miss Hanson smiled. "You will discover that Lady Alverley always does things on a grand scale. It is not for me or for you to question her ladyship's wishes."

Sarah was silenced. She finally saw that it was futile to try to persuade Miss Hanson not to put out such expense on their account, for the lady did not have the power to countermand Lady Alverley's orders. Sarah wished that she had realized it earlier in the day, for it must have seemed to Miss Hanson that she and Margaret had been badgering her unmercifully.

Sarah decided that she must speak to her grandmother and explain to Lady Alverley that she and Margaret had not come up to London to be a financial burden to her ladyship. Even one as rich as Lady Alverley must have a bottom to her purse. It seemed incredibly imprudent to Sarah to keep spending money like water until circumstances forced an end to it, and that is what she was afraid that Lady Alverley might be doing.

As for Miss Hanson, she was Lady Alverley's dependent and she acted solely at Lady Alverley's behest. It was useless to try to reason with her. Sarah said slowly, "Very well, Miss Hanson. I shall no longer question your decisions. Margaret, have you any thoughts on the matter?"

"Oh, I quite agree. Poor Miss Hanson! You look as though you have the headache. You must lie down when we are returned," said Margaret, reaching out to pat the older woman's arm.

Miss Hanson's face registered surprise. Then her expression smoothed to a slight smile. "Thank you, my dear. You are kind," she murmured.

Sarah received the distinct impression that Miss Hanson's needs and desires were not often noticed. She felt ashamed. She had been so wrapped up in her own frustrations that she had not seen what was so obvious now that Margaret had pointed it out.

"Yes, Margaret and I can well entertain ourselves for the remainder of the afternoon. We have all of these lovely things to put away and a score of things to talk about," said Sarah. "Perhaps we might take tea upstairs and then rest for a while. Unless, of course, our grandmother desires to see us."

Miss Hanson nodded. "That is a sensible plan, Sarah." There was a note of relief in her voice. "I do not believe that Lady Alverley will have returned from making her calls yet, so I see no reason why you and Margaret cannot do just as you have said." Miss Hanson sent up word to you when her ladyship returns." Miss Hanson paused and her brow creased in an anxious line. "I am persuaded that Lady Alverley will surely be pleased by our progress today. I hope that tomorrow will be just as successful."

Sarah and Margaret shared an astonished glance. "We are going shopping again tomorrow?" asked Margaret.

"Why, yes, of course! We have not nearly accomplished what we need to, my dear," said Miss Hanson with a smile.

Sarah said nothing, but she shook her head. It was all so very different from home, she thought. There, she and Margaret would have whiled away the cold winter hours with reading and sewing and pleasant talk and taking a brisk walk or ride in the afternoons. Or they might have taken the gig into the village to do a few errands for their cook and housekeeper, Mrs. Buddington, and while there paid a call on friends. There would have been occasional chats with their father when he emerged from his library at mealtimes, and in the evenings they would have played cards or sat at the pianoforte to sing together.

Sarah knew that their lives would have been considered dull by many people and, of course, it could be tedious at times. However, this frenzy that they had plunged into since arriving in London was so strange that she wasn't certain that she quite liked it. "I am beginning to realize that we are going to be very busy," she remarked to no one in particular.

Miss Hanson actually laughed. "My dear Sarah! What a humorous thing to say! Of course, you shall be busy. Lady Alverley shall see to that, I promise you. You will not have a moment to spare outside of all the entertainments that you will be attending. That is the hallmark of a successful Season, you know."

Margaret's eyes sparkled. "How exciting! Just think of it, Sarah! We shall be going to parties and routs and balls and the theater! It will be so amusing!"

Sarah agreed to it, keeping her reservations and questions to herself. After seeing what Lady Alverley and Miss Hanson considered to be essential just in her wardrobe, she could not help but wonder if a staid country miss like herself could ever adjust to this new life.

Margaret was different, of course. Sarah did not think that her sister would have any difficulty at all. Margaret was still very much a child in some respects, greeting every new experience with unabated enthusiasm. She was like a little darting fish, happily exploring a new pond, thought Sarah whimsically, with a slight smile, while I am behaving like a wary cat.

When they entered the town house, Miss Hanson bid them good afternoon and went along to her own bedroom. The footmen carried in all of the parcels from the carriage and took them up to Sarah's bedroom. At Margaret's direction, they piled up the packages on Sarah's bed.

When Holby saw the slipping piles of packages, she threw up her hands in amazement. "My goodness! Whatever have you gone and done? Why, it looks as though you have bought out the shops!"

"Not us, but Lady Alverley," corrected Sarah quietly, untying the ribbons of her bonnet and lifting it off her head. She laid the bonnet down on a chair, together with her kid gloves.

"This is not the half of it, Holby," said Margaret merrily. "Miss Hanson says that we are to go shopping again tomorrow." She threw off her bonnet and gloves and tossed them in the direction of a chair. One of the gloves slipped to the carpet, but she did not notice. She jumped up onto the bed and began breaking the strings and ripping the brown paper from various curious-shaped packages.

"Proper spoiling, is what it is," muttered the maid, eyeing the seemingly endless array of things emerging from their wrappings. She drew her hand across one of the Cashmere shawls, obviously approving of its silky feel.

"Yes, one might say so," said Sarah, chuckling. She unbuttoned her pelisse and slipped out of it. "Holby, I am famished. Is there any chance for some sweetened tea and biscuits being sent up?"

"Of course, Miss Sarah. I shall see to it at once," said the maid, taking the pelisse from her mistress and setting it aside. She glanced at the younger lady. "You should get out of your pelisse, too, Miss Margaret. You'll get too hot if you leave it on."

"Pooh! I shan't mind it a bit," said Margaret, never looking up as she lifted a lovely straw out of a hatbox. She set it on her head and tied the satin ribbons. Margaret bounced off the bed. "Oh, I must look in the glass!"

Sarah and the maid exchanged a glance. The maid shook her head and bustled away. "I'll be getting the tea set up in the parlor, Miss Sarah."

A small parlor had been set aside for Sarah and Margaret's use and a quarter hour later Holby returned to the bedroom to inform them that tea and biscuits had been laid out. Sarah had managed to get Margaret to pull off her pelisse, saying that she refused to sit down with her sister still dressed for the outdoors. "The tea shall grow cold and then I will be greatly annoyed with you, Margaret," she added.

"Very well! I shall take it off," said Margaret, unbuttoning the outerwear and laying it aside. She was very willing to follow Sarah into the parlor for refreshments and consumed several of the biscuits.

Afterward, Margaret stretched out on a settee. She arched her back contentedly before curling up on the silk cushions. She yawned and looked surprised. "How odd! I feel a little fatigued."

"And no wonder! We were gone more than half the day, being poked and prodded and pulled," said Sarah, laughing. Then her smile faded. "Margaret, what do you make of it? Are we imposing too much on our grandmother? I do not like to think that we are."

Margaret gave a careless shrug. "Why do you let it concern you, Sarah?"

Sarah looked at her sister with surprise. "Margaret, surely you have not forgotten what Papa said to us?"

"Oh, I remember as well as you do what Papa told us. But it seems to me that while we are here in Alverley House that Grandmama's wishes count more than do our father's. We haven't a thing to say about it, so it's not a bit of use making a scene, is it?" said Margaret.

"Yes, I suppose that you are right. Once I realized how we had badgered Miss Hanson about everything, I really felt quite sorry for her. She is placed very awkwardly. I can see that now. I should have held my tongue and taken it up with Grandmama instead," said Sarah.

Margaret eyed her. "You intend to make a fuss, then? I don't know that is at all the thing to do, Sarah."

"Perhaps not," said Sarah. "Nevertheless, I hope to have an opportunity to discuss it with her later this evening."

Margaret shook her head. "I tell you now that it won't do you any good, Sarah."

"Oh, do you think that Grandmama might cut up stiff? I admit, I do think that she is rather proud and probably set in her ways, as well. But surely, if I approach her with reason, she will not be offended," said Sarah.

"I've been thinking about everything quite a bit since this morning, Sarah. I don't think that this matter has anything at all to do with Grandmama's character," said Margaret thoughtfully. "What I do think is that since Grandmama invited us to stay with her here and offered to sponsor us for the Season, we really have not the least right to question how she intends to do it. We don't know what is required to be properly launched into society, after all. But Grandmama does, and I, for one, have decided to agree to whatever she wishes."

"Whenever did you become so practical, Margaret?" asked Sarah, a little surprised. She was used to her sister speaking whatever ridiculous whimsy came into her head. This proof of serious reflection on Margaret's part was something new.

"I have always been practical. You simply never noticed," said Margaret, covering another yawn. "And since you are the eldest and have been used to arranging everything, I never re-

ally needed to do anything too much. You and Mrs. Buddington always settled everything between you."

Sarah was taken aback. "Oh, Margaret, I am sorry! I did not
realize that I was so managing."

Margaret's eyes twinkled at her. "What a peagoose you are,
Sarah! As though I minded! I had my lessons and my stitchery
and Miss Spoonsby was such a dear. She taught me ever so
much about how to go on in a household, having been made to
fend for herself in the most dismal of circumstances. What stories she told me about her previous posts! I daresay I know
better how to do for myself than you do, for you had that
awful woman as governess before dear Miss Spoonsby came
to us."

"Yes; I was never more glad when Mrs. Buddington took
such a dislike to her that she insisted that Papa choose between
them," said Sarah, chuckling at the memory. "Of course, he
had no choice but to side with Mrs. Buddington, for she knew
just how to make him comfortable."

Margaret laughed, too, but then her smile faded a little. "I
wish that we still had dear Miss Spoonsby with us. I still miss
her awfully."

"How could we keep her with us, when Papa finally decided
that it was time for you to be emancipated from the schoolroom and that I was too old to have a companion?" Sarah
laughed suddenly. "Poor Papa! I don't believe that he thought
any further than that. He made up his mind that we were all
grown up and then he didn't know what to do with us."

"And so he sent us off to London for the Season," said Margaret contentedly. "I am very happy, Sarah. I am all excited inside, as though something terribly wonderful is going to
happen. Don't you feel it, too?"

Sarah shook her head. "I am not so fanciful as you, Margaret. You know that. I am glad to have this opportunity, naturally. If it was not for Grandmama, I suspect that we would
have remained with Papa all of our lives."

"How dull that would have been!" exclaimed Margaret,
bouncing upright. "Sarah, I want to travel and meet all sorts of
personages and have lovely dresses and horses. I don't think
that I could stand being stuck in one place all of my life."

Sarah laughed at her. "Well, you shall have at least some of those desires granted to you this Season, Margaret."

"Yes, and I think that is why I feel all anticipation," said Margaret, unexpectedly serious. "I feel that my whole life is about to change."

"Of course it shall. You shall become an accomplished flirt and no doubt break a great many hearts and in the end wed someone very dashing and romantic," said Sarah teasingly.

"Oh, fie! That is what I think of marrying," said Margaret, snapping her fingers.

Sarah laughed again. She was interrupted by a knock at the door. "Come," she called.

The door opened and a maid entered, curtsying. "Begging your pardon, miss, but Lady Alverley sent me to request that you wait upon her ladyship in the sitting room."

"We shall be right down," said Sarah. She looked over at her sister, raising her brows slightly. "Now what, do you suppose?"

"How should I know? Oh, do let us hurry, Sarah! I just know it must be something wonderful," urged Margaret.

Chapter Five

When Sarah and Margaret went downstairs and entered the sitting room, they discovered that Lady Alverley was entertaining a visitor. The woman was much younger than her ladyship and attractive. She was fashionably turned out in a well-cut walking dress, and over it a three-quarter-length, bottle-green pelisse with bugle trimming. On her head she wore a large velvet bonnet of the same color trimmed with a sweep of black and white egret feathers.

"Ah, here are my granddaughters now, Mrs. Jeffries. Sarah, Margaret, allow me to introduce you to Mrs. Jeffries. She has kindly assented to place her time at your disposal whenever you should wish to enjoy a ride in the park," said Lady Alverley.

Mrs. Jeffries held out her hand to each of the younger ladies. She showed them a pair of twinkling green eyes and a captivating smile. "How do you do! I am glad to make your acquaintance. Lady Alverley has been telling me that you wish to keep up your usual habit of exercise while you are visiting her. I am most willing to chaperone you on these outings whenever you should so choose," she said.

Sarah was at once drawn to the widow's friendly manner. As she shook hands, she said, "We regretted leaving our mares behind, certainly. We are used to riding every day, you see."

"Then you must continue to do so while you are here," said Mrs. Jeffries. As Sarah and Margaret sat down beside each other on a settee opposite, Mrs. Jeffries inclined her head to her hostess. "That is, if Lady Alverley approves?"

"Certainly. I would not have summoned you if I had not just that thing in mind, Elizabeth," said Lady Alverley.

"Of course not, my lady," said Mrs. Jeffries with a hint of constraint, casting down her expressive eyes for a moment.

At once, Sarah realized that Mrs. Jeffries's relationship with Lady Alverley was not precisely one of friendship. Lady Alverley had in essence employed Mrs. Jeffries to look after her and Margaret when they went out riding. She recalled that Lady Alverley had mentioned Mrs. Jeffries the previous evening, and that the widow was not well situated financially. What a terrible thing it was, thought Sarah, to be obliged to rely on someone else's largesse.

"Have you got mounts for us already, Grandmama?" asked Margaret excitedly, perched on the very edge of the settee.

Lady Alverley smiled. "Of course, my dear. I sent down to the stables and requested my head groom to choose suitable horses for you and Sarah. I instructed him to make certain that they are well-behaved but with some spirit in them. I hope that meets with your approval?"

Margaret jumped up to throw her arms around Lady Alverley. "Oh, dearest Grandmama! They sound perfect! When may we see them?"

"Tomorrow morning, Margaret. I shall have them sent round about ten o'clock. Naturally I shall not be up to witness your departure, but I trust Mrs. Jeffries to take good care of you," said Lady Alverley, patting her granddaughter's arm, before setting her firmly aside.

"And so I shall, my lady," said Mrs. Jeffries with a warm smile. She gathered her gloves and began to pull them on, indicating that she was drawing her visit to a close. Rising to her feet, she held out her hand to her hostess. "I know that you must have many other appointments, my lady, and so I shall leave you now. I shall come round about ten o'clock for your granddaughters tomorrow morning. I count it as my pleasure to be able to ride with them."

Lady Alverley extended her hand to Mrs. Jeffries. "Thank you, my dear. I knew that I could count on you. You know your way out."

Mrs. Jeffries said a few kind words to Sarah and Margaret and then exited.

Lady Alverley turned to Sarah and Margaret. "Well, my dears? What think you? Did you care for Mrs. Jeffries?"

"I thought her quite delightful, ma'am," said Sarah. "I appreciate your consideration in finding a pleasant companion for us."

"Oh, yes! It will be simply wonderful to be able to ride again," said Margaret.

Lady Alverley smiled at her granddaughters. "I am glad that you are pleased. It is my wish that you enjoy yourselves as much as possible this Season. That is why I am going to such lengths on your behalf. Your happiness is very close to my heart, you see. Sarah, I understand from my cousin that you in particular have had reservations over the expense that I am going to on your behalf."

"Indeed I do, Grandmama. I can see that we are already becoming a sore trial on your purse," said Sarah. "I have certain misgivings, naturally."

"Pray do not let that concern you, my dear. I am a very, very rich woman. I can well afford to spoil my granddaughters. And it is all for a good purpose, in any event. You will find that my wealth, coupled with your own attributes of birth and beauty, of course, will open many doors to you both that otherwise might remain closed," said Lady Alverley.

"I do not wish to sound ungrateful, for indeed I am not. It is just that we are not used to such extravagant living, my lady," said Sarah with a smile.

"I do hope that you and Margaret will be able to abandon these bourgeois notions. They do not become one of my blood," said Lady Alverley sternly.

"Margaret and I were just discussing the matter, ma'am. Margaret is of the opinion that we should simply place ourselves into your hands and refuse to be anxious for anything," said Sarah quietly.

"That is quite true, Grandmama," said Margaret. "We were talking about it not a half hour past."

"You have a very sensible attitude, Margaret. I am glad of it. I hope that your sister is clever enough to learn from you," said Lady Alverley in an annoyed tone.

Sarah inclined her head, the shadow of a smile on her lips. She could do nothing more and her conscience was clear of its anxiety. "Indeed I am, Grandmama. I shall not utter another word of protest, whatever you may suggest."

Margaret nodded, her expression earnest. "We are quite prepared to be guided by you in everything."

Lady Alverley smiled. She nodded approvingly. "I am happy to hear it. We shall all go along much more comfortably, I assure you." She glanced up at the ormolu clock on the mantle. "It is already five o'clock, so let us go in to dinner. It is a bore to be forced to dine at home, but I do not begrudge the sacrifice while we are awaiting your new gowns. My cousin informs me that by the end of the week we can anticipate some fittings. It is satisfactory, very satisfactory, indeed!"

"Will Miss Hanson not be joining us?" asked Sarah, surprised, as she and her sister followed Lady Alverley into the dining room.

"My cousin has a touch of the headache and has requested the favor of taking dinner in her rooms this afternoon," said Lady Alverley. A flicker of annoyance crossed her face.

"I am sorry to hear it," said Sarah quickly. "However, I am not surprised. Miss Hanson seemed to have the beginnings of it before we had returned this afternoon."

Lady Alverley shrugged. "I do not regard it, for I have already had an opportunity to discuss several matters with her. Since Mrs. Jeffries will be taking you riding in the morning, you will not start the day with shopping. Marie may as well fill in the time by writing out the invitations for your first gathering. She is preparing a guest list this evening to submit for my approval."

Sarah kept her thoughts to herself as the soup was served, but she reflected that it sounded as though poor Miss Hanson never had a moment off the leash. She wondered if that lady had ever regretted making her home with Lady Alverley. Then she decided, quite correctly, that Miss Hanson would probably have regretted more giving up the perquisites of elegant attire and a fashionable address.

"Miss Hanson was very kind and patient with us today, ma'am. She pointed out several points of interest to us, as well as a few of the notables around town," said Sarah.

"That is very good," said Lady Alverley, nodding. "You must both get your footing as soon as possible. By the by, I was pleased to find a note from Lord Eustace in my correspondence today. His lordship has very prettily asked my permission to call upon you one day. Naturally I have no objection."

"That is certainly a kind gesture on his lordship's part," said Sarah, surprised. "We met him quite by chance, after all."

"He has exceptional manners, indeed," agreed Margaret, nodding.

"My dears! What naive chicks you are, to be sure! A gentleman like Lord Eustace does not beg leave to pay his addresses to two young misses unknown to him simply because he possesses exquisite manners," said Lady Alverley, giving a tolerant laugh.

"Does he not, Grandmama?" asked Margaret curiously.

"No, my dear. I would rather say that one or the other of you has made a most agreeable impression on Lord Eustace. That is why he pursues the acquaintance so quickly," said Lady Alverley.

Sarah was startled by her grandmother's interpretation, but it was left to her sister to pose the astonished question that formed in her mind.

"Oh, my goodness!" exclaimed Margaret. "Do you mean that Lord Eustace wishes to become one of our suitors?"

"I should not be a bit surprised, Margaret," said Lady Alverley complacently.

"Surely you are making too much of it, ma'am! Why, his lordship does not even know us. We shared his carriage with him for no more than half an hour," said Sarah.

"However, that appears to have been quite long enough to have persuaded Lord Eustace that he wishes to become better acquainted with you and Margaret, Sarah," said Lady Alverley. "It will be most interesting to see what comes of it. It is such an understood thing that Lord Eustace is out of the lists that this development is quite in the manner of a minor miracle. Ah, we are having turbot this evening! How delightful! I do not regret dining *en familie* in the least, after all. Altogether it has been a most satisfactory day. Don't you think so, my dears?"

"Indeed, ma'am, it has been most instructive," said Sarah, meaning every word, as she was served a helping of the well-prepared fish.

* * *

After breakfast the following morning, Sarah and Margaret attired themselves in their riding habits. Carrying their gloves and whips, and holding the long skirts of their habits draped over their arms, they went downstairs to join Mrs. Jeffries. As they descended, the sisters discussed what Lady Alverley had said the previous day concerning the habits that they had brought from home.

Sarah and Margaret finally agreed that they looked perfectly presentable. Their habits were scarcely a year old, after all. It was surely Lady Alverley's aversion to anything that she considered to be provincial that had made necessary the ordering of new habits, not any lack in their present appearance. Lady Alverley had made her judgment without ever having seen the habits.

"That will not weigh at all with Grandmama, of course," said Sarah. "Nor with Miss Hanson, who is quite as much determined as our grandmother to transform us into London misses."

"Yes," agreed Margaret and laughed. "At least Grandmama and Miss Hanson are spared the sight of us dressed in something that wasn't made in London, since they haven't risen yet."

"I doubt that we appear that unfashionable, in any event," said Sarah confidently.

When Sarah and her sister joined Mrs. Jeffries in the drawing room, they at once saw that they were in error. Mrs. Jeffries greeted them cheerfully, sweeping toward them to catch their hands in hers. She wore a figure-skimming velvet riding habit ornamented with cord and braid down the front and on the cuffs. A rakish black top hat sporting an ostrich plume was perched on her head. The bodice of her habit had been left open to show off her shirt and the froth of lace at her throat. Tan leather gloves and black half boots completed her outfit. There was no doubt that Mrs. Jeffries was attired in the very height of fashion. Sarah felt that she looked dowdy by comparison in her russet brown riding dress.

"Grandmama was right, after all," said Margaret on a sigh.

Mrs. Jeffries looked at them, her expression inquiring. "What is this, pray? Have I offended in some way?"

"Of course not. It is just that our grandmother had told us that we would need new riding habits and we didn't quite believe her," said Sarah with a smile.

"Yes, and now that we have seen yours, we know it to be true," said Margaret, shaking her head. "You utterly outshine us."

Mrs. Jeffries laughed. "You look quite charming, I assure you. The horses do not mind what we wear. As for the rest of the world, I am certain that Lady Alverley will see to it that you do her credit! Now let us go try out the mounts that her ladyship has provided for you."

Over the next several minutes, as they slowly rode through the streets, the lady exhibited such twinkling good humor and wit that all dismay over their obviously countrified riding habits faded away. Sarah at once felt comfortable with the widow. Even though Mrs. Jeffries was ten years older than she and far more worldly, there began to develop a warm friendship between them.

Margaret, too, swiftly warmed to the lady. She went so far as to confide in Mrs. Jeffries that she was the nicest person that they had yet met in London.

"How sweet of you! But I daresay that you will meet scores of others whom you will like just as much," said Mrs. Jeffries, leading the way at a sedate pace through the gates of the park. She was placed between the sisters, while her own groom and Lady Alverley's followed at a discreet distance behind the ladies.

"Oh, no. There are those that one feels instantly comfortable with and one just knows that they are going to be great friends. And that is just how I feel about you," said Margaret.

Mrs. Jeffries laughed, her browned complexion pinkening a little. "Well, if we are to be friends, then we must certainly address each other by our first names. Pray call me Elizabeth."

"And you must call me Sarah. I, too, am quite persuaded that we shall be friends," said Sarah. She easily controlled the frisking of her mare with a firm hand, proving who was in authority. Sarah breathed in the chill early morning air. It was good to have a decent horse under her and to be able to ride through the park. Though town life was shaping up to be very different and exciting, Sarah was glad for the familiarity of the exercise.

"That is just what I have been saying," said Margaret, nodding. "Isn't this wonderful, Sarah! I do like my sweet mare. I must ask the groom to tell me her name."

She fell back to converse briefly with the groom in the distinctive green and russet and then spurred forward again. "She is called Cassie and yours is Ladylove!" she informed Sarah happily.

"That is very pretty," said Sarah, and she crooned to her mount so that its ears swiveled back toward her. Sarah also had been pleased by her grandmother's choice in mounts for herself and her sister. Lady Alverley had judged to a nicety just the sort of horses that would suit them. The mares had good lines and were smooth gaited. She had nothing to complain of, thought Sarah with a smile.

Mrs. Jeffries handled her own cavorting mount with ease. She had been critically watching for several minutes how her companions rode and now she complimented Sarah and Margaret on their horsemanship. "You both have excellent seats. It is easy to see that you are well taught and have a love for horses," she commented.

"Our father taught us when we were very young. He was always a fine rider. I adore riding, but it is Margaret who is the better rider. She never grows fatigued," said Sarah.

Margaret laughed gaily. "Yes, I am made of iron. I never tire. I don't think that I like anything half as well as riding."

"We rode at home every day. It is good to be in the saddle again," said Sarah with a flash of a smile. For the first time since they had arrived in London, she felt completely at ease. It probably had to do with their surroundings as much as the ride. The trees in the park were still devoid of leaves and the riding paths showed the effects of winter in broken branches and mudholes, but Sarah thought she had not seen anything as peaceful since they had arrived.

"You might not wish to ride as often while you are here in London. There will be parties and dancing until all hours for the duration of the Season. You won't feel much like rising early each morning, I promise you," said Mrs. Jeffries, guiding them down a bridle path that had a canopy of sweeping, starkly bare branches overhead. "But you'll like all of that, too, I expect."

"Oh, yes! Grandmama has already told us about all of the plans she is making for our amusement," said Margaret. "We will be ever so busy, won't we, Sarah?"

"Quite. But I trust that we won't abandon all of our familiar habits," said Sarah. She leaned over to pat the mare's neck. "I should like to spend time with this lady."

"You might find that it is not so easy, once the Season truly begins," warned Mrs. Jeffries. "You will become increasingly busy as the Season progresses. More than likely, we'll end by doing most of our riding in the afternoons at the fashionable hour of five o'clock, so that you can meet all the new friends that you will make. Then there will be times when Lady Alverley will wish you to drive with her in her carriage rather than ride," said Mrs. Jeffries. "Her ladyship will wish to make certain that she is able to introduce you to just such personages who will prove most advantageous to your social progress."

"I wish to make a great many friends," declared Margaret. "Then Sarah and I can invite callers to tea every day. That will be very agreeable."

"There will be gentlemen calling on you, too," said Mrs. Jeffries, throwing her a teasing glance. "We must not forget that. You'll wish to receive them."

"I shan't mind that," said Margaret cheerfully. "Grandmama had told us to expect several offers made for us before the Season's end. She wishes to see us credibly established, but I am in no hurry to be wed."

"Nor I," said Sarah, laughing.

"Are you not ready to wed?" Mrs. Jeffries looked at them in surprise. "That is the reason most young ladies come up to London."

"But you see, we have lived so very quietly that the very novelty of being out in society is treat enough for the moment," said Sarah.

"Yes, and so I wish to go to as many entertainments as I possibly can," agreed Margaret. "Grandmama may be thinking of marrying me off, but I shan't turn my thoughts in that direction any time soon. I am still young. Why should I be anxious to wed? Now Sarah is already turned nineteen. I suppose she must have given it more thought than I have."

Sarah felt her face heat up under Mrs. Jeffries's swift, appraising glance. "Margaret, you do have a knack for leaving one in an awkward way."

Mrs. Jeffries laughed. "Never mind, Sarah! There is no disparagement connected to wishing to have an offer made to one. On the contrary! It is understood. And no doubt you will have your choice of the gentlemen."

"Grandmama is giving a small dinner party for us in a few days," said Margaret. "Will you be coming to it, Elizabeth? I do hope so, for then we shall know at least one person there!"

Mrs. Jeffries shook her head. "No, I fear not. I am not so well acquainted with Lady Alverley that I figure as one of her bosom-bows," she said easily. "Ah, here is a good place for a canter! Let us try the paces of your horses, shall we?"

The time passed very pleasantly. When Mrs. Jeffries suggested that they ought to return to the town house, Sarah and Margaret were regretful. "I had no notion that the time has passed so quickly!" exclaimed Margaret.

"It always does when one is enjoying oneself," said Mrs. Jeffries. "And that is the neatest compliment that you could have paid me, Margaret." The three ladies conversed easily on a number of topics until they reached Alverley House. Then Lady Alverley's groom helped Sarah and Margaret descend to the pavement and took the horses in charge.

"We do thank you, Elizabeth," said Sarah, reaching up with her gloved hand. Mrs. Jeffries grasped her fingers for the briefest of moments. "We will ride together again soon, shan't we?"

"Tomorrow morning, if you like," said Mrs. Jeffries.

Sarah and Margaret agreed to it, each expressing anticipation and pleasure. Mrs. Jeffries promised to bring a friend or two with her when she came. "I do not wish you to become too bored in my company," she said, laughing at their quick protests. "And besides, it will make for a merry outing." She gathered her reins and waved a final good-bye before trotting off, her brown-liveried groom keeping pace behind her.

Chapter Six

As they entered the town house, Sarah and Margaret speculated about whom Mrs. Jeffries intended to include in their riding party on the morrow. "I imagine that it will be a couple of her friends whom she believes we shall like," said Sarah.

"I shan't mind that at all if they prove to be as friendly and open as Elizabeth," said Margaret as she began to pull off her riding gloves.

"No, indeed," agreed Sarah. "Quite the contrary, in fact. I shall enjoy meeting others who like getting out as much as we do."

The footman who took their whips and gloves informed Sarah and Margaret that her ladyship had risen and she had left instructions that her granddaughters were to attend her in her bedchamber whenever they had returned.

"Pray tell her ladyship that we have returned this moment, and that we shall do so as soon as we have changed," said Sarah.

The footman bowed in acknowledgment. "I shall do so, miss."

The sisters hurriedly went upstairs to their respective rooms to change out of their habits and put on suitable daydresses. "I asked Holby to see to a torn flounce earlier, so more than likely she is in my room. I shall send her to you as soon as I can," said Margaret, opening the door to her bedroom.

Sarah nodded and entered her own bedroom. She was surprised when she found a quiet individual, who introduced herself as Bordon, waiting for her.

"Her ladyship thought it best that each of you had your own maid, miss, and Holby deemed it to be her place to care for the younger miss," said Bordon woodenly.

"Oh, I see. Of course," said Sarah. And she thought that she did. Lady Alverley had directed things as she thought to be for the best and Holby, though undoubtedly torn about where her duty should take her, had chosen to take Margaret in hand. Though Sarah regretted losing the comfortable services of one whom she had known virtually all of her life, she nevertheless appreciated Holby's wisdom in remaining with Margaret. Her sister was lively and imaginative, and sometimes needed a firm hand to dampen her enthusiastic starts.

When Sarah and her sister presented themselves to their grandmother, Lady Alverley informed them that she had several calls to make that day and that they were to accompany her.

"I have decided to take you with me when I make my calls today, and I have drawn up a list of particular friends to whom I wish to introduce you before my little gathering," said Lady Alverley. Her ladyship was still attired in her silk wrapper and was sitting up in bed with a number of laced pillows supporting her. She wore a cap over her tinted hair and she was sipping at a cup of hot chocolate. Several sheets of note paper and a newspaper were scattered across her coverlet.

"We are honored, of course," said Sarah.

"So you should be," said Lady Alverley. She critically surveyed her granddaughters' appearances. "Is that all that you have to wear?"

Sarah and Margaret exchanged glances. "Yes, ma'am, I am afraid so," said Sarah, hiding a smile.

Lady Alverley sighed. "Well, I suppose it will have to do until the other dresses have come in. Actually, I suppose that you do not appear all that badly, considering that those gowns were made by some unknown provincial seamstress."

"We have some very pretty Cashmere shawls that Miss Hanson had us purchase," offered Margaret.

Lady Alverley's face brightened. She nodded. "Good, good! That will do admirably. Go retrieve them at once. I shall be readied in one hour. Pray do not keep me waiting. Now you may kiss me and go away. I shall see you again presently."

An hour later, Lady Alverley led the way down the steps of the town house. Her ladyship was handed up into the carriage and her granddaughters after her. Margaret looked wide-eyed at Sarah, and surreptitiously motioned at the entourage that Lady Alverley deemed necessary for driving about town.

As her granddaughters would shortly learn, Lady Alverley always drove out in state. Her ladyship's carriage was attended by two powdered footmen in her well-known green-and-russet livery and the bewigged coachman wore a three-cornered hat and French gloves. "I feel like the Queen must," whispered Margaret behind her hand.

Lady Alverley heard her. With a smile, she stated, "Her Majesty would never travel without an escort as I do."

Sarah glanced at her sister, and they smiled at each other. Town ways were very different, thought Sarah, and she knew that Margaret was thinking the same.

A whirling round of social visits began. The week passed virtually in a blur for Sarah. After the early rides with Mrs. Jeffries, occasionally in company with some of her friends, there were always social calls to make with Lady Alverley. During these social visits, Sarah and Margaret were introduced to their hostesses, who were pleased to pronounce Lady Alverley's granddaughters to be charming additions to the London scene.

Not many days later, Lady Alverley was able to produce vouchers for Almack's for her granddaughters and flourished them in front of their eyes. Her ladyship nearly purred with satisfaction. "Now you are well on your way to being established. I knew that my connections would not fail me."

Many of the dresses and gowns that had been promised by the modiste were delivered in the latter half of the week. Each had to be tried on and shown to Lady Alverley, who critically pronounced judgment on them all. Most were acceptable, but a few had to be returned to the modiste for small alterations. One of the gowns that Margaret put on had broad lime green stripes and was instantly and roundly condemned by her grandmother. "I don't know what you were about, Marie! Those stripes! And those furbelows and ribbons and laces! Why, she looks like something off the stage!" exclaimed Lady Alverley.

Miss Hanson bit her lip. "This was not my doing, my lady, I assure you! There must have been a mistake in direction." She completely ignored the fact that the gown fit Margaret perfectly.

"Yes, I can see that! Send it back immediately!" said Lady Alverley.

"I thought it was rather pretty," said Margaret, disappointed.

"It is not a debutante's gown," said Lady Alverley with finality.

Miss Hanson combined further dress fittings and shopping trips around town with gentle lectures on social niceties. She told Sarah and Margaret that on no account could they walk down Bond Street or St. James's Street in the afternoon, though it was permissible in the mornings if they were accompanied by a maid or other servant to protect them from the ogling of gentlemen.

"In addition, a lady must always be accompanied at least by her maid when she goes about town," said Miss Hanson, indicating the two maids who followed a few paces behind them.

"I can see the sense in that if one is going to be shopping," whispered Margaret to Sarah. "For otherwise how could one carry home all of these parcels?"

Sarah gave a gurgle of laughter. "Too true!" Both she and Margaret were carrying parcels and so were the maids.

"Margaret, attend to me, if you please," said Miss Hanson. She turned into a shop advertising itself as W. H. Botibel, Plumassier. Her charges followed her like obedient geese. Miss Hanson picked up a few sprays of artificial flowers. "These lovely bunches of flowers will look quite charming in your hair at a small ball. Oh, that reminds me! On no account must you dance three times in the same evening with the same gentleman. Otherwise you shall give rise to talk that you have become affiancéd to the gentleman."

Sarah shook her head, the ready laughter springing again to her hazel eyes. "How nonsensical! One could simply be enjoying that gentleman's expertise."

"Think what you like, Sarah, but do not forget!" admonished Miss Hanson, and turned to the proprietor to pay for her choices.

Sarah and Margaret quickly became patrons of Gunther's in Berkeley Square and indulged themselves in delicate pastries and sugar plums. They learned from Miss Hanson that St.

James's Street, Piccadilly, Bond Street, and the surrounding area was the most exclusive shopping district in London, and it was there that they began making a few small purchases for themselves. Sarah bought a charming straw hat for a guinea and thought it very well worth the price, while Margaret fell in love with a narrow, silver bangle bracelet and parted happily with a few coins.

However, more than all the rest of the fascinating places that they were steered through, Sarah and Margaret never grew tired of Regent Street. It was a wide, bright thoroughfare with arcades and shops that sported signs as big as a man, and stagecoaches piled high with people rumbled past constantly. It was not an unusual sight to see a horse rearing in front of a house as the rider saluted an acquaintance inside the building, or to see men carrying wooden advertisements for all sorts of entertainment. One particular day, the advertisements extolled the achievements of a troupe of performing cats.

"Oh, I do wish that we could see the cats," said Margaret. She slid a glance at Miss Hanson. "And Astley's Circus!"

"I have already told you, Margaret, these sorts of entertainment are best left to those too vulgar to appreciate a finer society or to feckless young men," said Miss Hanson reprovingly.

Margaret sighed. "It seems so unfair. I should still like to see the performing cats and the riding spectaculars. And I do not think that I am vulgar in the least."

"No, of course, you are not, Margaret," said Sarah on a gurgle of laughter. "I, too, am curious. What in the world do the cats do?" It was an unanswerable question, but that did not deter Sarah and Margaret from proposing every absurdity that came to mind. Miss Hanson rolled her eyes and shook her head, maintaining a patient expression.

When they returned to the town house, it was to be greeted with the intelligence that Lady Alverley was entertaining a visitor and had requested that her granddaughters join her if they should return in time. "You must go upstairs at once and put off your hats and gloves," said Miss Hanson. "Herbert, pray convey to her ladyship that we shall all be down again shortly."

"Of course, Miss Hanson," said the butler.

When Sarah and her sister returned downstairs and were

ushered into the sitting room, Sarah was a little disconcerted to discover that the visitor was none other than Lord Eustace. His lordship rose to his feet as she and Margaret entered. "My lord!" exclaimed Sarah.

Lord Eustace approached to take Sarah's hand. He smiled down into her astonished eyes. "Miss Sommers, I am happy that I was able to catch you upon your return. Miss Hanson has just come in and has been telling me that you and your sister have been extremely active since coming to town. I hope that you are adjusting well to town life?"

"Perfectly, Lord Eustace," said Sarah, smiling up at him. "My sister and I have found much to interest us."

"I am certain that must be true," said Lord Eustace, releasing her hand and turning to the younger miss. His smile was particularly warm as he greeted her. "What have you liked best, Miss Margaret?"

Sarah had quietly gone to take her seat beside Miss Hanson on the settee, while Lord Eustace escorted her sister to another settee. Her sister's vivid blue eyes gleamed as she returned the gentleman's smile. "Oh, I have liked everything, my lord! Gunther's and shopping and riding!" said Margaret with animation. "I should like to see Astley's Circus and the performing cats, too, but Miss Hanson says that only young gentlemen are allowed to go to those sorts of entertainments."

Sarah heard Miss Hanson utter a distressed murmur. At once, she realized that Miss Hanson thought that Margaret was being unbecomingly forward. Sarah glanced swiftly at her grandmother for that lady's reaction, but she saw that Lady Alverley's expression held only benign approval.

"Performing cats?" Lord Eustace sent an inquiring glance in Sarah's direction.

"We saw advertisements for them in Regent Street when we were out with Miss Hanson earlier. Our curiosity was not unnaturally aroused," said Sarah with a smile.

"Yes, I can see why." Lord Eustace laughed and turned back to Margaret. "I cannot recommend the performing cats, Miss Sommers, having never seen them. I suspect, too, that Miss Hanson is quite correct in her assessment of the probable audience. However, I have attended Astley's Circus several times and I have found nothing at all to object to in the perfor-

mances. The horsemanship is superb. My brothers and sister
and I have often attended through the years and we have never
tired of it."

"I believe that I saw the first performance ever given at Astley's. As I recall, I enjoyed the equestrian show very much,"
said Lady Alverley.

Margaret stared at her grandmother. "You, Grandmama?"

"Why, yes. What is there in that?" asked Lady Alverley,
raising her eyebrows.

"Nothing at all, ma'am," said Margaret hastily, casting a
quick glance at Miss Hanson.

Miss Hanson frowned at her.

"If Lady Alverley would permit, perhaps you and your sister would like to join my sister, Lady Frobisher, and I as our
guests. We are taking my nephews for their first sight of Astley's one day next week," said Lord Eustace.

"Oh!" Margaret's eyes rounded with excitement. She
clasped her hands in front of her bosom and turned to Lady
Alverley. "Oh, Grandmama, may we? Pray say yes!"

Lady Alverley smiled. "I believe that it would be quite an
unexceptional outing. I am well acquainted with Lord Eustace's sister, Lady Frobisher, and I can think of few whom I
could trust to better chaperone you. Certainly you may go,
Margaret. I am sure that you and Sarah will enjoy the treat."

"I shall have my sister get in touch with you with the details," said Lord Eustace.

Lady Alverley nodded. "That will be most delightful, I am
certain. Now, Lord Eustace, I have not had an opportunity to
ask yet about your lady mother. I trust that she is well?"

"Indeed she is, my lady. You are kind to inquire. In fact, I
am on an errand for her today. She has charged me with her
greetings and an invitation to your ladyship to take tea with
her tomorrow," said Lord Eustace, encompassing all of the
ladies in his smile.

"How nice! We shall be delighted, of course," said Lady
Alverley.

After Lord Eustace had left, Lady Alverley turned to her
granddaughters. Her expression was one of great satisfaction.
"You will naturally accompany me when I go to take tea with
his lordship's mother, Lady Eustace. It appears to me that

Lord Eustace has quite made up his mind to pay court to one or the other of you. Don't you think so, too, Marie?"

"Undoubtedly, my lady. It is without question. Why, whatever other reason could Lord Eustace have for volunteering his escort for an outing to Astley's Circus?" said Miss Hanson, nodding in a worldly fashion.

"Precisely," said Lady Alverley. "I am very glad that you brought up Astley's Circus, Margaret. It has worked out very well. You see how quickly Lord Eustace leaped upon the opportunity to further his acquaintance with you both!"

"But this is too absurd, ma'am!" exclaimed Sarah with an astonished look.

Lady Alverley raised her brows and looked at her coolly. "Why is that, Sarah?"

"You have built upon something that is so simply explained, after all," said Sarah. "I am persuaded that his lordship included Margaret and me into his party out of mere kindness. Anyone could see how much Margaret wished to go!"

"My dear Sarah, gentlemen as a rule do not involve themselves in such family outings. Astley's Circus and grubby nephews, indeed! I wish I might believe it," said Lady Alverley with a snort.

Miss Hanson gave a titter of laughter. "Indeed, my lady! One's imagination fairly boggles."

"But don't you think that Lord Eustace wants to go to Astley's Circus?" asked Margaret, puzzled by her grandmother's words.

"My dear, I would be greatly astonished to learn that Lord Eustace has patronized such tame entertainment in years. I would also be astonished to learn that Lady Frobisher knows anything at all about this projected outing as yet," said Lady Alverley. "I am quite certain that Lord Eustace is at this moment sending a note round to his sister to tell her about what he has already arranged with you and Sarah."

"That is undoubtedly true, my lady," said Miss Hanson, nodding.

"I think that I would rather believe that Lord Eustace is simply being kind," said Sarah slowly. Her grandmother's supposition was taking them too fast, she thought. She did not like to think that Lord Eustace was trying to fix his interest with either her or Margaret. Surely gentlemen did not rush into such things so heedlessly. It would make the outing so uncomfortable now that the suggestion had been planted in her head.

"Just as you will, Sarah. But let me point out that, as a rule, a gentleman does not pointedly issue an invitation for the young ladies' guardian to join his mother for tea," said Lady Alverley tartly.

"But is Lady Eustace not an intimate acquaintance of yours, ma'am?" asked Sarah, her brows drawing together. "I quite assumed that to be the case."

"Well, it is not. Lady Eustace and I know one another, of course, but we are scarcely intimates!" said Lady Alverley. She shook her head. "No; Lord Eustace is quite definitely intrigued. But I have not made up my mind which of you it is whom he prefers. He certainly showed no preference while he was here. You always have you an opinion to advance, Sarah. Which of you is it?"

Sarah frowned slightly, not at all certain that she liked this sort of speculation. Certainly that was all it was, too. Even so, Lady Alverley's observations had set her thinking. She recalled how captivated Lord Eustace had seemed to be with Margaret's vivacious conversation when he had given them a lift to the inn.

"All I can say is that from the first, Lord Eustace seemed to be quite taken with Margaret," said Sarah, throwing a speculative glance at her sister. She really did not give much credence to Lady Alverley's assertion that Lord Eustace had been enthralled by either of them, but it was true that he had enjoyed Margaret's chatter during the short time that they shared his carriage with him.

Margaret shook her head quickly. "Oh no, it cannot possibly be me. Why, Lord Eustace is far older than I am. It must be you that he likes, Sarah."

"Never mind, my dears! I see that you are both determined to deny anything is in the wind. It scarcely matters at this juncture, however," said Lady Alverley. "We must go carefully, of course. I do not wish to scare off Lord Eustace if he is beginning to consider marriage at last."

"Grandmama! How can you talk so? We scarcely know the gentleman and already you have Margaret wed," said Sarah.

"No, she's talking about you," said Margaret quickly.

Lady Alverley threw up her hand to put a stop to what appeared about to degenerate into a pointless argument. "I would be satisfied to welcome an offer from him for either of you. However, that is a premature hope as yet."

"I should say so!" exclaimed Sarah.

Lady Alverley frowned at her. "I charge you both to make yourselves agreeable while in his lordship's company. Lady Frobisher will naturally be wondering at her brother's inclusion of two unknown misses into a family party. She will also be aware that you have sat at tea with her mother at Lord Eustace's instigation. Naturally, she will be curious."

"Do you mean that she will ask us if we like her brother?" asked Margaret, appalled.

"I don't think that Lady Frobisher will cross that line just yet. However, she will be watching you and forming an opinion, you may be certain of that. So pray do make a good impression. I should not like to think that Lord Eustace's budding ardor was cooled because his sister happened to take an aversion to you," said Lady Alverley.

Sarah and Margaret looked at each other. Sarah could easily read her sister's expression of disenchantment, and Margaret's next words confirmed it.

"It almost makes me not want to go to Astley's Circus at all," said Margaret in a deflated tone.

Sarah tried to rally her sister. "Nonsense! You know how much you have longed to see it. We shall just make the best of it, Margaret," she said, with a reassuring smile.

"Very practical, Sarah," said Lady Alverley approvingly. "One's attitude is most important to one's success, as you will quickly discover."

"It seems that everything in the world has a bearing upon our success," murmured Sarah.

Chapter Seven

Lady Eustace received Lady Alverley's party in her boudoir. She was a pretty woman, with regular features and a very keen pair of gray eyes. A single streak of white, startling against her dark hair, winged back from her broad brow, disappearing under the ravishing lace cap that she wore. She welcomed her visitors graciously. "Forgive me for not rising," she said, smiling. "I am invalided, as you can see." She was seated in a wheelchair and a large shawl covered her lap and skirts.

Lady Alverley went up to take the slender hand that her hostess had extended. "I am happy to see you looking so well, however, my lady."

"Oh, yes. I am never ill," said Lady Eustace cheerfully.

Lady Alverley introduced her granddaughters. "This is my eldest granddaughter, Miss Sarah Sommers, and this is Miss Margaret."

Lady Eustace looked up at the younger ladies as they also politely shook hands. "How like your mother you both look! Though she was quite fair, fairer than you, Miss Margaret, you have both inherited the shape of her lovely eyes and her delightful profile."

"Then you knew our mother?" asked Sarah, surprised.

"Quite well. Pray sit down and make yourselves at ease," said Lady Eustace. She waited until Lady Alverley and her granddaughters had seated themselves before she continued. "I was already wed when Annabelle Alverley came out. She was barely seventeen and I was already a matron with two lively toddlers, so one might assume that there was too much of a gulf between us. But we became friends, of sorts. Do you recall, Lady Alverley?"

"Indeed. You and my daughter were often in one another's company," said Lady Alverley with a polite smile.

Lady Eustace easily read the questions in Sarah and Margaret's eyes that they were too polite to utter. She laughed and lightly touched her covered knees. "I was not as you see me now, of course. The hunting accident that robbed me of my mobility happened many years later. In those days, however, I danced and rode better than most. That was the real tie between Annabelle and myself. We enjoyed the same activities. She had few equals on the dance floor or in the fields on a hunter, did she, my lady?"

"No; no, she did not," said Lady Alverley in a somewhat strangled voice.

Lady Eustace looked swiftly at Lady Alverley and quick concern touched her face. She reached out to squeeze her ladyship's gloved hand. "Forgive me, Lady Alverley. I did not realize that such happy memories would bring pain to you."

Lady Alverley stiffened her carriage. "You need not apologize, my lady. I am perfectly all right, I assure you. I had forgotten so much and had not realized—"

Lady Eustace nodded. She picked up a silver bell from the occasional table that was next to her chair and rang it. "I have been terribly remiss. I have yet to offer refreshments to you. Allow me to do so now."

A door opened and two footmen entered, bearing trays. A lavish tea was spread before the ladies, and in a few minutes they were sipping tea and had accepted several biscuits and small cakes. Lady Eustace took only a cup of tea, laced generously with cream. She easily led the conversation in general topics, making inquiries about what the Season had in store for Lady Alverley's granddaughters.

Lady Alverley responded to her hostess's polite queries. Soon her ladyship was describing the many delightful plans that she had made for Sarah and Margaret, which included a grand ball, presentation at Court, and their debut at Almack's. "I have already procured the vouchers for Almack's, which you will no doubt understand has pleased me very much."

"Oh, yes, I can see how it must have," said Lady Eustace. "You are beforehand with the world, Lady Alverley, for many of our young misses are not so fortunate to begin the Season so situated."

Lady Alverley accepted the compliment with a smile. "I am beginning with just a small gathering, of course, just to see how they go on. Naturally I do not anticipate any difficulty, for Sarah and Margaret are well brought up due to the influence of a superior governess. However, I should like them to gain a measure of confidence in company before I fully launch them."

"Of course. That is very understandable. I have often thought it such a shame that so many of our young misses are simply thrown into society without having the advantage of getting their feet wet first. You are wise, my lady," said Lady Eustace. Lady Alverley bestowed a gratified nod on her, and Lady Eustace turned to her other two guests. "And what are your thoughts on all of this, Miss Sommers, Miss Margaret? I suppose that it must all seem to be rather overwhelming at this point."

"We have not had much leisure to think about it, my lady, and perhaps that is just as well," said Sarah with a smile. "Miss Hanson has taken us shopping and subjected us to measurings and fittings ever since we first arrived, while Grandmama has taken us with her when she makes her calls."

"And we ride most mornings with Mrs. Jeffries," said Margaret, nodding. "So we have already become very busy."

"And do you like this new schedule?" asked Lady Eustace.

"I like it very much. I am very happy to have to come up to London," said Margaret with bright eyes.

"And I, also," said Sarah. "Grandmama has been everything that is kind to us."

Lady Eustace chuckled. "I am glad for you, my dear. Lady Alverley, they are delightful."

"Thank you, Lady Eustace." Lady Alverley looked proud. "I have already enjoyed having them with me."

The door opened. Lord Eustace stepped in, but paused with his hand still on the doorknob. "May I join you, ma'am, or is it a private party?" he asked with a smile.

Sarah had hoped that Lord Eustace would be taking tea with them. When they had arrived and she had seen that he was not present, she had been disappointed. Now she felt an upsurge of gladness. His lordship was such a kind gentleman. It was a pleasure to see him again, naturally.

At her son's query, Lady Eustace at once held out her hand. "Gil! Of course you may join us. You do not mind, Lady Alverley, I hope?"

"Of course not," said Lady Alverley, smiling.

"Thank you, my lady," said Lord Eustace, closing the door and going over to salute his mother. He took her hand and bent down to kiss her cheek. "You appear delightfully, ma'am. Is it a new cap?"

Lady Eustace put her hand up to the scrap of lace on her hair. "You have noticed! How sweet of you, my dear! Yes, it is new. I had Martha purchase it for me only yesterday."

"Very fetching," said Lord Eustace approvingly.

Lady Eustace turned a laughing countenance toward her guests. There was a hint of pink in her cheeks. "You see how I am blessed in my son. He is quick to flatter me and pay just the sort of attentions to me that every lady prefers."

"You are fortunate, indeed, my lady," said Lady Alverley. She bestowed a nod on Lord Eustace as he turned from greeting his mother and took her own hand. "My lord, it is always a pleasure. I must always bear you a debt of gratitude for coming in so timely a fashion to the aid of my granddaughters."

"I did only what anyone would have done, my lady," said Lord Eustace easily. He turned to greet Sarah and Margaret. They were seated together on a settee. "I need not ask how you are, for it is evident that you are both in great beauty."

Sarah blushed. "Thank you, my lord."

Margaret flashed a bright-eyed smile at him. "Yes, thank you, Lord Eustace! You are quite one of our favorite acquaintances, for you have such divine manners."

Lord Eustace laughed, while his mother hid a smile behind her hand. "I think that I have had my compliment rather neatly returned to me," he commented.

"Margaret is wonderfully forthright, as you can see," said Lady Alverley smoothly. "She speaks but the truth, however. Lord Eustace has become a favorite of us all. I trust that we shall be seeing more of you in the future, my lord."

Lord Eustace pulled a wingback chair near the gathering, so that he was seated between his mother and the two sisters.

"Certainly you shall, my lady. I was telling my mother at breakfast of the delightful outing that my sister and I have planned to Astley's Circus. She was naturally very much in favor of my invitation to Miss Sommers and Miss Margaret."

"Yes, indeed," said Lady Eustace with a smiling glance toward the younger ladies. "I well recall how one can take the greatest delight in the simplest of entertainments. I was never more surprised—I mean, glad to hear that my son had decided to take my advice. I have urged Gilbert often lately to mingle with a livelier set, for he has grown too preoccupied with my concerns."

"Nonsense, ma'am. You know that I enjoy looking out for your interests," said Lord Eustace. He looked around at Lady Alverley and her granddaughters. "You probably do not know, for my mother does not like to exalt herself. My mother is a benefactress to several orphanages."

"No, I was not aware," said Lady Alverley, obviously surprised.

"But how admirable!" exclaimed Sarah.

"Thank you, my dear. I find it to be extremely satisfying," said Lady Eustace. She waved her hand around the beautifully furnished boudoir. "I am very comfortably cared for, as you can see. Since the accident, I have had much time to reflect and to read things about our world to which I previously had not paid much attention. Oh, one gathers impressions about things, of course. But one really does not know what is happening until one has the time to look around. I discovered that I did not like myself very well, for my life did not seem to count for much."

"That is not true," said Lord Eustace quickly.

Lady Eustace reached out and briefly squeezed his hand. "You are biased. I have told you so. Regardless, my feelings were quite the opposite. So I decided to involve myself in orphanages and providing schooling and training for the poor children who have been left to fend for themselves all over this city."

Lady Alverley was regarding her hostess with an open mouth. She seemed to have been struck speechless. Margaret also was looking at Lady Eustace with wide eyes.

"Are there a great number of such children, ma'am?" asked Sarah.

Lady Eustace nodded. "Regretfully, yes. So many have lost their fathers in the war and some are castoffs from families that are simply too poor to care for them. I am associated with several orphanages now, some in the city proper and some that have been established in the country. It is my hope that with proper food and shelter and training, these poor creatures will be able to better themselves, and to find employment when it is time."

"But surely—" Lady Alverley shook her head. "Forgive me, Lady Eustace, but it seems to me that it is a rather . . . daunting project. You cannot hope to save every dirty street urchin, surely. And those whom you do befriend, shall they not turn against all that you have attempted to do for them and return to the very squalor that bred them? It is breeding that tells in the end, is it not?"

"God willing, I trust and hope that Christian charity will overcome such disadvantages, my lady," said Lady Eustace, smiling. She reached out to her son again, lightly touching his sleeve. "I owe much of my present contentment to my son. He has been my faithful deputy in all ways."

"Indeed!" said Lady Alverley on a note of astonishment.

"I do not take to myself all of the glory. My mother's man-of-business handles all of the myriad details that are associated with such charities, but I occasionally visit the orphanages to be certain that all is being done as it should be. In fact, that is where I was headed when I came across the accident to your granddaughters' coach, my lady," said Lord Eustace.

Sarah thoughtfully regarded his lordship. She did not think that she would be surprised to discover that he had down-played his role in governing Lady Eustace's charities. She liked him the better for it, appreciating his innate modesty.

"Your previous engagement! That is why you could not stay to dine with us," said Margaret.

Lord Eustace suddenly met Sarah's gaze. "Precisely, Miss Margaret," he agreed.

Sarah smiled at him. She recalled very well that Lord Eustace had been taken aback by Margaret's innocuous invitation and that he had obviously understood her own attempt to shield her sister from possible censure. It was kind of him now not to reveal the particulars of that dinner invitation, for certainly Lady Alverley, at least, would be horrified to know how free Margaret's conduct had been.

"Have you and Mary decided upon a firm date to take my grandsons to Astley's Circus?" asked Lady Eustace.

"Indeed, we have. Has my sister yet contacted you, Lady Alverley?" said Lord Eustace.

"There was a very pretty note from Lady Frobisher in this morning's post," said Lady Alverley, nodding. "Lady Frobisher mentioned Tuesday next, I believe."

Lord Eustace nodded. "I hope that is agreeable, my lady?"

"Quite," said Lady Alverley, smiling at him. "Sarah and Margaret will be delighted to join your party that afternoon."

"Oh, yes! I shall look forward to nothing else all week!" exclaimed Margaret.

Sarah chuckled, her hazel eyes gleaming with fun. "Why, Margaret, how is this? I thought you had any number of things that you wished to do this week?"

"Well, perhaps only half as much," amended Margaret.

Everyone else laughed, while Margaret good-naturedly shook her head, not minding at all. Lady Eustace addressed Margaret. "After you have been, you must be sure to come to visit me again, for I shall want to hear all about everything."

"Oh, I shall do so indeed, my lady," said Margaret promptly. "I promise you! You are such a gracious lady that I know that I shall feel very comfortable in talking with you again."

"You are a good, kind girl," said Lady Eustace.

"Indeed, she is," agreed Lady Alverley, throwing a pleased glance at her youngest granddaughter.

While the other ladies talked, Lord Eustace had turned to Sarah. "I know that you do not look forward to the outing with the same enthusiasm as your sister, Miss Sommers. I hope that you will not be too bored."

"I do not think that I shall be, my lord," said Sarah, a little surprised by his statement. "I am very willing to be amused, I assure you."

Lord Eustace smiled. "My sister expressed some concern to me that I was dragging you into what is, after all, a juvenile party. I described you to her as a young lady of good understanding and that put her into a quake. She hopes that you will not find it too dull to be obliged to spend an afternoon with her children."

"I hope that I am not so starched-up that I cannot enjoy myself in whatever company I find myself, my lord!" exclaimed Sarah, laughing.

"You relieve my mind, Miss Sommers," said Lord Eustace.

"But now I have been put in a quake, my lord," said Sarah, twinkling at him. "What will Lady Frobisher expect of me?"

"My sister is excessively good-natured, as is her husband, Lord Frobisher. They are very much devoted to one another and to their children. I don't think that you need fear anything from their hands, Miss Sommers," said Lord Eustace reassuringly.

"I am already predisposed to like them," said Sarah.

Lord Eustace gave a slight bow from the waist. "And you will be well received by them, I assure you."

A moment later Lady Alverley announced that it was time to take their leave of Lady Eustace. "I have thoroughly enjoyed myself, my lady," she said, giving her hand to her hostess.

"I am glad. Come back at any time, my lady. And you, also, Margaret, Sarah! You will always be welcome," said Lady Eustace.

When the leave-takings were done, Lord Eustace offered to escort Lady Alverley and her granddaughters to the door. "Thank you, my lord. That is exceedingly kind," said Lady Alverley.

When they emerged from the town house, Lord Eustace himself helped all of them up into Lady Alverley's carriage. As the carriage rolled away, Lady Alverley said, "Well, I thought that went very well. Lady Eustace is charming, though I thought she has grown to be a bit odd, too. However, I understand it often happens thus with recluses and invalids."

"Why, what do you mean? I found Lady Eustace to be quite interesting," said Sarah.

"And I, also. It is such a wonderful thing that her ladyship is attempting to do," said Margaret.

"That is precisely what I meant when I said that Lady Eustace has become a bit odd," said Lady Alverley. "No one in their right mind spends literally a fortune on such charities! Why, it is absurd! What can one gain from it?"

"Obviously her ladyship enjoys the satisfaction of helping others," said Sarah.

Lady Alverley shook her head. "Ridiculous! In my opinion, Lady Eustace is casting away her substance to no good purpose."

"Why, don't you believe in helping the poor, Grandmama?" asked Margaret, astonished.

"Of course I do. But there must be limits, my dear," said Lady Alverley. "Individuals of our class have no business indulging such fanatical ideals. I am surprised that Lord Eustace so readily accepts his mother's folly."

"Would it be more acceptable if Lady Frobisher were to gamble away her fortune?" asked Sarah.

Lady Alverley narrowed her eyes, regarding her eldest granddaughter with a cold gaze. "That was both impertinent and stupid, Sarah. I believe that I have made perfectly clear my views on wasting one's fortune away with excessive gambling. This is not the same thing at all."

"It was fortunate that Lord Eustace came in. He was extremely obliging," said Margaret hurriedly.

Lady Alverley's attention was nicely diverted. Her ladyship nodded with sudden complacency. "Nothing could have exceeded his lordship's civility. What was Lord Eustace saying to you toward the last, Sarah?"

"He merely wanted to assure me that Lady Frobisher was anticipating our inclusion into her party," said Sarah.

Lady Alverley gave an amused smile. "Whatever may have been said to the contrary, I believe that this whole expedition was dreamed up by Lord Eustace. You cannot convince me that such an elegant gentleman has the least interest in spending an afternoon at Astley's unless he has other thoughts in mind."

"However that may be, ma'am, I am persuaded that Margaret and I shall enjoy ourselves famously," said Sarah.

Chapter Eight

Sarah liked Lady Frobisher on first meeting her. Lady Frobisher was a young matron in her early twenties, fashionably dressed in an azure-blue pelisse trimmed with ermine fur. A large upstanding velvet bonnet framed a pretty face and an inquisitive gaze. She came into the drawing room, escorted by her brother, and followed by her nanny and two small boys.

Sarah stared at the little boys in amazement. They were twins, each blond with large gray eyes and merry expressions, about three or four years old. They were dressed alike in belted smocks and pantaloons, and as far as Sarah could tell, there was not a distinguishing feature between them.

Giving her gloved hand to Lady Alverley, Lady Frobisher said with a laugh. "Do forgive me for bringing my little ones in with me, my lady! They objected to letting me out of their sight for even a moment. Edmund and John seem to think that I shall forget their treat if they are not with me to remind me."

"Perfectly all right, Lady Frobisher," said Lady Alverley graciously. She bestowed a wary glance on the two lively imps, who were tugging on their nurse's hands. "These are my granddaughters, Miss Sarah Sommers and Margaret."

"I am delighted to meet you. My brother has described to me the plight in which he found you. I am glad that neither of you took hurt," said Lady Frobisher.

"Thank you, my lady," said Sarah, smiling. "I am happy to make your acquaintance."

Margaret greeted Lady Frobisher also, but her attention swiftly returned to the twins. "And are these your sons? They are positively adorable!" she exclaimed.

Lady Frobisher and Lord Eustace laughed in unison. "You may change your opinion once you have been in their company for any length of time, Miss Margaret," said Lady Frobisher.

"They are hardened rapscallions," said Lord Eustace roundly. His nephews shot him gap-toothed grins, apparently delighted with this encomium.

One of them suddenly broke loose from the nanny. Promptly his twin emitted a cry of protest. Disregarding his brother's howl, the tiny boy ran over to grab Lord Eustace around the leg. He twinkled up at his uncle. "Up, Uncle Gil! Up!"

Lord Eustace bent down and swung him up onto his shoulder. He met Lady Alverley's incredulous gaze. "You see how I am used," he said.

"Indeed!" uttered Lady Alverley, her brows scaling into her hairline.

Lady Frobisher cast a glance at Lady Alverley as she took possession of her other son's hand. "Perhaps we should be going, Gilbert. I am certain that Lady Alverley has a myriad of things that she wishes to do this afternoon," she suggested.

Lord Eustace agreed, and in short order the party had taken leave of Lady Alverley and left the town house. "We are going in two carriages," said Lord Eustace. "It is impossible for all of us to fit into one. Who is riding with Mama?"

Both little boys vigorously rejected this option, giving it as their joint opinion that to drive with their uncle in his splendid curricle was much more entertaining than sitting with their mother. Lord Eustace gave way with good grace, laughing. "But I warn you, Edmund, John! Any fighting or one cross word and I shall put you down to ride with Nurse."

"We will be good, Uncle Gil," said one of the twins. The other nodded vigorously. "Yes, berry, berry good."

"See that you are!" said Lord Eustace in a menacing voice that sent his nephews into fits of giggling. He lifted them into the curricle.

Lady Frobisher picked up her skirts and entered her carriage. Sarah sat down beside her, while Margaret took the seat with her back to the horses. "I do hope that you do not mind this sort of family party," said Lady Frobisher anxiously.

"Not at all, my lady. We have never had the opportunity to

be much around children. I, for one, think that your sons are perfectly engaging," said Sarah.

"Oh, yes! They are such happy, merry little gentlemen," said Margaret. "I am going to sit next to them in Astley's Circus just so I can watch their faces. That is, if you permit, Lady Frobisher!"

Lady Frobisher laughed. "With my good will, Miss Margaret!"

Good relations thus being established, Lady Frobisher entertained her guests with little stories about her young family and amusing anecdotes about some of her friends in society. Sarah was not very long in realizing that Lady Frobisher was also subtlely eliciting information about her and her sister's backgrounds, as well. Sarah reflected that perhaps Lady Alverley had been more correct than she had given her ladyship credit for. Lady Frobisher did indeed seem inordinately curious about them.

Sarah and Margaret were amazed by their first glimpse of Astley's Circus. The building was built out of ships' masts and spars and a canvas ceiling was stretched on fir poles and lashed together with ropes. The rough interior was lit by a huge, brilliant chandelier, which Lord Eustace impressively informed everyone continued fifty patent lamps. Below the blazing chandelier, and in the midst of three tiers of spectator boxes, was the huge ring of sawdust. An orchestra was situated next to the ring and provided dramatic music for the performance.

For the next hour and a half, Sarah and the others were enthralled by superb equestrian feats and trick riding. Lord Eustace had to forcibly restrain one of his nephews from his announced intention to jump down into the ring and run after the horses.

"I agree, John, it is a very pretty horse," said Lord Eustace. "When you are older I will get you one just like it."

Instantly the other twin began to lobby his uncle, tugging imperatively on his coat sleeve. "Me, too, Uncle Gil! Me, too!"

"Yes, and one for you, too, Edmund," said Lord Eustace, laughing.

"How do you tell them apart?" asked Sarah.

"At the moment, I have only to count teeth," said Lord Eustace. At her disbelieving expression, he grinned. "I am perfectly serious, Miss Sommers. Currently Edmund has one more front tooth than John. When I am in doubt about which of them I am talking to, I demand to see their teeth."

Sarah choked on a laugh at the absurdity. "What shall you do when John gains another tooth?"

In a thoughtful voice, Lord Eustace said, "That possibility, Miss Sommers, haunts me."

Sarah laughed outright. "How absurd you are, to be sure!"

Lord Eustace affably agreed to it, also laughing.

Lady Frobisher looked around at them. She smiled, returning her attention almost at once to the equestrian show. She pointed for her sons. "Look, John, Edmund! See the lovely lady dancing on the back of the horse!"

"I can do vat," said one twin, critically watching the performance.

The other nodded. "Me, too."

When the performance was over, the twins exclaimed loudly and tearfully that they wanted the horses to come back. "It does seem as though the time has flown past," said Margaret regretfully.

Lord Eustace suggested getting an ice at Gunther's and his nephews' tears magically disappeared. "You spoil them terribly, Gilbert," said Lady Frobisher between laughter and irritation.

"That is what an uncle is good for," said Lord Eustace. He caught Miss Sarah's gaze upon him and smiled at her. "Do you not agree, Miss Sommers?"

"We did not see our own uncle very much as children, my lord, so how can I say?" said Sarah, amused. "However, I believe that I would have enjoyed such an uncle very much."

"There, Mary, you see? Miss Sommers approves," said Lord Eustace, winking at Sarah.

Sarah felt her face warming. She glanced up into his lordship's face, then away, uncertain what to make of Lord Eustace's friendly air. She was relieved when her sister created a diversion.

"And so do I! An ice at Gunther's!" exclaimed Margaret, clapping her hands just as enthusiastically as the twins.

Lady Frobisher laughed. "I am overruled, I perceive. Very well! An ice. But then I must return these two to the nursery for their naps or Nurse will be very irritable with me. Isn't that right, Nurse?"

"Aye, my lady. They'll be a handful if they don't have their nap," agreed the nanny with a benevolent smile.

Gunther's was a great success with the Frobisher twins. They happily consumed their ices under the supervision of their nanny while the rest of the party conversed at another table nearby. Eventually Lady Frobisher thought it best to bring the party to a close. She suggested that her brother escort their guests back to Lady Alverley's town house, while she went on her way with her sons and their nanny.

"For I see that Edmund is already nodding. He will fall asleep in a few minutes and John will not be far behind, so it is best that I take leave of you here," she said, holding out her hand in turn to Sarah and to Margaret.

"Thank you, my lady. We have enjoyed ourselves very much," said Sarah sincerely.

"Oh, yes! I have never seen anything quite like it," said Margaret with a bright, happy smile.

"I am glad. I trust that we will see each other again quite soon," said Lady Frobisher, also smiling. She turned to say something to Lord Eustace, who nodded. She went away to help the nanny with the twins. The small boys had wound down like slowing tops and they needed to be carried back to their mother's carriage.

Lord Eustace smiled at Sarah and Margaret. "Let me escort you out to my curricle. My sister has said her good-byes to me, also, preferring that I see that you get safely home."

Sarah accepted Lord Eustace's hand up into the curricle. She sat down and eased over to make room for Margaret. The vehicle rocked slightly when Lord Eustace climbed in and took up the reins. It was a tight fit on the seat. Sarah glanced at her sister's face. Margaret was in high spirits, her vivid blue eyes sparkling as she looked out over the horses' heads. She seemed oblivious that she was sitting close enough to Lord Eustace so that his shoulder occasionally brushed hers.

Sarah did not think that she would have been so insensitive if she were seated in her sister's place. That afternoon she had become aware of each nuance of Lord Eustace's voice and his every change of expression. She had very much liked sitting with him at Astley's Circus and exchanging cheerful observations about the performance. For her, it had seemed there had been a sort of rosy hue in the very air all afternoon.

"Did you enjoy yourself, Miss Margaret?" asked Lord Eustace, glancing at her with a glinting smile.

"There was never anything so wonderful!" exclaimed Margaret, turning her head and laughing.

Sarah saw a queer look cross his lordship's face, but then it vanished. He was laughing, too.

"I am glad," said Lord Eustace. He looked past Margaret and met Sarah's eyes. "And what of you, Miss Sommers? Was Astley's Circus everything that you had envisioned?"

"More, my lord, for I did not know what to expect," said Sarah. "I, too, found it a wonderful spectacle. I am glad that you included us in your party. It was extremely kind of you, for Margaret, in particular, wished to go."

"Not any more than my nephews, I daresay," said Lord Eustace dryly.

Sarah chuckled. "No, indeed!"

"Well, I did like it," said Margaret, tossing her head. "I daresay I will go back if I am ever invited by anyone to do so."

As Lord Eustace conversed with them, he guided his team expertly through the heavy traffic. The ribbons slipped through his fingers effortlessly, seemingly just a touch from them communicating everything necessary to the high-bred team of blacks that he drove. Sarah liked to watch his lordship's hands, for she appreciated the strength and skill that he was displaying as he drove.

"Here we are!" He pulled up at the curb in front of Lady Alverley's town house and snubbed the reins.

Lord Eustace jumped down to the pavement, then turned to help Margaret to descend. He put his hands around her waist and swung her down to the ground.

Margaret darted a laughing glance at him. "I am no featherweight, I believe, my lord!"

Lord Eustace only smiled and bowed. He turned to offer a hand up to Sarah. Guiding her with one hand, and the other supporting her elbow, he helped her to descend.

"Thank you, my lord," said Sarah, smiling up at him. "Will you come in?"

Lord Eustace escorted them up the stone steps to the door. At Sarah's query, he shook his head. "Thank you, but no, Miss Sommers. I have another engagement yet this afternoon. But be assured that I will call again." He lifted her hand to his lips for a brief salute. Then he turned to her sister.

Sarah watched as Margaret gave her hand to him, and how Lord Eustace lifted her fingers to his lips. It was not quite the same formal leave-taking that he had honored her with, Sarah abruptly realized. She glanced sharply at Lord Eustace's face. She saw that his lordship's eyes were fixed, with a queer sort of hunger in them, on her sister's bright countenance. With something of a squeeze in the vicinity of her heart, Sarah saw that Lord Eustace was very definitely interested in her sister.

When they entered the town house, Sarah was more than usually quiet. But Margaret did not notice. She continued to chatter away about the delightful outing that they had enjoyed.

Chapter Nine

The dawn of Lady Alverley's small gathering finally arrived. Days of preparations had gone into making a success of the evening. The pleasant scent of beeswax and the deep gleaming reflections of candlelight in the furniture attested to hours of polishing. Huge floral arrangements were delivered that afternoon and were distributed throughout the rooms, adding their delicate perfume to the air. Two hours before the guests were due to arrive, the gowns that Sarah and Margaret were to wear were delivered.

Sarah's gown was discovered to be too long for her, dragging on the floor. "What am I to do?" asked Sarah, casting an anxious glance at the clock. "There isn't time to send it back now!"

"Do not fret, miss. I'll have it fixed in a trice," said Bordon. The maid brought out a sewing basket and quickly set to work. She proved to be an excellent needlewoman, whipping up the hem in less time than Sarah thought possible.

After dressing, Sarah looked at herself in the looking-glass. She was attired in a simple round gown of palest pink that brought out the color in her cheeks and emphasized her dark hair and eyes. The dress had small slashed sleeves at the shoulders and a modest neckline. Sarah had put on a string of pearls, which had belonged to her mother, and a matching pair of earrings. Her hair was dressed in a knot on top of her head, wisps of natural curls softening her face.

"It is such a plain-looking gown, but I don't think that I've ever looked nicer," she remarked.

" 'Tis the making of the gown, Miss Sarah," said Bordon, expertly smoothing the long flowing lines of the skirt. "Her ladyship's modiste has a particular knack."

"And so do you, Bordon. I don't know what I would have done without you. Thank you," said Sarah.

The maid's stern face eased into a slight smile. "I am glad that I could help, miss."

The panel door in the corner of the bedroom opened and Holby came in. She nodded to Bordon, who stepped back to allow her full sight of Sarah's toilette.

"Well, Holby, how do I look?" asked Sarah, catching up her skirt and twirling round.

Holby's sharp gaze took her former mistress in from head to toe. She was not displeased by the efforts of her replacement. She nodded briskly. "You'll do very well, Miss Sarah. Bordon has done a very credible job."

"She performed a rescue, as well, Holby. The hem was too long and I was tripping over it every time that I took a step. Bordon shortened it almost quicker than I could blink," said Sarah, "She has a way with a needle."

"Aye, I can see that she does," said Holby.

There was a knock on the door and a maid entered to relay a summons to meet Lady Alverley downstairs. "I sent Miss Margaret off not a moment ago, Miss Sarah," said Holby.

"Then I must be close behind or her ladyship will wonder where I am," said Sarah. She allowed Bordon to slip her shawl over her elbows and arrange it in graceful folds. When she was ready, she smiled at her old retainer. "Wish me luck, Holby. I feel as though this might be one of the most important eves of my life."

Sarah descended the stairs and went into the drawing room. Her sister was already there with Lady Alverley. Sarah cast a fleeting glance at Margaret, wanting to see how her sister was turned out.

Margaret's gown was similar to her own, except that it was blue. The soft color caught the vividness of Margaret's blue eyes and brought out the honey blonde of her hair. A fillet of blue satin and pearls was twisted through her curls and a simple gold pendant hung around her slender neck.

Lady Alverley turned when Sarah entered. She inspected her eldest granddaughter's appearance with a critical eye while Sarah waited, smiling, for the verdict. Her ladyship nodded. "You'll do, Sarah."

"Thank you, Grandmama. I cannot hold a candle to you, however, ma'am," said Sarah, going over to kiss her grandmother's cheek.

"You are learning, dear child," said Lady Alverley. Her ladyship wore an emerald green satin with an overdress of Italian lace. A diamond set had been placed in her hair, holding a few esprits in place, and diamonds winked from her ears and around her wrinkled neck. Several bracelets graced her arms and rings circled every finger. A fine shawl dripped from her elbows.

"Margaret, you're beautiful! And Miss Hanson, too," said Sarah.

"Oh, I'm not half as pretty as you, Sarah," said Margaret admiringly. Her eyes sparkled. "Isn't it simply wonderful! I daresay I shan't sleep all night for the excitement."

Miss Hanson was elegantly dressed in a ruched crepe. She had adorned herself with several gold chains and wore carnelian drops in her ears and a carnelian bracelet. She opened an ivory fan and slowly fanned herself. "Naturally it will be quite exciting for you and Sarah."

"Sarah, when you came in I was telling Margaret what to expect this evening. I have invited an intimate number of my closest acquaintances," said Lady Alverley. "There will be a sprinkling of younger gentlemen, of course, but most of my guests come out of my own circle. This is because I wish more to generate invitations for you tonight than I wish to introduce you to any eligible partis."

"Dare I admit that I am just a bit relieved, ma'am?" asked Sarah with a laugh. "I confess the thought of facing a roomful of eligible gentlemen on our first evening had seemed rather daunting."

Lady Alverley nodded. "Quite understandable, but quite unnecessary. There will be time enough later to dazzle the male populace of London. Now come along! You and Margaret will stand in the receiving line with me for the first hour. Then you may be excused to join the rest of the company."

The musicians had arrived at seven-thirty and had already struck up. Sarah glanced around the drawing room, appreciating the flowers arranged everywhere. When Lady Alverley and her granddaughters stationed themselves at the door, it was eight and the first guests began to arrive. Most of the gentlemen wore cutaway coats and knee breeches. Their ladies were attired in elegant gowns, with plumes in their hair, and jewelry of every description on display.

The party filled the back drawing room and overflowed into the passage leading to the smaller room at the front of the town house. The harp and pianoforte accompaniment made a pleasant background to the flow of conversation and laughter.

Lady Alverley had already given permission for her granddaughters to be led away from the receiving line by portly admirers when Lord Eustace crossed the threshold. Lady Alverley at once greeted his lordship with a smile and an outstretched hand. "Lord Eustace! How good of you to come. I was not certain that you would honor me tonight with your presence, for the entertainment is only of modest fare."

Lord Eustace bowed over her ladyship's white-gloved fingers. "It is always a privilege, my lady. This early in the Season one has the leisure to choose invitations that are of particular exclusion."

Lady Alverley inclined her head, pleased with him. "Thank you, my lord. No doubt you would like to renew your acquaintance with my granddaughters. I must thank you again for coming so handily to their rescue, my lord. They told me that they would have been in dire straits indeed if you had not chanced by."

"I am glad that I could be of assistance," said Lord Eustace, slowly escorting her ladyship through the crowded company. They threaded their way, pausing often for Lady Alverley to acknowledge her guests and to bring Lord Eustace to the notice of the company. It was a coup for her to have been able to draw Lord Eustace to her first gathering.

Lady Alverley eventually guided Lord Eustace up to Sarah. "Sarah, Lord Eustace has honored us with his presence tonight. He desired in particular to renew his acquaintance with you."

Sarah cast a startled glance up at Lord Eustace's urbane expression and she murmured something appropriate. Lord Eustace bowed over her hand. As he straightened, he smiled down at her. "Will you honor me by taking a turn about the room, Miss Sommers?"

Sarah glanced toward Lady Alverley to gauge her reaction. Lady Alverley smiled and nodded. Sarah allowed only the slightest of smiles to curve her lips, but her hazel eyes gleamed with amusement. She could well read her grandmother's satisfaction at Lord Eustace's show of attention. "I shall be delighted, my lord," she said demurely, placing her gloved fingers lightly on his extended elbow.

Lord Eustace led Sarah slowly around the perimeter of the drawing room, nodding to various acquaintances as they caught his eye. He politely made conversation. "How are you enjoying this evening, Miss Sommers?"

"It is very bewildering and different from home. We lived very quietly," said Sarah honestly. "I have not quite gotten my social bearings, I fear. There are so many faces and names tonight that I have difficulty recalling them."

Lord Eustace smiled down at her. "I think it is the same for everyone who is used to living in the country. You will soon adjust, I daresay. How is your sister faring?"

"Margaret is quite happy whatever the circumstances. It is being in London for the Season, you see. She anticipates all sorts of excitements and wonderful happenings," said Sarah.

"And you do not, Miss Sommers?" asked Lord Eustace.

Sarah laughed and nodded her head. "Oh, yes, of course I do. But Margaret is far more excitable about such things than I am. She positively glows with enthusiasm whenever one mentions some new treat."

Lord Eustace's gaze traveled beyond Sarah's face to the young lady standing across the room. Miss Margaret Sommers was the center of a group of ladies and gentlemen and she was obviously enjoying herself. "Yes, so I perceive. Your sister is both lively and lovely. She will turn several heads this Season, I suspect."

"No doubt, my lord. My sister is a beautiful, charming girl," said Sarah warmly.

Lord Eustace looked back at her quickly. "There is an obvious affection between you."

Sarah nodded. "Yes, Margaret and I are very close. There is scarcely anything that we will not share with one another."

"Shall you share your admirers, too, Miss Sommers?" asked

Lord Eustace. When she looked up with a startled expression, he smiled. "Forgive me, Miss Sommers. I spoke out of turn."

Sarah was silent for a moment. "I suppose it is a natural question," she said thoughtfully. "I suppose that there usually is a certain rivalry between sisters, is there not? But I am persuaded that will not happen between myself and Margaret."

"Then you are fortunate. Such loyalty is rare and endearing," said Lord Eustace.

"Margaret and I could never be envious of one another," said Sarah positively.

Lord Eustace smiled again, more warmly. "I trust that it will remain so, Miss Sommers."

Miss Hanson walked up with a gentleman whom Sarah vaguely recognized from the receiving line. "Miss Sommers, I have brought over Baron Mittenger. He has expressed himself eager to be reminded to you," she said.

"Of course, baron. I remember you quite well from when we met earlier," said Sarah, smiling.

"I am delighted, Miss Sommers." The baron bowed over Sarah's hand. He was dressed very correctly in black evening attire. His coat fit perfectly a broad set of shoulders and he had a well-developed stocky physique. A broad silk riband crossed his chest and a foreign order was pinned to it. He wore no jewelry other than a heavy gold signet finger on his left hand, but several fobs and seals dangled from ribbons at his waist. Baron Mittenger was in his thirties, but his stiff bearing and the somberness of his dark-featured countenance made him appear to be older. The baron nodded politely to Lord Eustace. "My lord."

"Baron Mittenger." Lord Eustace lifted Sarah's hand to his lips in a brief polite salute. "Thank you for a delightful conversation, Miss Sommers. I look forward to furthering our short acquaintance," he said.

"And I," said Sarah, smiling. His lordship bowed and walked away. Baron Mittenger at once claimed her attention. Shortly thereafter, Sarah chanced to see Lord Eustace go over and seek out her sister.

Sarah and Margaret were drawn into conversation with a score of personages. Sarah did not enjoy her time with a couple of the elderly ladies. Mrs. Plummer was a sharp-featured woman with thin, gray hair. She had an irritating habit of hissing through her false teeth. Her sister, Lady Cromes, was short and extremely well-dressed. However, she had the bad taste to hang a multitude of gold chains around her neck, from which were suspended little charms, gold hearts, quizzing glasses, and watches.

"You look very like your mother, Annabelle Alverley," said Mrs. Plummer with a narrow, gauging look.

Sarah inclined her head. Smiling, she said, "Why, thank you, ma'am. That is a compliment indeed, for I believe that my mother was considered to be something of a beauty."

"Oh, she was a beauty! Of that at least there is no doubt!" snorted Mrs. Plummer. "A fine piece, indeed!"

Sarah stared at the lady, a frown drawing her brows together. "I beg your pardon?"

"Now, sister, you mustn't give Miss Sommers the wrong impression," admonished Lady Cromes. She wreathed her face in a smile. "We quite liked dear Adelaide's daughter. It was just such a pity that it all ended in such a horrid scandal. The elopement, you understand."

Mrs. Plummer hissed through her teeth, sounding much like a donkey. "Adelaide never quite overcame the disgrace. Annabelle Alverley, the toast of the Season! Every hope cut up and dashed to pieces. You look very much like your mother, Miss Sommers."

"Yes, but I think that her manner is not quite as free," said Lady Cromes in an aside to her sister, though her eyes remained fixed on Sarah's face.

Sarah was beginning to conceive a dislike for the ladies, but she retained her pleasant expression. Of all things, she detested gossip and there was nothing but malice oozing from these two. She wondered that her grandmother chose to call them her friends. Sarah glanced around, hoping to discover a gracious way to make her escape.

"I trust you are not so headstrong and so utterly lost to convention as your mother," said Mrs. Plummer. "A hoydenish piece if ever there was one!"

Sarah turned full toward the woman. Raising her brows, with ice in her voice, she said, "I beg your pardon."

With an affronted expression, Mrs. Plummer drew back and

hissed through her teeth. "Well! I don't know what to make of that, I'm sure!"

Sarah smiled, but there was anger in her hazel eyes. "Do you not? Perhaps your sister might explain it to you! Excuse me, Mrs. Plummer, Lady Cromes. There are several other guests whom I should like to speak with." She swept away, her head held high.

It was just before supper, and Sarah hoped that she was graced with a few moments to regain her temper before the guests were paired by Lady Alverley. Margaret came up to her and caught her elbow. "Sarah, what is it? I saw you just now, when you left those two ladies, and I don't recall ever seeing you in such a flame."

"That is Mrs. Plummer and Lady Cromes," said Sarah in a low voice.

Margaret nodded. "I remember them from the receiving line. I thought it odd how Grandmama simply pokered up when they arrived."

"Perhaps they had the audacity to make mention of our mother to her," said Sarah, her eyes flashing. She shook her head. "Really, Margaret, it is no wonder that our grandmother is still so affected by what happened all those years ago with our parents. Those two women actually had the audacity to slander Mama to my face and then turn about and ask if I was the same sort of hoydenish piece!"

Margaret eyes rounded and her pretty mouth quivered. "Oh! How horridly cruel!"

Sarah glanced quickly at her. She slid an arm around her sister's narrow waist and hugged her. "I am a selfish beast. I should not have told you. There! I am better now and we shall forget all about it, shall we?"

Margaret's smile wobbled. "You are always so sensible, Sarah! I wish I was more like you."

Sarah laughed. "And I wish that I was more like you! Why, you have had every gentleman in the room paying you such fulsome and lavish compliments that your head must already be turned!"

Margaret blushed. "Yes, it is quite, quite extraordinary! And Sarah, the awful thing is that I cannot remember any of their names!"

"You! Why, I am perfectly petrified about going in to supper," said Sarah.

"Oh, I had forgotten! What am I to do if I cannot remember how to address my supper partner?" asked Margaret, dismayed. "It will not do to mix up a lord with a plain mister!"

"Just so!" said Sarah. "I suspect that we shall be utterly undone when we go into the dining room."

"Oh, dear! I wish you hadn't said anything at all, Sarah," said Margaret.

However, their concern proved to be groundless. As Lady Alverley arranged for supper partners, she made certain that she reintroduced the gentlemen to her granddaughters before she sailed off again.

Sarah accepted the arm of the portly gentleman selected for her and followed the couples ahead of them into the dining room. She thanked him with a smile as he seated her. As she glanced around the crowded table, Sarah felt a little uncertain of herself in the company. Sarah glanced down the table at her sister and knew from Margaret's expression that she was experiencing the same twinge of insecurity. But supper went off without either of them making a serious faux pas in front of Lady Alverley's distinguished guests.

Lady Alverley signaled the end of the sumptuous three courses by rising and suggesting to the ladies that they retreat to the drawing room for coffee, leaving the gentlemen to enjoy their wine.

It was a pleasant half hour in the drawing room. Sarah and Margaret both studiously avoided any further conversation with Lady Cromes and Mrs. Plummer. Several of the other ladies encouraged Sarah and Margaret to play a duet on the pianoforte, having heard that the sisters had often entertained themselves in similar fashion at home. Their performance was well received.

When the gentlemen rejoined the ladies, Lady Alverley suggested that an interlude of sedate dancing was not out of form. "I do not pretend that this is a ball-and-supper, of course, but those who wish to indulge in such mild exercise may certainly do so." A few couples took advantage of Lady Alverley's impromptu suggestion, while the rest of the company mingled to exchange bright conversation.

Sarah wondered whether Lord Eustace would be one of those who would take to the dance floor, but he did not. Instead, he shortly took leave of his hostess.

Sarah regretted Lord Eustace's departure, for she saw him as a friend in a sea of strangers. Nevertheless, she managed to enjoy herself very much. Most of the guests were of an older generation, but she discovered that she had no difficulty in conversing either with the gentlemen or their ladies. She was used to speaking about many of the same topics from talks that she had with her father or with neighbors.

Sarah saw that her sister was not shy in company. She was pleased that Margaret was shining to such advantage, for Sarah did not believe that many young misses directly out of the schoolroom could have exhibited the same degree of poise.

Lady Alverley received several compliments on how prettily behaved her granddaughters were and accepted invitations on their behalf. At one o'clock, when the last of her guests had departed, Lady Alverley pronounced herself quite satisfied with how the evening had gone. "You did very well, my dears. I could not ask more from you, unpolished as you are. What do you think, Marie?"

Miss Hanson nodded in agreement with her ladyship's opinion. "I think Sarah and Margaret did quite well, my lady. With a little town bronze, I expect them to go far, indeed."

Lady Alverley smiled complacently. "That is just what I was thinking! I trust that you enjoyed yourselves?"

"I did, Grandmama, but I am not so certain about Sarah," said Margaret.

Lady Alverley glanced at her eldest granddaughter. Her brows rose slightly in inquiry. "Oh? Pray, what was amiss, Sarah?"

"Nothing, dear ma'am. I thoroughly enjoyed the evening," said Sarah. She was reluctant to bring her unpleasant experience to her grandmother's notice. The ladies in question were obviously well liked by Lady Alverley, since they had been invited that evening. It was not for her to criticize her ladyship's friends.

"Why, what a bouncer, Sarah! As though you were not put into a perfect flame by what those ladies said to you!" exclaimed Margaret.

Sarah shook her head, frowning a little at her sister. "It is not important, Margaret."

"On the contrary, Sarah. It is important to me. What is Margaret referring to?" asked Lady Alverley.

Reluctantly, Sarah said, "I was engaged in a conversation with two of your guests, the tone of which I disliked very much."

"Indeed! Am I to be forced to pull teeth to have it out of you, Sarah?" asked Lady Alverley impatiently.

Sarah chuckled. "No, ma'am! Very well, then. The gist of the matter was that there was something said about my mother to which I took instant exception. I am afraid that I was not quite civil when I left the two ladies."

"Oh, dear," murmured Miss Hanson, casting an anxious glance at Lady Alverley.

Her ladyship's face resembled a rouged mask, only her eyes showing glittering life. "Perhaps you will be good enough to furnish me with their names? Or might I guess. Lady Cromes and that reedy female whom she calls her sister, Mrs. Plummer!"

"That is exactly right, ma'am," said Sarah slowly. "But how did you guess?"

Lady Alverley gave a sharp laugh, but there was no amusement in the sound. Her fingers clenched and unclenched her chair's arms. "Their hatred is unparalleled. They have delighted themselves for years in dredging up the dirt in my past. I beat Mrs. Plummer out of Lord Alverley and they neither of them have ever forgiven me. When my daughter eloped, those two vicious tongues were at the forefront fanning the fires of scandal."

"If they dislike you so much, whyever did you invite them tonight, Grandmama?" asked Margaret in puzzlement.

"I can't think, Margaret!" Lady Alverley's mouth worked a moment longer; then she gave an abrupt nod. "Very well! I am done with them. Cross Lady Cromes and Mrs. Plummer from my guest lists, Marie. I will not have them setting foot in my house again to insult either me or my granddaughters! We shall see how well that is received!"

"I shall attend to it at once, my lady!" said Miss Hanson, rising with an agitated manner. She started for the door, exclaiming, "The effrontery! The gall! How dare they! Well! We shall see how they like being blackballed from my lady's entertainments!"

"I apologize for being the cause of all this unpleasantness," said Sarah quietly. She had been astonished by the reaction she had unleashed.

"My dear! You are scarcely the cause! I should have cut those two from my acquaintance years ago," said Lady Alverley. She had regained her smile. "Now, my dears, you must go up to bed."

Margaret covered a yawn behind her hand. "Forgive me, Grandmama. I am very tired all of a sudden."

"And I," said Sarah. "I shan't mind seeking my bed this night."

"You think that you are tired tonight; but you will soon discover that this little function is but the beginning," said Lady Alverley. "You must learn to pace yourselves, for I do not want that youthful bloom of yours to fade. The gentlemen like that fresh dewy appearance."

"Grandmama!" Margaret made a laughing face. "What a terrible thing to say!"

"Why? It is but the truth. Now kiss me, both of you, and go up to bed."

Chapter Ten

The next morning Lady Alverley's small gathering was reported in *The Morning Post*, which so pleased her ladyship that she decided to get out of bed at once and dress. She sailed downstairs to the breakfast room, the newspaper clutched triumphantly to her bosom. Her appearance surprised her granddaughters and Miss Hanson.

"Grandmama! I did not think that you ever came downstairs before luncheon," said Margaret.

Lady Alverley requested a cup of tea and dry toast from the butler and sat down at the breakfast table. "No doubt, my dear. However, I could not delay in telling you the good news. Already we are noticed." She read the pertinent piece aloud, and when she had finished, she looked up, beaming. "Isn't that simply marvelous?"

"Indeed it is, my lady," said Miss Hanson with a smile. "Of course, how could it be otherwise? You have always inaugurated splendid parties."

"Quite true," agreed Lady Alverley, sipping her tea. "And this Season must be no exception. I must immediately begin to make plans for a grand rout. It will take place after your presentation at court and your come-out ball, of course. Your court presentation will take place next week and your come-out the week after. Have all of our plans been set into motion, Marie?"

Miss Hanson nodded. "I have already engaged the services of the orchestra and ordered the lobsters for supper. The invitations are at this moment on your desk awaiting your signature, my lady."

"Thank you, Marie. I know that I may rely upon you to see that all is properly done," said Lady Alverley absently.

Miss Hanson turned quite pink from gratification. "Thank you, my lady!"

"Now the rout . . . I am not certain exactly what date I should choose. Marie, you must help me to decide, for you know my calendar even better than I do," said Lady Alverley.

"Yes, my lady," said Miss Hanson, nodding.

A note had been delivered a few minutes earlier to Sarah and Margaret and, in fact, they had been discussing its contents when Lady Alverley had surprised them. Margaret now remembered it. "Grandmama, we have been invited by Mrs. Jeffries to a small impromptu musicale which she is holding this afternoon. She says in her note that she has invited a talented singer to entertain her guests. I should like very much to attend the party if you do not object," she said.

"Let me see the note," said Lady Alverley, holding out her hand. When Sarah had handed it to her, she perused it swiftly. "A musicale. That sounds innocuous enough. Ah yes, Mrs. Jeffries mentions that Annette Lozanger and Mrs. Philby will be attending. Perfectly respectable!"

"Does not Mrs. Jeffries reside in Sloane Street?" asked Miss Hanson.

"As I recall," nodded Lady Alverley. "Very well, Margaret. Though I myself shall not be attending, you and Sarah may go. I have nothing of moment for you this afternoon and I know that you enjoy Mrs. Jeffries's company."

"Indeed we do, ma'am," said Margaret, her blue eyes shining.

"I see that you are wearing your new riding habits. They look well on you both," said Lady Alverley. "I assume that you will be riding with Mrs. Jeffries this morning. You may inform her then that she may expect you at her musicale."

"We shall do so," said Sarah. "Miss Hanson, will you be accompanying us?"

"I think not, Miss Sommers. Though there is nothing more that I enjoy than to listen to a fine singing voice, I do wish to take a look at her ladyship's calendar," said Miss Hanson.

"Yes, we must get busy, Marie. I wish my grand rout to be a crowning success," said Lady Alverley. She rose from the breakfast table. "I shall expect you to join me in my sitting room whenever you have finished, Marie."

"Yes, my lady," said Miss Hanson, nodding.

* * *

Mrs. Jeffries resided in Sloane Street, a respectable address for those who were well-born enough to mingle in society, but not rich enough to command the prestige that someone like Lady Alverley did. Sarah and Margaret entered the town house and looked around curiously. They were standing in a rather narrow hall, with a stairway at the far end. They allowed the porter to take their wraps. Then they were conducted upstairs by a footman attired in fawn-brown livery and shown into the drawing room.

Their entrance was instantly noticed. Mrs. Jeffries welcomed them with warm affection. "My dear Sarah! Margaret! I am so glad that you could come. Is Miss Hanson not with you?"

"Miss Hanson sends her regrets. She was needed by our grandmother this afternoon," said Sarah.

"What, no chaperone?" Mrs. Jeffries laughed merrily. Her green eyes danced. "This is something, indeed! But perhaps it is just as well. I suspect that my musicale is something quite beside the usual. But come, I shall introduce you to those whom you do not already know."

Sarah and Margaret were ushered by their hostess into the drawing room. Mrs. Jeffries's attention was at once claimed by an acquaintance and the sisters waited on her while she made a laughing reply. Sarah had the opportunity to glance around.

The room was full, mostly with younger ladies and gentlemen. Overall the company was a younger set than Sarah and Margaret had met the previous evening, but Sarah already knew many of them from the morning rides with Mrs. Jeffries and her friends. All were well-bred sons and daughters from established families.

Sarah was astonished, however, to see that several of the young men were lying on the carpet at the feet of the young ladies with their heads resting against the sofa cushions. It was a liberal atmosphere Sarah was utterly certain that Lady Alverley would have forthrightly condemned and would have made Miss Hanson turn pale. "Oh my," she murmured.

Margaret heard her and turned her head. Her own gaze was wide-eyed and wondering. "What do you think, Sarah?"

Sarah shook her head, not daring to reply because Mrs. Jeffries had turned back to them.

"Now, my dear ones, you must meet everyone whom you do not know," said Mrs. Jeffries. She drew them after her, gaily calling out various names as they proceeded through the room. Several individuals nodded or bestowed a smile of welcome on the Sommers sisters. Here and there a gentleman got to his feet to offer his bows.

Sarah was surprised and even relieved to see Mrs. Philby, whom she knew to be a friend of her grandmother's. "Ma'am, how glad I am to see you here," she exclaimed.

Mrs. Philby patted her hand. "I can see that you are. Pray do not look so anxious, my dear Miss Sommers!" She cast an amused glance around them and murmured, "It is not precisely what one is used to, of course, but I see no harm in it."

"There you are, Sarah. I seem to have lost you for a moment," said Mrs. Jeffries with a lively glance at Mrs. Philby. "But you have found a friend, I see."

"Oh, yes. Miss Sommers and I have enjoyed a brief chat," said Mrs. Philby, graciously waving them on.

"And now I wish you to meet my brother-in-law, Captain Henry Jeffries. He is in the cavalry and has gotten a short leave," said Mrs. Jeffries. "Henry, pray say hello to my friends, Miss Sarah Sommers and Miss Margaret Sommers."

A gentleman unwound himself from the carpet. He was very tall. He wore side whiskers and a mustache. His wiry, curly hair was cut in a military crop. He was lean and browned, and when he smiled, the corners of his gold-brown eyes crinkled. His gaze lingered longest on the younger Miss Sommers's face. Captain Jeffries bowed to Sarah and to Margaret. "I am pleased to make your acquaintance. My sister-in-law has told me that you are both bruising riders. Perhaps we shall meet in the park one day."

Sarah had to tilt her head back to look up into the cavalry officer's face. "I am glad to meet you, Captain Jeffries. I know that Elizabeth is very happy to have you visiting with her."

Captain Jeffries laughed. "Is she? She has not told me so! According to my sister-in-law, I am a great nuisance."

"And so you are! My cook despairs of ever satisfying your appetite at any one sitting. As for me, I am always tripping over your boots or the newspapers that you have flung down beside the chair when you come to see me," said Mrs. Jeffries, laughing with her brother-in-law. It was clear that there was an easy affection between them.

"Are you staying with Elizabeth for long?" asked Margaret.

"I am not staying with Elizabeth at all," said Captain Jeffries firmly.

"Oh! I quite thought that she said—" Margaret broke off in confusion, color rising in her face.

"Henry is staying at one of those hotels that cater so shamelessly to the military officers who are on leave. He swears that otherwise he would starve because I am not prepared to kill the fatted ox for him each day," said Mrs. Jeffries.

"Nothing of the sort. I require only to sit down to a well-cooked dinner with a good bottle of wine," said Captain Jeffries with dignity. He ignored his sister-in-law's derisive snort. He smiled, his lips curling in an utterly attractive manner. "Fenton's does very well for me, in any event."

"Oh, I see that Miss Smythe is ready to sing now. Let us find a place for you to sit, Sarah. Margaret, you may sit here. Henry, have a care for her hem! Sarah, you may share my place with me," said Mrs. Jeffries.

Sarah turned to follow her hostess once more, leaving her sister and Captain Jeffries exchanging a tangle of apologies and disclaimers. Sarah was amused by the gentleman's display of gaucherie, for she had thought that Captain Jeffries was extremely sophisticated. However, from the instant that he had trounced on her sister's hem, he had become almost tongue-tied in Margaret's presence. And Margaret was not unnaturally embarrassed, her heightened color betraying her.

The singer was dressed all in blue and had a fine voice. She sang several songs accompanied by a harp. The audience applauded each rendition with enthusiasm. It was a pleasant afternoon and when the musicale had ended, Sarah and Margaret took leave of their hostess with assurances that they had enjoyed themselves very much.

Captain Jeffries saw them out to their carriage and helped them inside. "I shall call on you one day, Miss Sommers," he said, looking at Margaret.

Margaret cast down her eyes, a smile quivering on her lips, but she did not offer a reply.

Sarah glanced at her sister, wondering at Margaret's rectitude. "Pray do so, Captain Jeffries. We would be delighted," she said civilly.

Captain Jeffries transferred his gaze to Sarah, his expression surprised. Then he smiled. "Thank you, Miss Sommers." He stepped back and closed the door of the carriage.

They rattled away. Sarah settled back against the squabs. "Was there ever such a thing! When we first entered the drawing room, I wondered whether it was just the sort of entertainment that we should be attending. But it was a very nice musicale, after all."

"Oh, yes! I enjoyed myself very much. But I don't think that I shall disclose to Grandmama just the sort of company that we found ourselves in," said Margaret. "I was never in my life more shocked to see all of those gentlemen lounging on the floor!"

Sarah laughed. "Nor I! I agree with you. Grandmama would not be amused by a detailed description of the company, though of course there was nothing that was truly vulgar. But can you imagine what Miss Hanson's reaction would have been had she walked in on that lackadaisical company? She would quite possibly have swooned away."

"I shan't breathe a word to her, either," said Margaret, her eyes twinkling.

"Captain Jeffries seemed to be a pleasant gentleman," remarked Sarah.

Margaret suddenly became inordinately interested in the strings of her beaded reticule. "Do you think so?"

"Oh, yes. It was plain that Elizabeth thinks highly of him," said Sarah. "But I suppose that he did not make a perfect impression on you, since he trod on your skirt."

Margaret looked up at that. Her face had warmed with remembered embarrassment. "Oh, Sarah! I felt ready to sink!"

Sarah chuckled. "I rather think that Captain Jeffries felt the same."

After Sarah and Margaret had returned to the town house and put off their bonnets, they were summoned by Lady Alverley. When they entered the sitting room, Lady Alverley waved her hand at the occasional table. "What did I tell you?" she asked in triumph. "There are more than forty invitations delivered today alone, five or six for each day! There is a soirée at Lady Cowper's, another at Prince Polignazc's, a private concert in Grosvenor Square, and several routs!"

"My goodness, ma'am. How shall we manage to go to them all?" asked Sarah wonderingly, picking up a few of the gilt-edged cards.

Lady Alverley chuckled. "My dear! As though I shall not winnow out those that are just a shade beneath our notice!"

"Are there any masquerades?" asked Margaret curiously, inspecting the cards in her turn.

"No, of course not! And if there were, I would not take you to them," said Lady Alverley. "Why do you ask?"

"Well, we have those quite lovely dominoes. I could not imagine where else one may wear a domino," said Margaret reasonably.

"My lady, I thought that there might be a riditto or perhaps an evening at Vauxhall with a private party," said Miss Hanson tentatively.

"Yes, of course. A private masquerade is one thing and quite unexceptional. I was thinking of a public masquerade, which is quite out of the question, naturally," said Lady Alverley. "We shall be attending Almack's this evening, by the way. Pray see that you are suitably dressed. Now you may kiss me. I shall not be seeing you again until dinner."

When Lady Alverley and her granddaughters arrived at Almack's, they found a large company already in attendance. The young misses were gowned in pale colors, as befitted debutantes, and the gentlemen were attired in formal wear. Sarah and Margaret had already been informed that no gentleman, even the Prince Regent himself, was allowed to come through Almack's portals unless he was wearing the required knee breeches.

Lady Alverley glanced around. "It is a very fair turnout," she said approvingly. "You will meet a score of eligible gentlemen this evening, no doubt. I will introduce you to a few personages."

Sarah and Margaret followed in their grandmother's wake.

Lady Alverley took them up to Mrs. Drummond-Burrell, who had the reputation for being the starchiest of the seven patronesses of Almack's. The two ladies exchanged pleasantries and Mrs. Drummond-Burrell unbent enough to give a gracious nod to Lady Alverley's granddaughters.

After that hurdle was successfully negotiated, Lady Alverley made a slow circuit of the ballroom, bringing her granddaughters to the notice of everyone with whom she was acquainted. Soon Sarah and Margaret had their dance cards nearly filled. Lady Alverley was shortly able to seat herself with the other matrons and look on complacently as her granddaughters were led out several times onto the dance floor.

The subscription balls at Almack's were always held on Wednesdays. The dancing was decorous and the refreshments, limited to lemonade and tea, bread and butter, and stale cake, were indifferent. It was a marvel to Sarah that anyone chose to attend at all. However, she recognized that Almack's had one thing that was prized above all else. Its membership was exclusive and entrance was gained solely through the good offices of one of the seven patronesses. If one was denied entrance to Almack's, one's social consequence was considered to be a shade beneath the best of *ton*.

Margaret struck up immediate friendships with a few of the younger misses, some of whom she already knew, and when she was not dancing, she sat with her new friends and chattered away in the most unconscious style. Sarah also was admitted to the circle of misses, but she was the eldest of them all and so she felt a little out of place. Later she mentioned it to Lady Frobisher, who had come without her husband that evening. "I am a graybeard compared to Margaret and some of the rest," she said with a twinkling glance.

Lady Frobisher laughed. "I can readily understand. Most of the debutantes are scarcely out of the schoolroom, while for the past two years you have been learning to manage a house. However, I assure you that does you no disservice in the eyes of sober-minded gentlemen, Sarah. I think that you will find it easier to converse with someone like Lord Dissinger or my brother, Lord Eustace, than would one of these chits. The gentlemen have been on the town for long enough to appreciate a level-headed, sensible young lady."

Sarah made a face. "How boring I sound, to be sure! Sometimes I wish that I was more like my sister. She is never happier than when she is able to throw herself into whatever merriment may be afoot. Since we have been to London, our entire lives have been turned upside down and I have yet to see Margaret at a loss, while I—" She shook her head as she laughed at herself. "Sometimes I feel so uncertain that I scarcely know what to say or do."

Lady Frobisher took hold of her hand and pressed her fingers. "My dear Sarah! No one would ever guess it, I assure you. Margaret has an effervescent charm that carries her well, but you possess that rarer quality: grace. You are kind and clever, too. I already count you as one of my dearest friends."

Sarah blushed. "Thank you, Mary. You have no notion how much those words mean to me." She made reference to something else that Lady Frobisher had said. "Will Lord Eustace be attending this evening? Surely it is getting too close to eleven o'clock to still expect him. The doors will soon be closed."

"Oh, I don't expect to see Gilbert here! He has seldom set foot in Almack's since—" Lady Frobisher stopped. She regarded Sarah for a moment. "I suppose it will do no harm to tell you, for you have probably heard certain rumors already."

"Do you mean about Miss Leander? I have heard that Lord Eustace was betrothed to her and that she was killed in a tragic carriage accident," said Sarah.

"Yes; it happened two years ago. My brother was devastated, I think even a little haunted, by her death. No one dared to speak about her to him, even his best of friends, for we could all see how awful it was for him," said Lady Frobisher. She slanted a glance at Sarah while she played with her fan. "Until Gilbert told me about you and Margaret, I did not think that he would ever begin to show an interest in another lady."

Sarah stared at Lady Frobisher. "Pray, what are you saying?"

Lady Frobisher closed her fan and smiled. "You are clever enough to take my meaning, Sarah. Ah, here is Lord Dissinger to lead you out in the cotillion! My lord, I am glad to see you this evening. Lord Frobisher was mentioning your name to me just yesterday. He has a hunter that he wishes to show to you."

The tall nobleman bowed over her ladyship's hand. "Lady

Frobisher, a pleasure as always. A hunter, did you say? I shall be certain to call on his lordship tomorrow." As Lady Frobisher excused herself with a smile, Lord Dissinger turned to Sarah. He smiled down at her. "It is my dance, I believe, Miss Sommers."

"Indeed it is, my lord," said Sarah, rising from her chair and putting her hand into his. She looked up into his pleasant face. "Do you hunt much, my lord?"

Lord Dissinger nodded, an eager light coming into his rather prominent brown eyes. "I am in the saddle morning to dusk during the hunting season. There is nothing like a good run to stir one's blood. Do you hunt also, Miss Sommers?"

"We lived so quietly in the country that I seldom had the opportunity, my lord. However, I think that I would like it very much. I enjoy sitting a good horse," said Sarah.

Lord Dissinger eagerly expounded on the manifold positive qualities of horses and hunting until they formed up in the set. Then the figures of the cotillion separated them too often to really converse. When the set ended, his lordship steered Sarah back to her chair and lingered for a moment. "I have enjoyed your company, Miss Sommers. Perhaps, if you do not dislike it, I shall call on you later in the week," he said.

"I shall not mind it in the least, Lord Dissinger," said Sarah with a smile. She gave her hand to him as he bowed farewell.

Lord Eustace came up to her, exchanging a nod with Lord Dissinger as his lordship left. He bowed to Sarah. "I hope that you kept a set open for me, Miss Sommers," he said.

Sarah felt a faint flutter in her breast as she consulted her dance card. "I do have one opening, my lord." She looked up with a smile. "I am free for the next reel."

Lord Eustace sat down on the chair beside her. "I shall wait with you until it strikes up."

Sarah looked at him. "I am surprised that you are here this evening, my lord. I did not think that Almack's was just in your line."

He looked inquiringly at her. "Why would you think that, Miss Sommers?"

Sarah's color rose. She could not very well disclose that she and his sister had been gossiping about him. For answer, she gestured at the crowded ballroom. "It is a younger company than you must really care for, Lord Eustace."

"Do you mean that I am past the age of my callow youth?" asked Lord Eustace, smiling.

Sarah chuckled. "Just so, my lord! I was informed that Almack's is commonly referred to as the Marriage Mart because each Season's newest crop of debutantes make their initial bows to society here. That explains my own presence, naturally, though I am a bit older than most."

Lord Eustace laughed. "Perhaps, Miss Sommers, but you are hardly an anecdote. I imagine that you have already excited the interest of several admirers this evening."

"You are kind, my lord. But I suspect that my sister is more likely to take the honors rather than I. I don't believe that I have been able to exchange more than two words with her all evening," said Sarah, nodding in her sister's direction.

Lord Eustace's gaze followed hers. "Yes, so I have noticed. Miss Margaret draws admiration like bees to honey. She has already made a mark for herself."

Sarah glanced at him, surprised by the reflective tone of his voice. "Do you disapprove, my lord?"

He glanced at her swiftly. "Of course not! What have I to say to anything? I was merely remarking upon your own observation, Miss Sommers." He stood up and held his hand down to her. "I believe that the reel is striking up, Miss Sommers. Will you honor me, ma'am?"

"Certainly, my lord," said Sarah, rising, and putting her hand into his.

The remainder of the evening went off very pleasantly. Sarah danced nearly every set. She knew that Margaret had, too. Neither of them was stigmatized as a wallflower, as happened to one or two unhappy maidens.

Chapter Eleven

Over the next few days it became obvious that Miss Sommers and her sister, Miss Margaret, had been favorably received by the new society that they had entered. A flattering number of posies and cards from admirers were left at the town house.

Lady Alverley graciously received some of the bolder gentlemen when they came to call, showing them a civil hospitality. Sarah and Margaret enjoyed the visits from their admirers. The attention lavished upon them was very pleasant for two country misses who were used to spending much of their time in a solitary fashion.

One afternoon, it seemed as though a dam had broken and the drawing room was filled with so many visitors that the gathering almost resembled a private party. Mr. Lawrence, a fine gentleman of dandified tastes, came with his sister, Miss Penelope Lawrence. Miss Lawrence was a particular friend of Margaret's. They had met at Almack's and it was Miss Lawrence's praises for her new friend that had originally piqued her brother's interest in meeting the young beauty. Mr. Lawrence had accompanied his sister to Almack's the following Wednesday and upon first sight of Miss Margaret Sommers had promptly declared himself to have been knocked for a loop. He had subsequently become one of Margaret's most faithful of swains.

Sir Thomas Eppherd, who was known for his powerful showing in several private curricle races, was also patently smitten with Margaret. When he entered the drawing room and realized that Mr. Lawrence had arrived before him, he virtually ground his teeth. Thereafter the two eyed one another with jealous gazes and jostled for position in winning Margaret's dazzling smiles.

The rivalry between Mr. Lawrence and Sir Thomas did not perturb Margaret. She preferred those two youthful gentlemen to Lord Mittenger, whose serious mien was rather daunting. Casting the baron a thoughtful glance as he crossed the room toward her sister, Margaret confided behind her hand to Miss Lawrence, "I never know quite what to say to the baron."

"Nor I," agreed Miss Lawrence in a whisper. "My brother says that he is rather stiff-rumped."

Margaret went into a peal of laughter. Her admirers begged to be let in on the secret, but she only shook her head. "No, no! It is a private joke between Penelope and myself."

Captain Jeffries also seemed to have found favor in Margaret's eyes, though she was more likely to address her funning remarks to Mr. Lawrence or Sir Thomas. Captain Jeffries did not seem to mind being slighted in such a fashion. He reposed at his ease in a nearby wingback, stroking his mustaches with one finger as he listened to the heated exchanges between the other two younger men. He watched Margaret with an intent gleam in his eyes, joining in the conversation only as it suited him.

The baron's sister had come with him and Mrs. Braddon had at once ensconced herself in a corner with Miss Hanson. The ladies were of similar age and tastes and were thoroughly enjoying a comfortable cose together. Lady Alverley was in deep conversation with one of her own cronies, Mrs. Philby. Her ladyship was learning for the first time precisely what sort of musicale that her granddaughters had enjoyed at Mrs. Jeffries's home and her brows scaled into her hairline.

"Well! I am vastly disappointed in Elizabeth Jeffries. I thought she had more sense than to allow such loose conduct," said Lady Alverley. "And you and Annette Lozanger countenanced it! I am amazed, utterly amazed."

Mrs. Philby chuckled. "Oh, do come down off of your high ropes, Adelaide. It is the fault of the younger set, particularly the military. We live in such uncertain times that a certain wild streak surfaces now and then. Fortunately, Elizabeth Jeffries knows just where she should draw the line. I watched particularly and I saw no real misconduct."

"I trust that my granddaughters did not encourage any gentlemen to lay their heads on the cushions beside them," said Lady Alverley repressively.

Mrs. Philby laughed, shaking her head. "My dear Adelaide! They are as starched-up as you are yourself! You should have seem their expressions when they entered the drawing room. For an instant, I thought that they might bolt."

Lady Alverley at last smiled. "I am glad to hear it. It gives me a very comfortable notion of their characters."

"Quite," said Mrs. Philby, nodding. "You need not be anxious on their accounts. They will not give you a single fretful moment, I am certain."

Lord Eustace was announced and he advanced to make his bows to Lady Alverley. He exchanged civilities for a few minutes with both her ladyship and Mrs. Philby, who was naturally known to him.

Sarah noticed his lordship's entrance and she exchanged a smile and a civil nod with him before she turned back to her own companion. She had much enjoyed talking to Lord Dissinger. He had made her laugh more than once during his visit and she felt at ease with him. Since meeting his lordship, she had heard someone refer to him as being rather jingle-brained and she had to admit that there was some truth in the description. There was not much on his lordship's mind but his hunters and how he was best going to entertain himself that Season. He related to Sarah several wild schemes as they chanced to rise out of his fertile imagination, causing her to exclaim once, "My lord! You must not be so foolhardy. I would not like to hear that you have had an accident."

Lord Dissinger appeared gratified. "I wouldn't wish to cause you any anxiety, Miss Sommers. So perhaps I shan't do it, after all."

Lord Mittenger had come over and he listened to the conversation with a slightly disdainful expression on his face. He was a proud man and felt himself to be beyond the wasteful extravagances of youth. "Certainly that is the better part of wisdom, my lord. One hopes that this flash of steadiness takes permanent root."

Lord Dissinger looked at the baron with dislike. "Your expression of concern is touching, sir."

The baron smiled gravely and bowed. "Not at all, my lord. I would offer the same advice to my young nephew. He is five years of age and prone to equally fantastical notions."

Lord Dissinger's pleasant features stiffened. "Indeed! Poor little whelp. I should think he would run and hide whenever he caught sight of you."

Lord Mittenger puffed out his cheeks and glared at Lord Dissinger.

Hostilities were fairly joined and Sarah glanced around for help. She met Lord Eustace's amused expression. "Lord Eustace, pray come join us. I believe that I overheard you saying a moment ago that you have commissioned a new phaeton to be built. Is it of your own design?"

Lord Eustace said a word to Lady Alverley, who smiled and bestowed a nod on him, before he stepped over. "Yes, Miss Sommers. I decided that I wished to extend the shaft, as well as make a few other minor changes."

In short order, Lord Mittenger and Lord Dissinger had forgotten their antagonism and began plying Lord Eustace with questions. Sarah was relieved. She knew that Lord Mittenger had a hobby of designing anything and everything that took his fancy, and that nothing would excite Lord Dissinger's interest more than to discover that Lord Eustace meant to try racing the phaeton once he had acquired a superior team.

"A four-in-hand?" Lord Dissinger frowned thoughtfully. "Tricky, my lord, very tricky!"

Naturally, when Sir Thomas realized what was being discussed, he was also drawn into the conversation. He had several words of advice for Lord Eustace on the different courses that were generally used for carriage racing. "If you like, I would be happy to take you over what I consider to be the most challenging of roads," he offered.

Sarah detached herself unobtrusively and went to sit with Lady Alverley. Mrs. Philby had just taken her leave and the place beside her grandmother was empty. Her ladyship nodded to her and murmured, "You managed that very adroitly, my dear."

"Thank you, ma'am. Poor Lord Eustace! I have quite callously thrown him into the breach," said Sarah quietly.

Lady Alverley laughed. "Oh, you need not worry overmuch

about Lord Eustace. A more suave gentleman I have yet to meet. Tell me, my dear, what think you of Margaret's various beaus?"

Sarah glanced over at her sister. Margaret was seated on the settee opposite them, Miss Lawrence on one side of her and Mr. Lawrence on the other. Captain Jeffries had left his chair and was leaning over the back. Margaret was laughing merrily at something that had been said and both gentlemen were smiling. "Why, I think that they are a pleasant enough set, Grandmama."

"Quite. However, those gentlemen who seem to be particularly taken with Margaret are almost as young as she is herself," said Lady Alverley. Her ladyship shook her head. "I do hope that Margaret attracts a number of more sober, settled gentlemen before the Season is out."

"Is it so unnatural that Margaret is drawn to the younger gentlemen and they to her, Grandmama?" asked Sarah.

"Of course not. In fact, I would have been greatly astonished if it had been otherwise. Margaret is still such a child. She enjoys pranks and jokes and gaudy uniforms. It is no wonder that she prefers those two over there and Sir Thomas instead of an eminently suitable parti such as Lord Mittenger," said Lady Alverley.

"If it is any consolation, ma'am, Margaret also prefers to surround herself with young misses of her own age, such as Miss Lawrence," said Sarah gently. "I don't think that she has actually given any thought to the future just yet, or the connections that she is in the process of making. She is enjoying herself too much for such sober reflections."

Lady Alverley nodded. "Just as I was thinking, also. Once Margaret has acquired a little town bronze, she will settle down and her natural good sense will assert itself. I am confident that she will make a suitable match when all is said and done."

"I am sure of it, Grandmama," agreed Sarah, keeping her reflections to herself. She knew that Lady Alverley had expectations of seeing both her and her sister betrothed before the end of the Season. Margaret had maintained from the first that her primary ambition was simply to enjoy the Season. If a suitable offer was made to her, she might well consider it, but it was not to be taken for granted that she would accept it.

For herself, Sarah wondered what she would do if an offer were made to her by any of her current admirers. Though she enjoyed the attentions from other gentlemen, she had already discovered that she had a preference for Lord Eustace's company. It was unfortunately clear to her, however, even if to no one else yet, that his lordship had his gaze firmly fixed on her sister.

Lord Eustace was circumspect. He observed all of the polite conventions, always paying the same amount of attention to any lady within his orbit. But there was a queer hunger in his lordship's eyes whenever he looked at Margaret that betrayed emotions that he did not harbor for any other lady. Sarah had seen that expression a number of times, perhaps because she was peculiarly sensitive where Lord Eustace was concerned. She had observed that Lord Eustace never had that look except when he was in Margaret's company.

Sarah loved Margaret. She had never envied her sister for anything, until now. Sarah felt a certain bleakness in the vicinity of her heart. She again glanced over at her sister, who was at that moment receiving Lord Eustace's bows.

Sarah pinned on a smile. It made for good practice. No one must ever know that she had fallen in love with a gentleman who preferred her sister.

As Sarah and Margaret became fully launched, Lady Alverley contemplated their successful progress with satisfaction. Invitations continued to pour in at the town house. She and her granddaughters were scarcely ever at home. Accompanied almost invariably by Lady Alverley and Miss Hanson, Sarah and Margaret attended routs, card parties, soirées, suppers, and private breakfasts. A water party was spectacularly successful, (earning Lady Alverley's envy and that of every other hostess, as well), consisting of a ride in a carpeted boat with a choice supper from Gunter's. At Vauxhall Gardens, they enjoyed the splendor of an outdoor fireworks display. Madame Tussand's waxworks in the Strand was worth one visit, but Sarah and Margaret agreed that the horrific sight of the victims of the French Revolution was enough to last a lifetime.

Every Season, Lady Alverley and Miss Hanson attended performances of the Philharmonic Society Orchestra. Sarah and Margaret accompanied them when they went to the next concert at Hanover Rooms in Hanover Square. The music was well done and was greatly appreciated by the audience.

Sarah was as much entertained by those in the audience as she was by the musical program. One gentleman in particular stood out in sharp relief to his neighbors. There were several empty seats all around him, with just a handful of others inside the circle. It was obvious that the center was the short thin gentleman. His coat was ridiculously padded and so were the calves of his stockings. He wore spots of rouge on each cheekbone and he kept flourishing an oversized, lace-edged handkerchief, carrying it often to his mouth or long sharp nose. His fingers were covered with several large, flashing rings.

As the evening ended, Sarah leaned toward her grandmother. "I must ask you, Grandmama. Who is that extraordinary creature?"

Lady Alverley glanced round. She smiled slightly and with a hint of distaste in her voice, said, "That is the Marquis of Yarwood. He is a prominent patron of the arts."

"Why is he seated in such haughty seclusion, ma'am?" asked Sarah.

"Those are the marquis's confidantes. No one else is allowed to sit near his lordship. He is a hypochondriac and fears that he might catch some disease from the crowd," said Lady Alverley.

Sarah stared at her. "You cannot be serious, ma'am!"

"Am I not? The marquis is very rich and so his paranoias are tolerated. I am rather surprised to see his lordship, actually. He is so rarely seen in society these days because of his fears. He remains unmarried for the same reason," said Lady Alverley.

Sarah shook her head, confused. "I am not certain that I understand, Grandmama. Why has the marquis remained unmarried?"

Lady Alverley's smile grew wider as she watched her granddaughter's expression. "The marquis has stated on several occasions that he cannot bear the thought of having a wife around him for fear of catching some disease."

"What an object of pity," murmured Sarah.

"You need not waste your compassion, Sarah. The Marquis of Yarwood is an entirely selfish creature. Come, I shall introduce you," said Lady Alverley, taking Sarah's elbow and sweeping toward the gentleman. He had risen and, surrounded by his entourage, was slowly making his way out of the concert rooms.

Lady Alverley hailed the marquis as she approached him. He took a hurried step backward and waved his handkerchief in agitation. "No closer, my lady! I beg you, no closer!"

Lady Alverley stopped. "As you wish, my lord. Allow me to present my eldest granddaughter, Miss Sarah Sommers. She was quite taken with the performance this evening. I have told her that you are a great patron of the Philharmonic Society Orchestra."

"Indeed, I thought the performance very fine, my lord," said Sarah, somewhat at a loss. She had been disconcerted by Lady Alverley's rush to introduce her to the marquis and was not certain how to respond to her ladyship's gambit.

Even at a distance, Sarah could smell the heavy scent that the Marquis of Yarwood favored. He had apparently doused his person, and each time that he waved the handkerchief, a fresh wave of oppressive scent wafted toward her. Sarah disliked it excessively.

The Marquis of Yarwood waved his handkerchief again in a dismissive gesture. "Oh, the Philharmonic does its best. But it cannot be compared to the Continental orchestras, of course. A pity that the Continent is undergoing such barbaric turmoil or we could bring truly great musicians to our shores."

"Perhaps one might appreciate the foreign artists better on their own soil," suggested Lady Alverley with a malicious glint in her eyes.

The marquis shuddered. "Pray do not even suggest it, my lady! I would die in a fortnight of stepping foot outside our dear London. I am very susceptible to any change in my immediate environment. And now I really must go, my lady. I have been too long amongst this crowd. Ah, I have been so imprudent tonight! I daresay that I shall take an infection of the lungs."

"Let us pray not, sir," said one of the marquis's hangers-on.

"Indeed! Just so," said the marquis. He did not bow or say a departing word, but simply walked away. Sarah thought she had never seen anyone half as rude.

The marquis put his handkerchief up to his nose. As he leaned on the shoulder of one of his confidantes, he said, "Did you see, Trevalyn? Did you see how close they came? I actually felt the touch of their breaths! I must have myself purged as soon as I arrive home. And these clothes must be burnt. A pity, for I liked this coat."

Sarah turned to her grandmother. She shook her head. "Extraordinary!"

"Quite." Lady Alverley shrugged in dismissal. "It is a worthless creature. Painted and padded and full of formless fears. But exceedingly rich, and because of that, though he is caricatured and disliked, the marquis is also catered to and tolerated. Pah! He is never on my guest lists, I assure you."

"I am unsurprised, ma'am," said Sarah, reflecting that even if Lady Alverley did choose to send out invitations to the marquis, that gentleman would most assuredly not attend. She had never met an odder personality.

Lady Alverley glanced around her with irritation. "I cannot imagine where Margaret and Marie have gone. It is quite annoying when I wish to go home."

"Perhaps they have gone to call the coach, Grandmama, knowing that you do not like to wait," suggested Sarah soothingly.

Lady Alverley's expression cleared. "Of course! I know that you must be right, Sarah. Let us join them at the curb at once."

Chapter Twelve

Surprisingly for one who seemed so thoroughly focused on her social obligations, Lady Alverley made a practice of attending early morning church services every Sunday. She was always accompanied by Miss Hanson and her granddaughters. Her ladyship bowed and nodded to all of her acquaintances, and exchanged pleasantries with those who could claim a firmer footing with her.

Lord Tottenham made a point of coming across to greet Lady Alverley and her ladyship's party. He bowed over each lady's hand in turn, saying all that was civil and generally making himself agreeable. He was a middle-aged gentleman past his prime, but was always extremely well-turned out in his attire. He did not aspire to dandyism, perhaps because he was aware that his thickened figure would not appear to advantage in the exaggerated fashions adopted by some of the more dashing gentlemen.

"It is a particularly beautiful spring, is it not? I am often tempted to drive in the park, for I enjoy taking the air. I count myself fortunate whenever I chance to meet you or your lovely granddaughters, Lady Alverley," said Lord Tottenham with a grave smile.

"You are too kind, my lord. For my part, it is always a pleasure to run into a close acquaintance such as yourself," said Lady Alverley. "I trust that you will come take tea with us again one day this week?"

Lord Tottenham's deeply creased face eased into another grave smile. "Certainly I shall do so, my lady."

"Ah, here is my carriage! We shall look forward to it, my lord," said Lady Alverley, holding out her hand to him. Lord Tottenham took leave of the ladies and walked away to enter his own carriage.

After the service, her ladyship often consented to go walking in Kensington Gardens, where the lilacs were coming into bloom. That particular Sunday, Lady Alverley and Miss Hanson took only one or two slow turns about the paths before seating themselves on a bench. Sarah and Margaret continued to stroll at a sedate pace.

Margaret said suddenly, "Did you notice how Lord Tottenham looked at us this morning? It made me wonder what he was thinking."

"I, also, noticed the peculiar intensity of his lordship's gaze. And I am positive that he actually squeezed my fingers ever so slightly," said Sarah, reflecting for a moment. She chuckled suddenly. "Margaret, I have the most lowering suspicion that his lordship has decided to actually offer for one or the other of us."

"No!" exclaimed Margaret, her eyes rounding. "Why, he is quite old and a father besides! Oh, Sarah, what if he makes me an offer? What must I say?"

"Say what you will, Margaret," said Sarah. She laughed at her sister's reproachful expression. "I admit that I, too, shrink at the thought of having to turn down some gentleman's offer. However, at least in Lord Tottenham's case, I don't think that it shall actually come to that. His lordship is so correct in his manners that I feel positive that he shall apply first to our grandmother before he would speak to either of us."

Margaret's expression cleared magically. "Then it will be quite all right, for Grandmama can easily turn down Lord Tottenham's suit."

"We shall have to make it quite clear to Grandmama that is what we wish her to do," said Sarah.

"Quite! Lord Tottenham is not the gentleman for either of us," said Margaret positively. With very little effort, she banished all thoughts of Lord Tottenham from her mind and began to entertain her sister with several observations and anecdotes that she had already garnered since their debut into society. Shortly thereafter, they rejoined Lady Alverley and Miss Hanson and returned to Alverley House. They forgot to mention Lord Tottenham to their grandmother, but as it would shortly be revealed, it was completely unnecessary. Lady

Alverley was experienced enough to recognize the signs of increasing interest in her granddaughters.

Lady Alverley was particularly pleased that the gentlemen who called at the town house or sent in their tokens of admiration had swelled in number. There were those who had to be discounted, of course. Lady Alverley had high requirements that must be met in order to win her approval. Gentlemen of low birth or insubstantial income or of unsavory reputation were not encouraged. Then there were those who were tolerated because they were of good *ton* and it would not do to slight them. Lady Alverley had no intention of insulting families which she had known for decades. However, Lady Alverley privately considered certain of these gentlemen to be totally ineligible, also, and so they were subtlely discouraged from dangling too ardently after her granddaughters.

By the time that her ladyship's grand rout took place, Lady Alverley had already determined which gentlemen she considered to be acceptable partis for her granddaughters' hands.

Lady Alverley's rout was attended in such numbers that the guests could hardly find standing room on the staircase and had to push their way through into the drawing rooms. Several bunches of candles shed a bright blaze of light in the hot rooms, but melted so rapidly in the heat that drops of warm wax splattered on the company below.

An hour after it had begun, Lady Alverley dismissed her granddaughters from the receiving line. Margaret was escorted away by Mr. Matthews, a tall thin young gentleman whose taste in dress was dandified. His closely curled hair was brushed forward from the crown so that locks shadowed his high forehead. His starched shirtpoints touched his cheekbones. His cutaway coat sported huge brass buttons and his frilled shirtfront was fixed with an enormous diamond stickpin. His tight-fitting pantaloons were strapped under the arches of his Spanish leather pumps. Sarah thought that Mr. Matthews always looked a shade overdone. However, the gentleman did have an elegant bow and he was an excellent dancer, which was why Margaret liked his company.

Lord Eustace claimed the privilege of escorting Sarah away from the receiving line. Sarah smiled up at him, her spirit soaring.

Sarah was wearing a high-waisted decolleté gown of gold tissue. The skirt fell full and long to the floor with a demi-train and the slippers that peeped out from under her hem matched the fabric of her dress. Delicate plumes had been set into her curly locks and she carried a gilt-edged ivory fan. Her hazel eyes sparkled and the heat had put a blush of rose into her face. She appeared stunning, as more than one admiring gentleman had already told her. Sarah hoped that Lord Eustace had noticed and approved of her appearance.

As they slowly made their way through the crowd into the drawing room, Lord Eustace nodded toward Mr. Matthews and Margaret, who were preceding them. "Your sister is in remarkable spirits this evening, Miss Sommers," he observed.

"Yes, Margaret is always happy when she is with friends," said Sarah quietly. Her own happiness in being singled out by Lord Eustace was dimmed. It was very lowering to discover that a gentleman could be thinking about someone else, rather than the lady whom he had on his own arm.

Sarah made up her mind that she wasn't going to allow Lord Eustace's indifference toward her to spoil her evening. She knew that she was looking her absolute best and there was no reason to feel or behave like a wallflower. And if Lord Eustace wanted to pay court to someone else, why, then he could go with her good will.

Sarah paused to chat with several personages known to her. She and Lord Eustace quickly became part of a lively group. Eventually Sarah had the doubtful satisfaction of accepting Lord Eustace's civil excuse that he had seen a friend whom he had not yet greeted. She watched him walk away, a queer tightness in her throat. But then she shook off the pall of depression that threatened to overtake her and turned back to her other companions. She laughed and conversed with unusual vivaciousness.

Several minutes later, Sarah found herself cut out of the group by Lord Mittenger. When his lordship had drawn her a little apart, he raised Sarah's hand and pressed his lips to her fingers. The light of admiration was in his dark eyes. "Miss Sommers, you are incomparable. My admiration for you is without bounds. My heart leapt within me at first sight of you tonight. In short, I am your most obedient servant." He kissed her fingers again.

Sarah's eyes widened at the baron's unexpected show of devotion. The gentleman had always behaved in such a correct fashion that this display was almost alarming. The thought fleeted across her consciousness that Lord Mittenger had by degrees been growing more attached. Perhaps the gentleman was toying with the notion of offering for her.

Sarah's heart quickened, almost in panic, and she glanced around for a distraction. She pointed with her fan. "Look, my lord! There are Lord and Lady Frobisher. I haven't had the opportunity to greet them yet this evening. Will you be good enough to escort me through this crowd, my lord?"

"Certainly, Miss Sommers. I count it as my joy to perform any service on your behalf," said Lord Mittenger, offering his arm to her. He smiled with a greater degree of warmth than was his usual custom.

Sarah smiled in acknowledgment, at once forming the intention to disengage herself from the gentleman as soon as possible. Lord Mittenger was acting so uncharacteristically that Sarah feared he might actually press his suit in public. She had not the least desire of encouraging the baron in his apparent course.

Sarah greeted Lord and Lady Frobisher with enthusiasm. "How glad I am that you were able to attend, my dear friends. The evening would have seemed rather flat without you."

Lord Frobisher's eyes crinkled as he bowed. "Very good of you, Sarah."

"Indeed it is, my dear." Lady Frobisher embraced Sarah lightly, and as she did so, murmured in her ear, "You look quite hunted. Perhaps a rescue is in order?"

As they parted, Sarah's glance at her ladyship was eloquent. "Of course, you know Lord Mittenger?"

"Indeed we do," said Lady Frobisher, at once holding out her hand to the baron. "How do you do, my lord? It was only last week that we saw you, I think, though it seems longer. Lord Frobisher was telling me earlier that he has read about a most fascinating steam engine that has been developed."

"Indeed, my lord? Where did you read of it?" asked Lord Mittenger, his attention at once riveted.

Lord Frobisher looked startled. He cast a swift glance down at his wife, who gave him a significant nod. "Oh, I say. Let me think for a moment. It was written up in one of these scientific journals. Of course! I have it now."

As her husband began telling Lord Mittenger about the steam engine, Lady Frobisher said, "Oh, Sarah, I believe that Lady Alverley was looking for you a moment ago. Her ladyship was in the front room."

"Thank you, Mary. I shall go to her at once," said Sarah. She quietly made good her escape, leaving Lord Mittenger deep in conversation with Lord Frobisher.

It was difficult making a path through the tightly packed company, but Sarah managed it at last and entered the front room. She found Lady Alverley engaged in conversation with several personages.

When Lady Alverley saw Sarah, she turned aside with a polite word. "Well, my dear! How are you enjoying the evening?"

"It is a marvelous function, dear ma'am. I think everyone who was invited has come tonight," said Sarah.

Lady Alverley smiled, very well pleased. "I believe you are correct, Sarah. I have had an excellent turnout. Now, my dear, was there something in particular you wished of me?"

"Lady Frobisher had said that she thought you might be looking for me," said Sarah.

"If I said so, I cannot recall why now," said Lady Alverley, glancing at her sharply.

"Perhaps she was mistaken," said Sarah with a smile. "I am sorry to have pulled you from your guests, Grandmama."

"Quite all right, my dear," said Lady Alverley with a smile and a nod.

As Sarah stepped away, she overheard one of Lady Alverley's friends. "Such an attentive girl, Adelaide. You are fortunate."

Almost immediately Sarah was drawn into conversation with acquaintances and she remained talking with various personages for the next hour and a half. The crush of people, the blaze of the candles, and the pervading heat all began to take their toll. Sarah used her fan incessantly, directing a constant eddy of the heated air into her face. She started to develop a headache. But she continued to smile and exchange witticisms with Lady Alverley's guests. The evening began to seem interminable.

Sarah tried to edge her way toward the refreshment tables. She thought if she could just have something to drink she would begin to feel better. But the crowd was so heavy that she could not push her way through at any speed. She began to despair of ever winning through. The headache was pounding in earnest now.

Sarah's head spun. The heat was so oppressive that the air seemed dead and she suddenly felt as though she couldn't breathe properly. Sarah swayed.

A large hand grasped her elbow, steadying her. "Miss Sommers, are you quite all right?"

Sarah recognized Lord Dissinger's voice. She looked up and with difficulty focused her eyes, meeting his concerned gaze. "Lord Dissinger. I-I fear that I am about to be ill."

His lordship looked alarmed. "Don't do that, Miss Sommers! Here, I'll take you out on the balustrade. A little fresh air is just the thing you need."

Sarah scarcely heard him. The headache was pounding so viciously that she was blinded. She felt the gentleman's hand under her elbow, supporting her and urging her forward. There was the sound of a bolt being drawn back and then a rush of cooler air.

Sarah drew in a deep breath. Her vision cleared and she saw that she was standing on the balustrade that overlooked the moonlit gardens. Lord Dissinger was still holding on to her elbow and he was gazing down at her with an anxious frown. Sarah sought to reassure him. "Thank you, my lord. I am much better now."

"Are you absolutely certain, Miss Sommers? For you looked whiter than paper just now," said Lord Dissinger.

"Oh, yes. The night air has completely revived me. It was just the heat. I started to get the headache and then I felt so ill all of a sudden," said Sarah. "But the nausea has quite passed off now."

Lord Dissinger nodded and let go of her elbow. He shook his head. "That is the drawback of these routs. There are always such crowds and the windows are nearly always all closed. Even the staunchest of us fellows feels the heat. I am happiest when I can leave town and go into the country. I am glad that you are feeling better, Miss Sommers. Do you wish to go back inside?"

Sarah shook her head. "Not just yet, my lord. Oh, I know that it is terribly fast of me to ask, but will you take a turn about the gardens with me?"

Lord Dissinger looked astonished, but he made an instant recovery. "Of course, Miss Sommers. I would be delighted." He escorted her down the stone steps onto the flagstone path. They had only walked a little ways when they heard the sound of weeping.

Lord Dissinger stopped dead. "Perhaps we should go back, Miss Sommers," he muttered uneasily.

"Nonsense, my lord," said Sarah, urging her companion on. A turn in the path brought them upon a bench, on which sat a disconsolate figure. The lady turned quickly when she heard the gravel crunch beneath their feet. Sarah instantly recognized the lady's features in the moonlight. "Why, Miss Darton! How is this?"

Miss Darton surreptitiously brushed her hands over her cheeks. She stood up quickly. "Miss Sommers, Lord Dissinger! I-I—"

"Did you come out for a bit of air, too?" asked Sarah gently.

"I-I . . . yes, that's it exactly," stammered Miss Darton. She cast a half-frightened look about the shadowed gardens.

Sarah did not miss that quick glance. Obviously Miss Darton had not come out alone. At once Sarah decided that the young girl must not be left to reenter the drawing room by herself. If it had been noticed that Miss Darton had left the rout in company with a gentleman, it would certainly cause comment if she returned without escort. "We are about to return inside. Perhaps you will join us? Lord Dissinger, your arm, if you please," said Sarah.

Lord Dissinger instantly offered his other arm to Miss Darton. "My pleasure, Miss Darton!"

Sarah did not ask any questions of the girl. Instead she kept up a gentle flow of conversation that was designed to put Miss Darton at ease. By the time that they reentered the drawing room, Miss Darton had begun to laugh at some of the things that Lord Dissinger was saying.

Sarah left Miss Darton with Lord Dissinger, easily excusing herself when she saw her sister. She walked up to Margaret and greeted her and her companions. "It is an awful squeeze, isn't it?"

"Oh, yes! A splendid success for Lady Alverley," exclaimed one lady.

Captain Jeffries was standing beside Margaret. His gold-brown eyes crinkled as he smiled at Sarah. "I was flattered to be included on her ladyship's guest list. If I had not gotten a short extension of my leave, I would almost certainly have missed this rare treat."

Margaret glanced up quickly at her companion. Her eyes were sparkling. "Oh, I am glad, then. We would have missed you dreadfully, wouldn't we, Sarah?"

"Indeed we would have," agreed Sarah, smiling. "I know that Mrs. Jeffries must be here this evening, but I have not seen her as yet."

"My sister was at the refreshment tables a few moments ago. If you desire an escort, I will be most happy to go with you in search of her," said Captain Jeffries.

"Thank you. I must confess, however, the moment you mentioned the refreshments that nearly all thought of Mrs. Jeffries fled my mind. I am very, very thirsty," said Sarah, accepting the cavalry officer's arm.

Captain Jeffries threw back his head and laughed. "There is no need to apologize, Miss Sommers! The heat is blistering." He flashed a smile at Margaret and the others. "I shall return anon, I daresay."

Sarah was glad of the tall cavalry officer's escort. The crowd seemed to part before him with very little effort, whereas before she had scarcely made any headway at all. Before too many minutes, she and Captain Jeffries arrived at the refreshment tables. As Sarah picked up a glass of lemonade, she said, "Thank you, sir! The cavalry always comes to the rescue, does it not?"

Captain Jeffries laughed again. "We do our best, Miss Sommers. And here is Elizabeth! I have brought Miss Sommers to you, my dear. She was wanting to greet you." He bowed and retreated.

Mrs. Jeffries held out her hand to Sarah. Her expression was welcoming. "My dear! I, too, was hoping to be able to speak with you tonight. It is a lovely turnout. I have already said so to Lady Alverley. I expect that it shall go quite late, however. Shall I expect you and Margaret in the morning?"

"Oh, I hadn't thought about it! I suppose that it will be awfully late before everyone leaves, won't it?" said Sarah. She shook her head, smiling. "Is it bad of me not to commit myself? I wouldn't want to stand you up if I was to oversleep."

Mrs. Jeffries laughed. "No, of course not! Well, why don't you send a note around to my house tomorrow when you have risen and let me know. I shan't be going out before ten o'clock, in any event."

Sarah agreed to it, and then she and Mrs. Jeffries were interrupted by mutual acquaintances. Sarah enjoyed the remainder of the evening, especially as the company slowly began to be reduced in numbers as various personages began to take their leave. Afterward, when she and Margaret were going upstairs to bed, she recalled her conversation with Mrs. Jeffries. "Margaret, Elizabeth Jeffries inquired whether we would want to meet her this morning to go riding. I told her that we would send a note round to her if we had risen at a decent hour."

"Oh, of course we must go! I wouldn't miss a chance to go riding for worlds," said Margaret, covering her mouth as she yawned.

"But it is almost dawn now. You can't possibly wish to go riding," said Sarah.

"I am not in the least tired," said Margaret. She stumbled on the step and caught herself by reaching out for the balustrade.

Sarah laughed at her. "You are half asleep even as we speak. Very well, we shall go. But I, for one, intend to rest a bit in the afternoon."

"Just like a frail old lady," said Margaret, giggling.

"You have got an impudent tongue, miss," said Sarah.

Chapter Thirteen

The following afternoon, Lady Alverley perused the newspaper. Its pages contained a brief piece on the rout that she had given the previous evening. The affair was pronounced a sad crush, a description that gratified her ladyship no end. Lady Alverley basked in her social triumph. "Just think of it, my dears! No less than four ladies fainted dead away from the overcrowding in the rooms and on the stairs," she said.

"At one point, I felt very faint myself. If Lord Dissinger had not taken me out to the gardens for a breath of air, I might have disgraced myself entirely," said Sarah. "His lordship was very understanding, however."

"Lord Dissinger is exceptionally well-mannered." Lady Alverley glanced over at her granddaughter. With a suggestive tone, she said, "I suppose that you have not begun to form an attachment in that direction?"

Sarah chuckled and shook her head. "No, Grandmama. I consider Lord Dissinger to be a pleasant companion, but nothing more."

"A pity. His lordship is very well-breeched. You could do worse, Sarah," said Lady Alverley. She gestured at the bouquet of yellow roses in a vase on the mantel. "And he is so very considerate, besides."

"I concede all of it, ma'am. However, Lord Dissinger has failed to snare my heart," said Sarah firmly.

"You might as well give over, Grandmama," suggested Margaret, her chin propped in her hand as she turned over the pages of a fashion magazine. "Sarah is far too sensible to accept Lord Dissinger's suit when Lord Mittenger has made her the object of his admiration."

"Margaret!" exclaimed Sarah, heat rising in her cheeks. She

had confided to her sister earlier that morning how Lord Mittenger had seemed to be on the point of offering for her. It was horrid of Margaret to tease her about it.

Lady Alverley bolted upright on the chaise upon which she was reclining. "Mittenger! Why, Sarah, you sly boots! I had no notion that you had such game in your sights."

"The baron is said to be fabulously rich," said Miss Hanson in a congratulatory tone. She was carefully embroidering her initials on a lace handkerchief and peered closely at her work.

"I am not entertaining a suit from Lord Mittenger, either," said Sarah, sending a scorching glance at her sister.

Margaret went into a peal of laughter. "Oh, Sarah! You are such a funny when you are put to the roast. You have daggers in your eyes."

Sarah threw a cushion at her. "There, Miss Sauce-box!" Her sister ducked, giggling.

"And what of you, Margaret? Is there a gentleman who has found particular favor in your eyes?" asked Lady Alverley.

Margaret looked startled and suddenly wary. "Me?" she faltered. "Why, what can you mean, Grandmama?"

"I've noticed that the Honorable Timothy Matthews is growing markedly attentive. There are also Lords Darton and Tottenham," said Lady Alverley. "We have also seen rather a lot of Sir Thomas Eppherd, Captain Jeffries, and Mr. Lawrence."

"Well, yes. But there is nothing in that, for they are my particular friends," said Margaret. "Penelope Lawrence and Barbara Darton are my closest bosom bows, besides. And I like Mrs. Jeffries very well, too. When we all go riding together we have such fun. Don't we, Sarah?"

"Yes, indeed. Lord Eustace and Lord Dissinger often escort us, as well," said Sarah.

"Nevertheless, perhaps it is time that we have a serious talk, Margaret," said Lady Alverley.

Alarm showed in Margaret's expression. "Whatever about, Grandmama?"

"I do not mind that you show a degree of friendliness toward any of those whom I have mentioned. However, I wish you to become aware that not all of these admirers of yours are eligible suitors," said Lady Alverley.

"Are they not?" Margaret shot a quick, anxious glance at Sarah. "Am I not to associate with them, then?"

"I don't think that is exactly what our grandmother means," said Sarah reassuringly.

"Certainly not. I well understand how much you enjoy the company of these young gentlemen, and that of their sisters, as well," said Lady Alverley. "I merely wished to point out certain truths, in the event that you began to form a *tendre* for any of them. For instance, Lord Darton is completely ineligible. He delights in gaming and is far too gone in Dun Territory to be thought to be the least provident. And Lord Tottenham, though better placed than Lord Darton in my estimation, is not right for you, I think."

"Lord Tottenham likes Sarah just as much as he does me," offered Margaret.

"Yes, and so my warning is for both of you. Lord Tottenham is a widower, as you know, and he already possesses a nursery of hopeful heirs. If either of you were to wed his lordship, your children would naturally be last in line for the succession," said Lady Alverley.

"Very bad," commented Miss Hanson, shaking her head. "It is not at all the situation that one could wish."

"You have our assurance that we do not consider Lord Tottenham to be a possibility, Grandmama," said Sarah. "In fact, if his lordship should make an offer for either of us, we would be grateful to you if you would decline it."

"I perceive that you have discussed this matter between you," said Lady Alverley, amused.

"Oh, yes. Sarah and I noticed how particular Lord Tottenham's attentions have become," said Margaret, nodding. "His lordship is not at all acceptable to us, Grandmama."

"Quite. I am glad that you both have such sensible heads on your shoulders. I should perhaps tell you that you should not be surprised if you lose Lord Darton as an admirer. I heard only yesterday that he shall soon be forced to look to the ranks of the heiresses for a bride if he is to survive his penurious embarrassments," said Lady Alverley.

"What a pity. He is such an excellent dancer," said Sarah flippantly.

Margaret giggled, but Miss Hanson looked up to frown at

them. "It is not a laughing matter, Sarah, Margaret," she said reprovingly.

"I am happy that you have no great attachment in that direction," said Lady Alverley dryly.

"I apologize, ma'am. You were saying?" said Sarah.

"Thank you, Sarah. There are also Mr. Lawrence and Captain Jeffries to consider. Younger sons, both. Completely ineligible," said Lady Alverley, waving her hand in a dismissive gesture.

"Do you mean . . . like Papa was?" asked Margaret tentatively.

Miss Hanson looked up, quick alarm entering her expression. "Margaret, I beg of you!"

Lady Alverley's face tightened. Her eyes had become cold blue flames and her lips had thinned in a narrow line. At Miss Hanson's sharp interjection, her ladyship's countenance abruptly relaxed. "Exactly so, Margaret. I trust that you will remember it. Now we shall not say anything more about it, if you please."

Margaret gave her grandmother a long, thoughtful look. She was unusually reticent, not offering her thoughts as she was wont to do.

"What of Mr. Matthews?" asked Sarah curiously. She had not liked the tension that had entered the atmosphere with her sister's question, but she was not one to back down from an unpleasant encounter, either. It seemed odd to her that Lady Alverley had not included Mr. Matthews in her list of ineligibles and she wanted to know why. "Is he not also a younger son?"

"Oh, but he is Cardell Matthews's heir," said Miss Hanson.

Lady Alverley nodded. "Exactly."

Sarah and Margaret looked to her ladyship for enlightenment. Margaret was frowning. Sarah knew that her sister was bothered by the seeming inconsistency in Lady Alverley's judgment, as was she.

"I do not perfectly understand, Grandmama," said Sarah.

"Cardell Matthews is Mr. Matthews's great-uncle. He is said to be a veritable nabob. Mr. Matthews may not be in line for the title, but he shall be quite fabulously rich," said Lady

Alverley. "And that, coupled with his unexceptional birth, renders him perfectly eligible."

"Yes, but he hasn't any chin," objected Margaret.

Sarah spluttered a laugh at her sister's candid observation. "Yes, that is quite true, the poor man!" Margaret's countenance lightened in response and she giggled.

"Quite unfortunate, but one must make allowances," said Lady Alverley, glancing reprovingly at her eldest granddaughter.

"And so we have neatly dealt with Lords Darton and Tottenham, Mr. Lawrence, Captain Jeffries, and Mr. Matthews," said Sarah, counting the gentlemen off on her fingers. For her, it was an exercise in absurdity. "We already know that Lord Dissinger and Lord Mittenger are favorably situated. Is there anyone else, Grandmama?"

"Lord Eustace seems to like us both," said Margaret.

"Yes," said Lady Alverley thoughtfully. She shook her head. "It is strange. I have not yet been able to decide which of you it is that continues to draw Lord Eustace to us. He pays compliments to you both and does not reveal a preference. His lordship is seemingly just as content spending time with you, Margaret, as he is with Sarah."

Sarah thought that she could enlighten her grandmother, but she chose to keep her own counsel. She truly did not want to delve into a discussion of how often Lord Eustace had talked to her about her sister. It was already difficult enough to play the friendly confidante.

"His lordship is a bit of a dark horse," suggested Miss Hanson.

"Quite so," agreed Lady Alverley. "You are perfectly correct, Marie. Lord Eustace has not made anyone the sole object of his admiration since his unfortunate entanglement with Vivian Leander."

"Yet his lordship does seem to enjoy Sarah and Margaret's company," said Miss Hanson.

Lady Alverley nodded reflectively. "I do not discount him entirely, for he has been flatteringly attentive. However, in my opinion it would be to greater advantage to encourage Lord Dissinger, Lord Mittenger, Sir Thomas, and Mr. Matthews."

"You make it sound almost like a military campaign, ma'am," exclaimed Sarah.

"Well, and so it is. A betrothal does not simply fall into one's lap, Sarah. One must labor to appear to constant advantage and to continually keep oneself in circulation. It would be fatal to simply sit at home and hope for the best," said Lady Alverley.

"If you do not mind, Grandmama, I would prefer to leave Lord Mittenger to Sarah," said Margaret. "I do not understand what he is thinking. He is too somber for my tastes."

"Well, really, Margaret, as though that is not the outside of enough! I do not think that I am so lacking in animation that it follows that I must have a preference for someone who is described as somber!" said Sarah, laughing.

"Oh, I do not mean it that way, Sarah. As you very well know! But you do understand what the baron means by what he says much better than I do," said Margaret. She slid a sly glance at her sister. "And lately he does seem to prefer you to me."

"Oh, we are back to that again, are we?" said Sarah. She picked up another cushion, menacing her sister with it. Margaret squealed in laughter. They engaged in a mock battle with the pillows, disregarding Miss Hanson's repeated admonitions to behave themselves with more decorum.

"Oh, let them be, Marie. It is harmless enough play," said Lady Alverley indulgently.

The door opened and Lady Frobisher entered. She stopped short at sight of the two sisters, who had turned startled faces. "My word! I did not realize that you indulged in cap-pulling," she said in amusement.

Sarah and Margaret straightened up their slightly disheveled hair and gowns. They hurriedly tried to smooth their appearance, while Miss Hanson covered her eyes with her hand.

Lady Alverley smiled and the glance that she cast at her granddaughters was a shade on the wicked side. "It is quite lowering, to be sure. They are fighting over an admirer, my lady."

Miss Hanson looked up at that and squeaked an agitated denial. "Oh, my lady! Pray do not say so! The implication!"

Lady Frobisher looked astonished. Sarah started laughing and rose to her feet, holding out her hand. "My grandmother is perfectly right, my lady. However, what she has not made

plain is that Margaret and I are each trying to give the gentleman in question away to the other!"

Lady Frobisher also laughed. "Oh, I understand perfectly
now! It is a case of too many suitors. Or perhaps, one who is
not so well-favored?"

"That's it precisely. How glad I am to see you, my lady,"
said Sarah.

"Indeed, we always enjoy your visits," said Lady Alverley,
also shaking hands with their visitor. She glanced behind Lady
Frobisher. "Er-you did not bring your delightful children with
you today, my lady?"

Lady Frobisher's eyes twinkled. "No, my lady."

"What a pity. Pray sit down, Lady Frobisher," said Lady
Alverley.

Lady Frobisher sat down. "Thank you, Lady Alverley. The
truth of the matter is that I have stopped by for just a moment.
I was on my way home when it occurred to me to inquire
whether any of you would be interested in a small outing late
this afternoon. There is a lovely exhibition of watercolors
being shown at those splendid showrooms in York Street.
Please understand that I have not gathered a large party, for
this is quite an impromptu. It will be only Lord Frobisher and
myself, my brother, and perhaps one or two others."

"It sounds quite delightful, my lady. However, I usually lie
down to rest in the afternoons and so I shall decline. But certainly Sarah and Margaret may go if they so desire," said Lady
Alverley.

"I should very much like to accompany you, my lady. I have
heard of the exhibition and had hoped to be able to see it," said
Sarah.

"Wonderful! And you, Margaret? Will you accompany us,
too?" asked Lady Frobisher, turning to the younger lady.

Margaret shook her head, a smile touching her lips. "Do
pray excuse me, my lady! I had already made plans to go
shopping with some of my particular friends."

Sarah glanced at her sister, a little surprised. It was the first
time she had heard that Margaret was going out. But then,
Margaret often traipsed off with Penelope Lawrence and Barbara Darton, so really it was not so unusual. She supposed that
Margaret simply had forgotten to mention it to her.

An amusing thought suddenly occurred to Sarah. She knew that Margaret was not keen on such outings as Lady Frobisher had proposed. Margaret preferred to participate in more active amusements. Perhaps this shopping trip was but the inspiration of the moment to free her from the obligation.

Lady Alverley directed a penetrating, thoughtful glance in Margaret's direction. "You will naturally take your maid with you, Margaret."

"Yes, Grandmama."

"I am sorry that you are unable to join us, Margaret, but I perfectly understand. As I said, this is quite an impromptu party. Miss Hanson, I would be delighted to take you up in my carriage as well," said Lady Frobisher.

"I appreciate your thoughtfulness, my lady. However, I believe that I should remain here and finish some correspondence this afternoon," said Miss Hanson.

Lady Frobisher nodded. She smiled at Sarah. "I shall return for you in about a half hour, if that is acceptable."

"Perfectly acceptable, my lady. I am looking forward to it," said Sarah.

Lady Frobisher started to her feet. "I must be going now. No, pray do not get up, Lady Alverley! I know my way out, I assure you." She gracefully took her leave.

Lady Alverley looked over at her eldest granddaughter. Her expression was almost derisive. "A high treat indeed, Sarah!"

"Yes, I shall enjoy the exhibition," said Sarah, flashing a smile. "I used to watercolor often and I miss my paints."

"Well, I am glad that I have something else to do. I cannot imagine anything duller than walking about looking at a great lot of watercolors," declared Margaret.

"Perhaps that is true, Margaret, but Sarah will also be enjoying Lord Eustace's company," said Lady Alverley. She turned again to Sarah. "I am certain that you will make the most of your opportunity, my dear. Now kiss me and run upstairs, for I know that you will wish to change into a more appropriate gown."

"Yes, Grandmama," said Sarah, obediently kissing her grandmother's cheek.

"I am going upstairs also, Grandmama. I must tell Holby that she is to accompany me," said Margaret. She bent to kiss her grandmother. There was bright laughter in her eyes. "Then I must send a note round to Penelope and Barbara to inform them that they are to go shopping with me!"

"Minx," said Lady Alverley indulgently.

Margaret had already left the town house before Sarah returned downstairs to the drawing room. Sarah had attired herself in one of her new walking dresses, a pale lemon gown that complimented her coloring. The upstanding bonnet charmingly framed her face and was tied with matching ribbons under her chin. A deep-fringed paisley shawl was arranged over her elbows. Soft kid gloves and a knitted reticule completed her outfit.

Sarah did not have long to wait before Lady Frobisher arrived. The ladies greeted one another and then went out to the carriage. Sarah held out her hand to Lord Frobisher with easy friendliness, having discovered in weeks past that she was comfortable in his lordship's company.

Sarah turned then to Lord Eustace and smiled as she gave her hand to him. "Lord Eustace, I was glad to hear that you were making one of this party. Do you like watercolors, then?"

"Yes, I do, Miss Sommers. Does that surprise you?" he said, glinting a smile at her.

Sarah thought that he looked every inch the gentleman. There was nothing pretentious or dandified about his lordship's dress. His well-cut blue coat perfectly fit his broad shoulders and was open to reveal a silk waistcoat and frilled shirt. The biscuit-colored pantaloons that he favored were smoothed into glossy top boots.

Sarah laughed. "I have ceased being surprised by what anyone in London likes or dislikes, my lord! In all honesty, I leaped at the chance to see this exhibition, for watercolors has always been a passion of mine."

"Then I am certain that you will enjoy this outing," said Lord Eustace. He handed her up into the carriage.

There was another lady besides Lady Frobisher, a Miss Justin, whom Sarah had briefly met a number of times during the Season. Miss Justin was a cousin of Lord Frobisher's. She had recently accepted an offer and was going to be wed in June.

Sarah and Miss Justin greeted one another civilly. "I have

not previously had the opportunity to offer my good wishes on your approaching marriage," said Sarah.

"Thank you, Miss Sommers. I am very happy, indeed," said Miss Justin, a blush of attractive color coming into her face

Lady Frobisher entered the carriage after her guest and gaily told her driver that they were ready. The two gentlemen rode behind the carriage.

The exhibition was located only a short distance away and was quickly reached. The ladies were handed down from the carriage and the gentlemen escorted them inside. Lord Eustace gallantly offered an arm both to Sarah and to Miss Justin. However, in a very few minutes Lady Frobisher had called Miss Justin's attention to a particularly lovely piece and effectively detained her while Lord Eustace and Sarah walked on.

The watercolors were beautiful and Sarah enjoyed slowly walking past each of them, discussing the pictures with her companion. She was at first conscious that she and Lord Eustace had been skillfully paired by Lady Frobisher, but very soon her faint sense of embarrassment faded away. His lordship was a very agreeable companion. Sarah discovered that they had many similar tastes in art and politics. Their opinions on any number of subjects were substantially the same and when they did differ, it was without rancor.

For virtually the first time since she had known him, Lord Eustace did not make mention of her sister. Sarah was therefore able to put out of her mind the fact that he had a preference for Margaret and simply enjoyed herself. It was a very rare afternoon.

When it was time to return to the town house, Sarah was regretful. She did not think that she had ever enjoyed anything more than the opportunity to bask in Lord Eustace's attentions. Of course, she knew that Lord Eustace, as a gentleman of honor, was bound to be considerate and polite and attentive. But just for a little while, Sarah pretended that he had another, more personal motive. Just for the duration of the afternoon, she pretended that she was entertaining a suit from Lord Eustace.

Sarah knew it was foolish. She knew that she was indulging in a dangerous fantasy. But just for a little while, she allowed herself to dream. Then when she walked up the steps and entered the town house, she let the dream slip away.

But the memory of it was one that she meant to treasure for a very long time.

Chapter Fourteen

The weeks flew by. The dismal winter gray had entirely disappeared. Spring burst into bud with fluttering green leaves and sweet-smelling flowers. The red and brown chimney pots of London, once hidden by thick fog and weather, now contrasted sharply with the blue sky. Everywhere colors glowed in the sun and the shops gleamed. Ladies put off their velvet bonnets, preferring instead the large upstanding straw hats adorned with flowers and ribbons.

Through the weeks it slowly dawned on Sarah that a vague discontent had begun to settle in Margaret's expression. Sometimes her sister made odd little comments that also pointed to dissatisfaction. It surprised Sarah because her sister had always been of a sunny disposition. It was unlike her to fall into these bouts of moody reflection.

When Sarah asked Margaret about it, her sister looked at her, her expression almost startled. Then Margaret laughed. "Why, nothing is wrong, Sarah. How could it be? We are so very busy and happy."

"I thought that perhaps you were not enjoying yourself as much as you did at first," said Sarah.

Margaret shook her head, a smile on her lips. There was a guarded look in her eyes. "Oh, I like it as much as I ever did, Sarah. It's just that I get the headache from the oppressive heat at these routs. And I feel a bit tired some days."

Sarah accepted her sister's explanation. She nodded. "It can be frightfully hot, can it not? I feel it myself."

Margaret shifted restlessly on the settee. "I only wish that I could go riding more often. I feel so stifled. We seem always to be indoors."

"Why do we not send a note around to Elizabeth this very moment?" asked Sarah. "I don't believe that Grandmama will mind if we slip away for an hour or two. We are usually shopping at this time, in any event."

Margaret's face lit up magically. "Oh, that would be lovely, Sarah!"

Sarah sent round the note to the town house in Sloane Street, with the request of a reply. In short order, they received word that Mrs. Jeffries would be delighted to join them for a ride. Margaret bounced up from the settee with all of her old enthusiasm and dashed upstairs to change into her habit. Sarah followed more sedately, glad that she had been able to provide such a simple solution for her sister's obvious bout of boredom. She paused only to leave word with the butler about their plans before she also retired to her bedroom to change.

With a groom accompanying them, Sarah and Margaret rode over to Sloane Street. They did not need to dismount, for Mrs. Jeffries was obviously on the lookout for them. That lady came out of the front entrance, the hem of her riding habit thrown over one arm and her whip and gloves clutched in her hand. "I am very glad to see you!" she called. "My groom is bringing round the horses now. Henry was sitting with me when your note arrived and he has asked to be included as our escort. I hope that you do not mind?"

Captain Jeffries stepped out behind his sister-in-law. "Pray do not hide your true feelings behind any false civilities, I beg you."

Sarah laughed. "You may join us with our goodwill, Captain Jeffries. Isn't that right, Margaret?"

"Oh, yes. Quite," said Margaret, offering her hand to Captain Jeffries as he came up to them. Her vivid blue eyes were bright and her smile swift.

"Thank you, Miss Margaret," he said, smiling up at her and then at Sarah. "I was bored this afternoon. I now see how fortuitous it was that I decided to pay a visit to Elizabeth."

The groom brought up horses for Mrs. Jeffries and Captain Jeffries. They were swiftly mounted and the party started out. The park was reached and the riders turned into its gate, the two grooms coming sedately behind. At first they all rode abreast, but then as the bridle path narrowed, Mrs. Jeffries and

Sarah dropped back and left Captain Jeffries and Margaret conversing with merry abandon.

Mrs. Jeffries nodded toward her brother-in-law's broad back. "I am exceedingly proud of Henry. He was telling me only a few minutes before your arrival that he is shortly to be promoted."

"That is wonderful news!" exclaimed Sarah.

"Yes, it is. Henry is an up-and-coming officer. If this war continues, and he is fortunate to get through it unscathed, I have great hopes for his continued rise," said Mrs. Jeffries. "Of course, Henry already possesses a comfortable living, so that is not really a major consideration. He could easily support a wife if he so chose."

"Has he expressed an interest in anyone of late?" asked Sarah, her gaze traveling to her sister. Margaret was turned in the saddle to look up into Captain Jeffries's face and she was laughing at something he had said. Sarah had noticed that her sister seemed to enjoy being in the dashing cavalry officer's company perhaps more than that of any of her other admirers.

Mrs. Jeffries shook her head. "If Henry does have anyone in mind, he has not confided it to me, which makes me think that he has not given thought to any such thing. Henry and I are very close. I am confident that I would be the first to know."

"No doubt," murmured Sarah, still regarding at her sister. She wondered what Margaret actually thought about the cavalry officer. Margaret had commented now and again about certain admirers, but she had never mentioned Captain Jeffries.

Mrs. Jeffries noticed the direction of Sarah's gaze. She laughed. "My dear Sarah! As though Margaret has ever entertained any such notion. Why, she is a babe yet! And Henry knows it. Believe me, he is too experienced not to recognize the signs of a schoolgirl crush and know, too, just how to gently set aside such inappropriate overtures. Has Margaret ever said anything to you about Henry or, indeed, any other gentleman?"

Sarah's brow creased slightly. "No, she has not. She has made an observation here and there about our admirers, but she has never appeared particularly attached to any of them.

Though I do think that she harbors a hint of partiality for Captain Jeffries."

"Is it any wonder, Sarah? Henry is ambitious and strong and honorable, everything that his brother Ambrose is not," said Mrs. Jeffries, with a sudden twist of her lips.

"Ambrose?" asked Sarah, looking at her companion in inquiry.

Mrs. Jeffries glanced quickly at her. "Surely you have met the scion of our house by now, Sarah, the Marquis of Yarwood?"

Sarah was shocked and astonished. "The marquis is Captain Jeffries's elder brother?"

"Yes; and he was also the elder to my departed husband. A pretty gentleman, is he not?" asked Mrs. Jeffries, her nose wrinkling in distaste.

"I own, I did not care overmuch for the marquis when we met," said Sarah. She glanced again at the gentleman riding ahead of them. She found it difficult to associate Captain Jeffries with the heavily scented fop whom she had met so very briefly.

"Ambrose is not well liked," said Mrs. Jeffries. "He is a ridiculous poultroon." There was an undercurrent of revulsion and bitterness in her voice. "When my husband was wasting away with his last lingering illness, Ambrose scarcely acknowledged our existence. He feared contagion. When I had exhausted all of our own resources, he refused my appeals and would not send monies to enable me to pay for the doctors."

Captain Jeffries gave a loud crack of laughter and Mrs. Jeffries smiled suddenly. With a warmer note in her voice, she said, "Dear Henry did what he could, of course. He was overseas, but still he managed to send funds to me whenever he could. I don't know what I would have done without him."

"I can understand why you hold Captain Jeffries in such high esteem," said Sarah quietly.

Mrs. Jeffries gathered her reins and set spur to the side of her horse. "As I said before, it is a pity that he was not the heir. Of course, Ambrose has not married and is not likely to, so one may hope, can't one?" She started forward to catch up with the couple ahead of them. Sarah followed suit, very thoughtfully.

* * *

That week, a stir was caused by the introduction of the waltz at Almack's. The waltz had already become established on the Continent and certain sophisticates privately learned its steps. But none had yet dared to flaunt their skill in the new dance when Lord Palmerston and Madame de Lieven, one of the patronesses of Almack's, took to the floor. Until Lord Palmerston and the haughty Russian countess seized the initiative, the waltz was considered to be too risque for polite society. However, once the waltz had invaded the inner sanctums of Almack's, it swiftly and inevitably became all the rage.

Lady Alverley was scandalized. It was her ladyship's opinion that the waltz was outrageous. "The gentlemen actually encircle their partners' waists," she exclaimed disapprovingly. "I cannot countenance it."

Mrs. Philby shook her finger at Lady Alverley. "Adelaide, you simply must give way. Your functions will soon be considered too insipid for words if you do not allow the orchestra to strike up a waltz or two during the course of the evening. And as for Sarah and Margaret—why, at least think of them! They will be left as wallflowers each time a waltz is played if you continue to forbid them to dance it."

Annette Lozanger had called in company with Mrs. Philby and she added her voice. She was a forthright personality who had no difficulty speaking what was on her mind. "You will not like to damage their chances with the gentlemen, Adelaide."

Lady Alverley frowned, rather annoyed by the unsolicited advice. But she prided herself on being an intelligent woman. As well as anyone, she knew how fickle was the favor of the society in which they lived. Reluctantly, she accepted the validity of her friends' arguments. "Since it is obvious that the whole world has gone mad and embraced this—this scandalous dance, I suppose that I am forced to concede. Margaret has already appealed to me for lessons any number of times."

"I am planning a dancing party this very Thursday to introduce some of the younger misses and gentlemen to the waltz. It was my thought that if they are properly taught the dance, then we shall not see it degenerate into a romp," said Annette

Lozanger. "If you do not mind it, I will be most happy to include Sarah and Margaret in the group."

"A very good notion. Thank you, Annette. I shall inform Margaret and Sarah," said Lady Alverley.

She did so on the afternoon in question. Margaret squealed in delight. "Oh, Grandmama! Thank you so much!"

Lady Alverley noticed that her eldest granddaughter did not exhibit the same excess of excitement as her sister. "And what of you, Sarah? Are you not as mad for the lessons as Margaret?"

"I have a black confession to make, ma'am," said Sarah with a half-guilty expression. "I already know how to waltz."

"No!" exclaimed Margaret, her eyes opening wide in astonishment.

Sarah laughed. "Well, yes, I do."

"How could you know the waltz, Sarah? We scarcely went anywhere," said Margaret.

"Do you recall Maggie Price's brother?" asked Sarah. When her sister nodded, she turned to give an explanation to Lady Alverley and Miss Hanson. "Markham Price is the son of a neighbor of ours. He was on leave last year from the diplomatic corps, from a post in St. Petersburg, I believe. In any event, he taught both Maggie and myself to waltz."

"You sly thing! You never said a word," said Margaret reproachfully.

"No, I didn't. It was great fun, but scarcely a dance that I wished to bring home to the schoolroom," said Sarah, laughing.

"At least you retained some shred of sense!" said Lady Alverley austerely. "And what, pray, had Miss Price's parents to say to their son's decadent behavior?"

"Actually, it was Mrs. Price who played the pianoforte for us," said Sarah. She saw the next question that was forming in Lady Alverley's eyes and said hurriedly, "Papa never knew."

"Absolutely scandalous!" said Lady Alverley.

"Quite, quite scandalous," agreed Miss Hanson with a sniff.

"However much I may decry such lax supervision over your activities, Sarah, I admit that it proves fortuitous now," said Lady Alverly. "Margaret, you may go to the waltzing party. I shall be making a few calls this afternoon and I can set you down."

"Thank you, Grandmama!" Margaret threw her arms around Lady Alverley and kissed her.

"Really, Margaret! Such a want of proper conduct. Anyone walking in might think you little better than a hoyden," said Lady Alverley reprovingly, but with the faintest of smiles.

An affection had grown up between Lady Alverley and Margaret that Sarah did not quite fully share in. Her ladyship had become fond of Sarah, too, but it was obvious that she did not engender the same depth of warmth in Lady Alverley that Margaret did.

Quite dispassionately, Sarah thought that the difference stemmed out of Margaret's own kind, affectionate nature. Margaret's emotions were so easily read and close to the surface, ready to bubble over at any time. It was difficult to hold Margaret at arm's-length. She was like a friendly and active pup, always willing to leap into whatever situation that presented itself. In short, Margaret possessed a *joie de vivre,* while Sarah herself was more reserved.

"If you do not mind it, ma'am, I shall remain behind this afternoon. I thought that I would write to my father," said Sarah.

Lady Alverley considered for a moment, then nodded. "Very well, Sarah. Pray do just as you wish. I have no particular agenda in mind today, after all. If anyone should call here, Marie shall be able to chaperone you."

"I shall be delighted," said Miss Hanson.

Within a few minutes, Lady Alverley and Margaret set off in her ladyship's carriage for Annette Lozanger's town house.

Sarah sat down at the secretary in the drawing room and penned a short letter to her father. She had developed the habit of writing a few lines each month about her own and Margaret's activities and the people they had met, feeling that it was her duty to keep Sir Francis informed about their lives. Sarah had been surprised and pleased when Margaret had announced a few weeks before that she, too, had recently written to their father.

Of course, Sir Francis had yet to honor them with anything but a single, brief page. It almost made one wonder whether he was actually reading their letters. But Sarah cherished the hope that the housekeeper was seeing to it that all of the letters from his daughters were propped up just where Sir Francis would be most likely to see them, so that he would pick them up and read them.

When she had finished, Sarah gave the letter to a footman to be posted. Then she went upstairs to retrieve her most recent acquisition from Hatchard's bookshop in Piccadilly. She had discovered that the front drawing room had better light than either the library or the sitting room and she had begun to take her books downstairs.

Margaret liked nothing better than curling up with either *La Belle Assemblee* or *The Lady's Magazine,* but Sarah's reading tastes were broader. When she had discovered the bookshop, she had made a habit of stopping in to browse and to select a few titles.

Miss Hanson looked up from her embroidery when Sarah reentered the drawing room. She saw the volume and shook her head. Though sympathetic to Sarah's craving for something more to read than the latest *on dits* and hints on fashion, Miss Hanson had very mixed feelings about some of Sarah's purchases.

"Be very careful, my dear Sarah. You mustn't get the reputation for being a bluestocking. Reading a romance or two cannot hurt you, but if it became widely known that you liked such things as Plutarch's *History,* it would quite shock some of your friends," said Miss Hanson. "Believe me, there are any number of gentlemen who would think less of you for displaying an unwelcome academic bent."

"I shall be circumspect, I promise you," said Sarah, as she opened the heavy volume. She quickly found her place, which she had saved with a velvet marker. "If anyone comes to call, I shall hide Plutarch under the cushions."

"Surely an ignoble necessity for such a weighty gentleman," said Miss Hanson, and chuckled at her own joke.

Sarah laughed and agreed.

A half hour passed with unusual quiet. Neither Miss Hanson nor Sarah minded. It was so rare to have a slice of peace. Miss Hanson began to hum softly. Sarah glanced over the top of her book at her companion, and smiled, before turning her attention back to the page.

There came a knock on the door, swiftly followed by the butler's entrance. "Lord Eustace."

Exchanging a quick look with Miss Hanson, whose expression was horrified, Sarah swept the thick volume under a pillow. She looked up to meet Lord Eustace's gaze. A half-guilty smile entered her hazel eyes. "My lord, what an unexpected pleasure."

He walked over to bow over her extended hand, then turned politely to take Miss Hanson's trembling hand for a brief instant. "I trust not an unpleasant one?"

Miss Hanson tittered. "Why, what a thing to say, my lord! I was just remarking to Miss Sommers that we were too quiet. Your visit is well-timed, indeed!"

Lord Eustace inclined his head to Miss Hanson, acknowledging her profuse welcome. "I am honored by the compliment, ma'am." He turned and sat down beside Sarah on the settee, shifting the pillows away. As he did so, his fingers came in contact with the hardbound cover of the book and he drew it out of hiding. Glancing curiously at the title, Lord Eustace's brows rose in surprise. "Plutarch's *History*? Who has a penchant for such weighty reading?"

Chapter Fifteen

Miss Hanson made a distressed sound and shielded her eyes behind one hand.

Sarah cast an apologetic glance at her. "I'm afraid that it is mine, my lord," she confessed. A challenging gleam came into her eyes. "I hope that this discovery does not give you a disgust of me."

A stifled moan escaped Miss Hanson's lips and she peeped from between her fingers to observe his lordship's reaction.

"On the contrary." Lord Eustace was amused. He said with a smile, "I often enjoy the classics. Have you read Euripedes or Cato, Miss Sommers?"

"I have dipped into Cato, my lord, but my father once told me that the Greek playwright was a bit shocking and that he did not recommend those works to me," said Sarah.

"Quite right. Euripedes's plays are considered fast even in our day," said Lord Eustace. He regarded her curiously. "You have an unusual parent, Miss Sommers. It is rare that females are allowed such a liberal education. What is his name?"

"My father is Sir Francis Sommers. Perhaps you have had occasion to read some of his work," said Sarah tentatively.

Lord Eustace's face lit up with recognition. "Sir Francis Sommers! Of course I have read his work. I should have guessed your relationship by the name, but it never occurred to me that you and your sister were the daughters of one of the eminent scholars of our times."

"Is he, indeed?" asked Sarah on a note of surprise. "I knew that Papa's work had been well-received, but I had no notion that he was held in such high esteem."

Lord Eustace smiled. "He obviously kept himself very

close. Perhaps he did not wish to appear the braggart in your eyes."

"I think it far more likely that he forgot to say anything to us," said Sarah dryly. "Papa is quite absent-minded about practical things, you see. He is always thinking about his books. He is a bit of a recluse, actually."

"I should like to meet Sir Francis one day. I am an admirer of his work, just as I am an admirer of his daughters," said Lord Eustace.

Sarah shook her head. "You are complimentary indeed, my lord. However, I suspect from what you have already said that neither my sister nor I can hold a candle to our respected parent in your eyes."

Lord Eustace laughed again. "I protest the slur to my character, ma'am. I see that I must prove my devotion. Therefore, I shall reveal to you now that I have called in hopes of persuading you and your sister to go riding with me this afternoon."

"I would be delighted, Lord Eustace. However, my sister is unavailable. She has gone to join friends for a dancing lesson," said Sarah.

"A dancing lesson?" asked Lord Eustace. He looked both surprised and skeptical. "How is this? Miss Margaret has always appeared to advantage on the dance floor."

"But she does not yet know how to waltz, my lord," said Sarah, twinkling up at him. "And now that we have both been given permission to waltz, Margaret doesn't wish to appear behind."

"I understand, of course. The waltz has swept the town from one end to the other. I have never seen anything like it. And did you not wish to join the other young ladies, Miss Sommers?" asked Lord Eustace.

"It is very lowering, but I must confess that I learned the waltz before I ever came to London," said Sarah, casting down her gaze.

Lord Eustace laughed. "You are beforehand of the fashion, I perceive! I hope that you save a waltz for me, Miss Sommers, when next I see you during a function. I would like to take a turn with you about the floor."

Sarah smiled at him. Her heart thumped. "I shall certainly do so, my lord."

Lord Eustace rose to his feet. He cast a glance at the mantel clock. "I have left my horses standing, so I hope that you will excuse me. I shall return about a quarter to five, if that is agreeable, Miss Sommers."

"Quite, my lord," said Sarah, giving her hand to him again.

Lord Eustace took his leave of her and of Miss Hanson before exiting the drawing room.

Miss Hanson looked over at Sarah. "My dear, you handled that very well."

"I scarce know what you mean, Miss Hanson," said Sarah, retrieving her book.

"It is a coup to have elicited a promise from Lord Eustace for the waltz, as well you know. I shall inform Lady Alverley of it when she comes in. Her ladyship will be most gratified, I assure you," said Miss Hanson.

She smiled at Sarah's level stare. "You do not like me to extol your conquest! Very well! I shall say nothing more. I shall go up to rest a bit before dinner."

Miss Hanson gathered up her embroidery and rose to her feet. Before leaving the room, she paused to say, "You will naturally take a groom with you this afternoon."

"Of course," agreed Sarah.

Though Sarah tried to focus on the book in her hands, she found it difficult to rekindle her interest in it when all she could think about was the coming ride with Lord Eustace. She glanced up at the clock. It was terrible of her, but she really hoped that Lady Alverley and Margaret would not return before the time appointed for her ride with Lord Eustace. Sarah acknowledged to herself that she wanted to ride just with Lord Eustace, not share the time with her sister.

"I am horrid, truly horrid," she said aloud. Snapping the book closed, Sarah got up and left the drawing room. She was going to go upstairs and change into her habit at once. And hopefully she would be gone before Margaret returned.

It happened just as Sarah had guiltily hoped. She and Lord Eustace went riding together in the park, unaccompanied except by a respectable groom, who kept a discreet distance between himself and the two riders. It was a very pleasant hour. They saw several personages known to both of them, but almost by tacit agreement Lord Eustace and Sarah kept from becoming joined with any other party.

A quick gallop down a grassy verge lent color to Sarah's face and put laughter into her eyes. "Marvelous!" she exclaimed as she rode up beside her companion. "I have needed to have the cobwebs blown out of my head."

Lord Eustace looked at her, his eyes gleaming in appreciation. "You are remarkably beautiful today, Miss Sommers."

Sarah's eyes widened in startlement, before she colored up. She looked away in sudden shyness. "Thank you, my lord."

He gestured to the beds of flowers that were in bloom. The air was filled with their scent. "It is a beautiful time of year, is it not?"

Sarah was glad of the change in conversation. She needed a moment to recover her countenance. She was flustered and absurdly happy. Lord Eustace had not before paid her such a forthright compliment. "Yes, yes. Quite beautiful."

Lord Eustace turned his horse and began walking it back the way they had come. Sarah followed his lead and paced her mare to match his horse. Lord Eustace glanced at her, a slight frown on his face. "It occurs to me, Miss Sommers, that we have not often spent time together. We are generally surrounded by other people."

"That is true, my lord," said Sarah tranquilly. She wondered what he was thinking, but he did not elaborate. A companionable silence fell as their horses sedately crossed the park toward the gate.

"I have enjoyed your company, Miss Sommers," said Lord Eustace abruptly.

Sarah was astonished. She looked over at him. "Why, thank you, my lord. I have enjoyed the ride, also."

"It is more than that. You and I have many tastes in common and similar intellects. I cannot recall ever becoming bored in your company. In short, Miss Sommers, I have grown to recognize that your friendship means much to me," said Lord Eustace.

Sarah looked across her horse's twitching ears. "I am honored, my lord," she said, speaking past the constriction in her throat. She didn't know whether she should laugh or cry. On the one hand, it was wonderful to receive such a compliment from someone like Lord Eustace; on the other hand, she very much wished that he felt something warmer for her than mere friendship.

As they turned out of the park, Sarah heard her name called. She turned her head, pulling up her horse. Lord Mittenger was waving to her from his carriage, which he had stopped.

"Here is Lord Mittenger, my lord," said Sarah, regarding the baron's appearance with relief. The distraction was welcome to her.

"Yes, so I see," said Lord Eustace shortly.

Sarah walked her horse over to the baron's carriage. "Well met, my lord!" she said, holding out her hand to him.

Lord Mittenger made a short bow over her fingers, clasping her hand only briefly before he acknowledged Lord Eustace's presence. "Lord Eustace, your obedient servant."

Lord Eustace nodded. "Mittenger."

Lord Mittenger turned back to Sarah. His dark eyes held a warmth of expression. "My dear Miss Sommers, how fortunate it is that I have run into you this afternoon. I would like permission to call on you tomorrow, if I may."

"But of course, Lord Mittenger," said Sarah with a faintly surprised inflection in her voice. His lordship had often called to visit or to take tea with them. Surely he had grown used to his welcome by now, and she said as much. "You are always a welcome visitor, my lord."

"I had hoped that you would say so, dear ma'am," said Lord Mittenger, a smile lighting his features. "I shall call on you tomorrow then, perhaps at one o'clock?"

"I shall look forward to it, my lord," said Sarah. She backed her horse as Lord Mittenger shook out his reins and with a flourish continued on into the park.

"You are on a familiar footing with Lord Mittenger," commented Lord Eustace.

Sarah glanced at her companion swiftly, her ears having detected a slightly censorious note in his voice. "Why, yes. Lord Mittenger is one of our oldest friends here in London," she said.

"I see," said Lord Eustace. His expression slightly bored, he introduced another topic and they did not mention the encounter with Lord Mittenger again. Lord Eustace saw Sarah to the steps of Alverley House, where the groom helped her to dismount and took her horse. Lord Eustace declined Sarah's invitation to come in for refreshments. "No doubt I shall see you at the soirée later this evening?" he asked, smiling down at her.

Sarah returned the smile. Her hazel eyes sparkled. "Of course, my lord. We are never home on any given evening. I am sure that you must have noticed that by now."

Lord Eustace laughed. "Yes, quite frankly, I have. Didn't I predict just that sort of success when I first met you and Miss Margaret?"

"Indeed, you did, my lord," agreed Sarah. He took his leave of her and rode off. Sarah lifted the hem of her riding habit, and whip in hand, entered the town house.

When Sarah went upstairs to change out of her habit, she was surprised to find Holby waiting for her rather than her new maid, Bordon. "Holby! Why, what is this? Where is Bordon?"

"She was given the afternoon off, Miss Sarah. I told her to go on and I would help you whenever you came in," said Holby.

"I am glad. I miss you, my old friend and confidante," said Sarah with a quick smile as she stripped off her gloves and laid them aside with her whip and hat.

Holby helped her out of the habit. "Miss Sarah, there is something that I have been wanting to talk to you about."

"Whatever is it, Holby? You know that you may say anything that you please to me," said Sarah, glancing at the maid's somber expression.

"It's Miss Margaret, miss. I am concerned for her," said the maid.

Sarah turned completely around. "What is wrong with Margaret?"

The maid shook her head. "I'm not certain, Miss Sarah. But I hear her sometimes at night, crying herself to sleep. And nights when she is too tired except to fall straight into bed, I can't help but think that she has deliberately gone the pace too fast so that she is too exhausted to stay awake."

Sarah frowned, saying slowly, "I, too, have been concerned about her, Holby. I suspected weeks past that she was not enjoying herself as she was wont to do. Oh, she is very willing to go anywhere and begs to be allowed to attend even those entertainments that Lady Alverley would pass on because her ladyship wishes us to rest. I've spoken to Margaret about it, but she laughed it off. She said that she was tired and often got the headache from the heat at the routs."

"That's as may be, Miss Sarah. But there's more to it. I am sure of it. Something is bothering Miss Margaret terribly, but not a word will she say to me," said Holby.

"Perhaps I should talk to her again," said Sarah, still frowning.

"I wish you would, miss. I see the awful strain that she is trying to hide, and I tell you now that it bodes no good," said Holby.

Sarah was a good deal bothered by the maid's disclosures. As an old family retainer, Holby knew both herself and Margaret perhaps better than anyone. Certainly better than anyone else in London. Sarah resolved to speak to her sister at the earliest opportunity.

When Margaret returned from the dancing party, she was full of high spirits. She began to strip the kid gloves from her hands. "Oh, Sarah! You should have been there! It was such fun."

"I am glad that you had a nice time, dear Margaret." Sarah hesitated, then made the plunge. "Margaret, I should like to discuss something with you."

Margaret looked around quickly at her sister. "Oh, dear! You have that serious expression in your eyes. What is it, Sarah? Has Grandmama decided that she has had enough of us?"

"Nothing like that," said Sarah. "Actually, I wished to talk about you. I expressed concern to you some weeks past and—"

"I told you, Sarah, you need not be anxious on my account," said Margaret with a gay laugh. She got up from the settee, holding her gloves tightly in one hand.

Sarah reached out and caught her sister's wrist. Earnestly,

she looked up into her younger sister's face. "Margaret, Holby tells me that you cry yourself to sleep some nights. Oh, my dear! Pray confide in me. What affects you so?"

Margaret stared down at her. There was anger and fear in her eyes. Both of her fists were clenched. "Nothing, I tell you! Now let me go." She wrenched free and ran to the door.

"Margaret—!"

The door slammed and Sarah was left staring at it, more perturbed than ever. Several minutes passed while she sat in thought. It was obvious that Margaret did not want her to pry. But Sarah had seen that underneath her sister's anger was a desperate unhappiness. She could not shut her eyes to it. Margaret was her sister and she loved her. She could not simply shrug and walk away.

Sarah concluded that she had to get to the bottom of whatever was bothering her sister. She was determined to make another opportunity to speak to Margaret again.

That evening at the soirée, someone else had occasion to mention her sister to Sarah. "Far be for me to pry, my dear. But I must tell you that this afternoon at my dancing party, I saw something in Margaret that was quite uncharacteristic," said Annette Lozanger. "When she thought that no one was looking, she would get almost a woebegone expression on her face. She actually looked weary. But whenever someone addressed her or glanced in her direction, she instantly began laughing and chattering quite in her usual manner."

"I am grateful for your concern, ma'am. I have also noticed lately that Margaret is not herself, but I cannot quite put my finger on it," said Sarah. "Have you spoken to my grandmother about Margaret?"

"I have not had the opportunity to do so yet this evening, but rest assured that I shall," said Annette Lozanger. "It is my belief that the girl is going the pace too fast. She should be reined in."

"Believe me, ma'am, I hope that we can do just that," said Sarah.

"See that you do. She will sicken with something if she is not forced to rest," said Annette Lozanger. She gestured with her fan. "Look at her now! One would never know that she is in the least physical distress. But I have sharper eyes than most. I saw the shadows under her eyes, and those speak more eloquently than all of her appealing ways." With a nod, she passed on.

Sarah stood where the lady had left her. A frown of concern was on her face as she looked across the floor at her sister. Margaret was dancing with one of her admirers, Mr. Matthews. She was laughing and her eyes sparkled, but Sarah thought that she could detect almost a feverishness in her sister's gaiety.

"A penny for them."

Sarah was startled and quickly looked around. She met Lord Eustace's smiling gaze, and colored faintly with embarrassment. "My lord! I am sorry. I was not aware of your approach."

"You were obviously in deep reflection," said Lord Eustace. "Have I disturbed you, Miss Sommers? Shall I go away?"

Sarah shook her head, laughing. "No, of course not! I am always happy to see you, my lord."

"There was trouble in your expression. Is there anything that I can do to help?" asked Lord Eustace quietly.

Sarah glanced upward, dismayed that he had read so much in her face. He knew her better than she had supposed. She shook her head. "No, my lord. There is nothing that you can do."

"Ah, I was right. You are troubled. And you were looking in the direction of your sister," said Lord Eustace. While Sarah stared at him, he regarded the lively lady on the dance floor. "She is partnered by Mr. Matthews. Is that what troubles you, Miss Sommers?"

"Of course not! I have no objection to Mr. Matthews at all," said Sarah quickly. When he turned an inquiring expression upon her, she started to laugh. "I cannot confide in you, you must know that I cannot!"

"Friends may share what others cannot," suggested Lord Eustace.

There was a short silence, while Sarah grappled with what he had said. Finally, she looked up at him. "Very well, my lord. I shall tell you that I do have concern for my sister. Margaret seems to be under a strain of some sort. Annette

Lozanger was just telling me that she has noticed it, as well. But Margaret claims that she is simply tired. I don't doubt it, for she always throws herself so wholeheartedly into everything!"

"There is something about your sister—" Lord Eustace shook his head, his eyes straying again to the young girl on the dance floor. "I can't explain it. Sometimes when I look at her, it's as though I see someone else. A trick of expression, a gesture—"

Sarah was surprised by what he had said. She waited for Lord Eustace to continue, but when it became obvious that he had become lost in his reflections, she prompted, "Someone else, my lord? What do you mean?"

Lord Eustace started. He looked around at her swiftly. Color rose under his tan. "Forgive me, Miss Sommers. I was woolgathering. I did not intend to be such dull company. Let me escort you to the refreshments table."

"No, not just yet, if you please," said Sarah, laying a detaining hand on his sleeve. A startling suspicion had entered her mind and she had to satisfy herself that it was not true. She looked up at him earnestly. "My lord, I wish you will tell me! I heard some time ago about your betrothed, Miss Vivian Leander and—"

Lord Eustace regarded her with a hardening expression. "This is not a subject that I care to discuss, Miss Sommers."

"I am sorry! I do not mean to pry into painful memories," said Sarah hurriedly. "But does my sister somehow remind you of Miss Leander? Is that whom you see when you look at her?"

He looked away for a moment. When he returned his gaze to her, he said harshly, "Yes, Miss Sommers, she does! She is vivacious and lovely and entirely captivating. I am haunted by the resemblance."

"Forgive me, my lord. But is it my sister or Miss Leander whom you pay court to?" asked Sarah, greatly daring. Her heart was pounding as she awaited his answer.

Lord Eustace stared at her, a stunned expression in his eyes. Then his face flushed with anger. "You go too far, Miss Sommers!" He turned on his heel and strode swiftly away.

Sarah watched him go, a horrible sinking feeling inside of her. It was confirmed when Lord Eustace avoided her for the remainder of the evening. Not once did he speak to her, even to take leave of her as he was wont to do. Sarah scarcely recalled what the rest of the evening was like, except that she had seldom spent a worst one anywhere.

Chapter Sixteen

The following day Lord Mittenger called as he had promised. He requested a private word with Sarah. "I know that I am breaking all the conventions, Miss Hanson. However, I am persuaded that you shall allow me five minutes," he said with a grave smile.

There was uncertainty in Miss Hanson's expression. "I don't quite know what to say. Lady Alverley is out and—"

"I promise you that I shall be completely circumspect," said Lord Mittenger.

Miss Hanson glanced toward Sarah. Her gaze was anxious. "Sarah?"

"I don't think that her ladyship will fault you, ma'am. If you wish to remain within call, you might wait just outside the door," said Sarah. Her thoughts were not really engaged by the conversation except in a fleeting way. She kept thinking about what she had said to Lord Eustace and wishing that she could undo it.

"Yes, I am persuaded that will be all right," said Miss Hanson. "Very well, my lord. Five minutes by my watch."

"Thank you, Miss Hanson." The baron showed the lady out of the drawing room. He shut the door before returning to seat himself beside Sarah on the settee. He lifted her hand. "Miss Sommers, you cannot be unaware of my purpose in requesting this interview. I have made my admiration known to you. Indeed, I have been hoping to speak to you on this topic for some weeks. Miss Sommers, will you do me the honor of becoming my lady wife?"

Sarah's attention was at last fully captured. "What?" she asked in liveliest astonishment.

Lord Mittenger was taken aback by her reaction. "Why, I have just offered to you my heart and my hand, Miss Sommers. Surely you realized that was my intent?"

Sarah colored. "I—forgive me, my lord. You have caught me off guard."

Lord Mittenger began to frown. "How is this, Miss Sommers? I thought I had made my meaning perfectly clear when I stopped you at the park."

Sarah shook her head, flushing still more hotly. She withdrew her hand from his clasp. "I suppose that I am unnaturally naive, my lord. I am sorry. I did not understand."

"I have been too forward. I knew it and yet I rushed in. Now see what has come of it! I have caused you unwarranted confusion and embarrassment. Forgive me, Miss Sommers," said Lord Mittenger contritely.

Sarah covered her cheeks with her hands. She managed a shaky laugh. "Oh, dear! What am I to say?"

Lord Mittenger seized his opportunity. He recaptured one of her hands, not without difficulty. "My dear Miss Sommers! Your maidenly confusion does you no discredit in my eyes. Indeed, it but reinforces my certainty that you are the lady whom I wish to make my own. I ask that you consider my suit for your hand."

"My lord. Dear Lord Mittenger, I fear that I cannot," said Sarah regretfully. "You have done me a great honor today, but I would be less than honest if I were to accept you. You have offered your heart and your hand to me, while I can offer only my hand in return."

Lord Mittenger was silent for a moment, his eyes fixed on her face. Gravely, he said, "I understand you, Miss Sommers. Believe me, my regard for you is higher than ever before. I only wish that you could return my feelings." He stood up, carrying her hand to his lips as he bowed over it. When he straightened, he managed to smile down at her. "I shall leave you now. Miss Hanson will no doubt be waiting for me. Good-bye, Miss Sommers."

"Good-bye, Lord Mittenger," said Sarah in a low voice.

He walked quickly to the door, opened it, and exited. Sarah heard a brief exchange between Lord Mittenger and Miss Hanson, before that lady reentered the drawing room.

Miss Hanson's eyes were bright with curiosity. "My dear! What happened with Lord Mittenger? He left here with such a grave expression. I hope that you did not offend him?"

"Offend him? Not intentionally, ma'am," said Sarah quietly, rising from the settee and going over to the window. She lifted the curtain so that she could look down into the street. Lord Mittenger was just then emerging from the town house. Sarah watched him descend the steps toward his carriage.

"Oh, then everything is all right," said Miss Hanson with a note of relief. "For an instant I thought—but all is quite all right, after all."

Sarah did not reply. She watched as Lord Mittenger climbed up into his curricle and took up the reins. As he drove away, she wondered whether she was allowing her best chance for happiness to exit her life. She could not have Lord Eustace, whom she loved. She did not love Lord Mittenger, but she knew that the baron would have done his best to make her happy. "Perhaps I am a fool," she murmured.

"What did you say, my dear? I did not quite hear you," said Miss Hanson.

Sarah turned. "I think that I shall go upstairs and lie down for a while, Miss Hanson. Pray excuse me."

"But of course, Sarah! Do just as you wish."

As Sarah left the drawing room, she wished that she could do just that. Unfortunately, it was not in her power to obtain the one thing that she most desired.

Over the next several days, Lord Eustace made it a point to continue to avoid Sarah. When he chanced to encounter her at a function, he was merely civil. Gone was the friendly smile, the polite inquiry into her well-being, the occasional burst of candor and comradery. Lord Eustace offered only a cold bow and a nod before moving on to greet someone else. Sarah was hurt more than she could ever have imagined that she could be. She had lost her friend.

Lady Frobisher asked Sarah about Lord Eustace's sudden about-face. "Have you and my brother had a falling out, Sarah?" she asked gently.

"Not precisely," said Sarah. She managed to smile. "You will no doubt tell me what a fool I have been and indeed I have already thought it, Mary. I asked Lord Eustace as boldly as you please whether Margaret reminded him too much of Vivian Leander."

"My dear!" Lady Frobisher stared at her. Then a thoughtful expression came into her eyes. "Sarah, I think you have hit upon something. Margaret and Vivian Leander . . . yes, there are similarities. How strange that I did not see it before! Both beautiful, both lively and captivating. Poor Gil! I did not realize that he was still carrying the torch for her!"

"Then you do believe that his lordship is still in love with Miss Leander?" asked Sarah anxiously.

Lady Frobisher looked at her quickly. "You are concerned for Margaret? Of course you are and little wonder! You are wiser than you know, Sarah. It would be a very good notion for you to warn Lady Alverley of what you suspect. You may tell her that she may apply to me for corroboration. Lady Alverley will know how best to protect Margaret."

"Protect her?" repeated Sarah quickly. "What do you mean?"

"Unless Lady Alverley is a fool, she will not wish to encourage my brother to dangle after Margaret," said Lady Frobisher forthrightly. She shook her head. "Much as it distresses me to say it, it would be an ill wind, indeed, for any young woman to be forced to compete with a dead woman."

"Yes, I understand," said Sarah unhappily.

Lady Frobisher touched Sarah's arm in sympathy. "I am sorry, my dear. I know what good friends that you and Gil have been. It must be difficult for you since he has turned away. But perhaps it is for the best just now."

Sarah felt tears start into her eyes, but she blinked them back. "It is always painful to lose a friend, of course. But I shall manage."

"Good girl," said Lady Frobisher. "Now I see that my lord is signaling to me. We will shortly be leaving, I suspect. Good night, dear Sarah."

Sarah said good night and Lady Frobisher swished away. Sarah was left prey to her emotions. She was confused and dismayed. Everything was horrid. She had not only lost Lord Eustace's friendship, but she had virtually driven a spoke through the wheel of her sister's future happiness. She had an obligation to inform her grandmother of what Lady Frobisher had said and when she did so, Lord Eustace would most likely not be considered a good candidate any longer. Sarah knew that if her sister was in any way emotionally attached to Lord Eustace, Margaret would feel pain at the separation. Yet if she said nothing, and Margaret did indeed accept an offer from Lord Eustace, then her sister would experience disillusionment and pain of another sort.

By the time that the long evening was over and they had returned to Alverley House, Sarah was worn out. She made no demur when her maid insisted that she go straight to bed.

However, after the candle was blown out and the room was darkened, Sarah could not sleep. She stared into the shadows of the bed canopy overhead, her thoughts giving her no rest. Finally, she tossed back the covers and got out of bed. She had to talk to Margaret about Lord Eustace, even as late as it was. She had to find out just how strongly Margaret felt about him, and perhaps drop a gentle warning in her sister's ear.

Pulling on a wrapper and slipping her feet into slippers, she crept out of her bedroom and down the hallway to her sister's door. Easing open the door, she slipped inside. There was enough light from the glow of the dying fire that she easily made out the sleeping form under the bedclothes.

Sarah went over to the bed to waken her sister. "Margaret? Margaret, are you awake?" When there was no response, Sarah gently pulled down the covers. She straightened, shocked, for there was only a bolster and a pillow where her sister should have been.

Margaret was not in her bed. With a sickening feeling, Sarah realized that her sister had sneaked out of the town house. Panic licked at her thoughts, but Sarah got control of herself. It was obvious that Margaret had made her plans carefully. Her gown that she had worn that evening was draped over a chair. The wardrobe door was open, so that meant Margaret had taken something else that she could put on by herself. Finally, Margaret had carefully made it appear that she was safely in bed in the event that her maid peeped in on her during the night. All of it pointed to a spirited young girl's escapade from which she fully intended to return.

Thoughtless, dangerous, mad! Sarah could think of a number of labels for her sister's adventure. It was quite obvious that Margaret had not gone off on her own. She had an accomplice. A gentleman, of course! There could be no other explanation.

Sarah's first inclination was to rouse the household and go in search of her sister. But she instinctively shrank from the inevitable repercussions of such a course. If she did that, Margaret's clandestine assignation would become common knowledge to the entire staff of servants. The tale would be all over London before sundown the next day. The resulting scandal could possibly destroy Margaret's reputation. As for Lady Alverley, Sarah thought that she could imagine well enough what a blow it would be for her ladyship to stand by helpless while her favorite granddaughter was shredded by such heartless individuals as Lady Cromes and Mrs. Plummer.

Sarah shivered. She had begun to grow cold as she stood there in hurried reflection. Sarah knew that she had to confront Margaret, but she decided that it was silly to freeze while she was waiting for her. Taking off her slippers, Sarah crawled into her sister's bed. Even if she fell asleep, she would know when Margaret returned.

Sarah never knew later how much time had passed before the tiniest creak of the door roused her. She had been dozing lightly and fitfully, but at that insignificant sound she came fully awake. Sarah remained quiet, her body tense, while she listened to the brushing of skirt across the carpet and the unmistakable sounds of someone undressing.

Then the covers of the bed were lifted. Sarah sat up. "Hello, Margaret."

Margaret leaped back, uttering a frightened squeak.

"Shh! Do you wish to rouse the whole house?" asked Sarah in a whisper.

Margaret slid into the bed. She drew her knees up to her chest and clasped them round with her slender arms. "What are you doing here, Sarah?"

"I think it is I who should be requiring answers," said Sarah. "Where have you been, Margaret? I came in to talk to you and discovered that you were gone. And pray do not spin some farrago of nonsense, for I know that you have been out with someone!"

Margaret tossed her head. "Very well, Miss Snoop! If you must know, I have been to a masquerade."

"With whom?" demanded Sarah. Her sister did not answer at once and she grabbed her arm. "With whom, Margaret? Was it some worthless cad whom you are too ashamed to introduce to our grandmother? Is that it?"

"No! It was Captain Jeffries! Let go of me, Sarah, do! You're hurting me," said Margaret, pulling her arm free and rubbing it.

"Captain Jeffries!" Sarah was stunned. She could not imagine the cavalry officer lending himself to something so potentially damaging as escorting a young girl to a public masquerade.

"You need not sound so amazed, Sarah," said Margaret sullenly.

"I supposed that Captain Jeffries at least would have had more sense," said Sarah in a curt tone.

"What would you know about it?" asked Margaret angrily. Then her voice changed. "Oh, Sarah, if you had only been there! I know that you would have liked it. It was so much fun. And then we drove past the Thames and all of the lights on the ships were bobbing and reflecting on the black water. It was so beautiful."

"Margaret, why? I don't understand! Why would you risk yourself in this fashion when you can see Captain Jeffries anywhere?" asked Sarah. An appalling thought suddenly hit her. "Margaret, is this why you have been so tired lately? Have you been out like this before? Have you acquired a taste for-for illicit affairs?"

"No, of course I haven't! Why, Sarah, what are you thinking? I am not some vulgar hoyden!" cried Margaret.

"Of course you are not," said Sarah quickly. She was ashamed of her suspicions. Surely she knew her own sister better. Margaret was simply spirited and wanted to enjoy life. It had been a harmless enough excursion, as it went. Margaret had been more interested in telling her about the masquerade and the lights on the Thames than she had been in her escort.

Margaret took urgent hold of her wrist. "Sarah, you are not going to tell Grandmama, are you? Oh, pray do not! I could not bear it if she were to be angry with me!"

"No, I-I don't think that I shall," said Sarah hesitantly. She wasn't certain that she was being perfectly wise in yielding to her sister's entreaties, but she could perceive that Margaret was genuinely distressed. "But you must promise me, Margaret! No more of these clandestine excursions with anyone!"

"Oh no! I shan't do it again, I promise," said Margaret, throwing her arms around Sarah.

After a few minutes more of whispered assurances between them and another fond embrace, Sarah left her sister's bedroom and softly reentered her own. As she slid into her own bed, she suddenly realized that she had not said one word about Lord Eustace to her sister. Her former concern had completely faded under the shock of discovering what her sister had been up to. Now Sarah thought that everything else could wait at least until morning.

However, as the days slowly passed one into another, Sarah began to realize that Margaret was just as determined not to be engaged in any kind of conversation with her. Margaret took care never to be alone with Sarah, and whenever Sarah did try to say anything to her, Margaret instantly made some excuse and whisked herself off. There were no more exchanged confidences between them.

Even on Sunday, when Sarah hoped that their usual perambulations in Kensington Gardens would grant her the opportunity that she needed, Margaret again thwarted her. Margaret claimed that she preferred to sit with her grandmother and Miss Hanson. "I have been drawing the bustle too much this week," she told Lady Alverley with a bright smile.

"I have noticed that you appear more tired than usual, my dear," said Lady Alverley. "I trust that you are resting well at night, Margaret. Perhaps you should lie down more often in the afternoons."

Margaret glanced away, only to meet Sarah's steady gaze. She flushed hotly. "That isn't necessary, Grandmama. I am certain that I shall soon feel more the thing."

"We don't need to attend every function, ma'am," said

Sarah. "Surely we are well enough established to be a little more discriminate in choosing which affairs that we should grace with our presence?"

"You may be right, Sarah. I have often said that you girls must learn to pace yourselves," said Lady Alverley. "Perhaps I shall scale back the number of invitations that we accept."

"But I don't wish to stay home!" exclaimed Margaret hotly. "I want to go to every party and entertainment that I can!"

"Margaret, pray be sensible. It would be best, at least for a time," said Sarah gently.

Margaret rounded on Sarah with an angry expression. "How dare you, Sarah! You have no notion what is or isn't best for me!" She leaped up and fled to the carriage.

"Annette Lozanger had told me that Margaret was looking pulled. I should have paid closer attention, for I begin to think that Margaret is actually burnt to the socket. I cannot recall ever seeing her indulge in a tantrum," said Lady Alverley, frowning as she gazed after her granddaughter.

Miss Hanson shook her head, pursing her lips. "No, indeed, my lady. Margaret is always so cheerful and energetic. One wonders whether she is sickening from something."

"I trust not. I have not made allowances for illness of any kind. Margaret must simply get over whatever ails her as quickly as possible," said Lady Alverley with finality.

"Just so, my lady," said Miss Hanson, nodding in agreement.

Sarah had listened with only half an ear. She was still shocked by Margaret's attack. She was also bewildered and frustrated. She could not understand her sister's about-face. It was almost as though Margaret now looked upon her as a stranger, or worse, an enemy.

"I have made my decision," announced Lady Alverley, rising to her feet. "Margaret must remain at home this evening. I wish her to rest. Marie, I would like you to remain behind, as well, so that I can be certain Margaret does just as I will tell her."

"Yes, my lady. I will do as you request," said Miss Hanson.

"What of me?" asked Sarah. "Should I not remain behind also? I can help Miss Hanson persuade Margaret—"

Lady Alverley snorted. "My dear Sarah! From what I saw a bare moment ago, you could not persuade Margaret to anything to her good. She obviously resents you, though I haven't a notion why."

"Nor I, ma'am," said Sarah in a low voice.

Lady Alverley looked sharply at her. "Have you and Margaret had a falling out, Sarah? Perhaps over one of your admirers?"

"Of course not!" exclaimed Sarah. "We haven't exchanged a cross word between us of any sort!"

"I choose to believe that you have told me the truth, Sarah," said Lady Alverley.

"So I should hope, ma'am," retorted Sarah, regarding her grandmother with a shade of anger.

Lady Alverley nodded. "Let us be off, then. Lady Frobisher's ball will no doubt be a lovely affair."

Sarah's heart was not in going out that evening. Especially to Lady Frobisher's, where she would be certain of encountering Lord Eustace and have to endure his lordship's cold snub.

Chapter Seventeen

The Frobishers' ball was a gala affair. A full orchestra had been hired and there was constant dancing. One entire wall of the ballroom was mirrored, so that the ladies' dazzling gowns and the formal dark evening clothes of the gentlemen were reflected under a blaze of chandeliers. Off the ballroom were two small salons devoted to card playing for those who preferred games of chance to the exertion of dancing. At the opposite end of the long ballroom, a drawing room had been made over for refreshments.

Sarah danced nearly every set. Lord Dissinger was one of her first partners and he confided during the course of the reel that he had made an offer for Miss Darton. "I wanted you to be one of the first to know, Miss Sommers, for you are a good friend," said his lordship with an eager expression.

"Indeed, my lord, I am exceedingly happy for you and Miss Darton!" said Sarah, surprised but genuinely pleased.

"I knew that you would be glad for us," said Lord Dissinger, nodding. "It was you who brought us together in the gardens that evening. Before then, I had not really gotten to know Miss Darton, but we talked together for several minutes and discovered that we have many things in common. Why, Babs is just as mad as I am for hunting!"

As the reel separated Lord Dissinger from her, it occurred to Sarah that she had been instrumental in steering away one of her most respectable admirers. She started chuckling because she knew that if Lady Alverley ever learned of it, her ladyship would want to give her a blistering scold.

Lord Dissinger's confidences enlivened Sarah's spirits. She was able to set aside some of her dread over encountering Lord Eustace and take pleasure in the evening. She had already seen Lord Eustace, of course. Upon arrival, her eyes had automatically sought out his well-built familiar figure. Lord Eustace was naturally attired in evening clothes, a black coat and knee breeches, white stockings, and black pumps. She thought that he had rarely appeared handsomer.

Sarah did not go up to Lord Eustace as she might once have done, nor did she expect him to acknowledge her. Sarah was therefore surprised when he came up to her halfway through the evening. She had just sat down for an interlude between dance partners, plying her ivory, gilt-edged fan gently to stir the air against her warm face. She had not even seen his lordship's quiet approach, so that his sudden appearance came as something of a shock. She met his gaze, her own startled.

"Miss Sommers, good evening."

Sarah inclined her head, held mute by surprise. She had not exchanged more than a polite word or two with him since that disastrous evening when she had asked him about his former betrothed, Miss Vivian Leander.

Lord Eustace indicated the empty chair beside her. "May I?"

Sarah felt her heart begin to race. She could not imagine why he had sought her out. She gestured permission with her fan. "Certainly, my lord."

Lord Eustace sat down. His expression was somber. "Miss Sommers, I owe you an apology. I spoke harshly to you. I am sorry for it."

"I understood it, my lord. I offended you by prying into private matters that should not have concerned me," said Sarah quietly. "I shouldn't have done so. I, too, apologize."

"Miss Sommers, you have heaped coals on my head," said Lord Eustace with a wry grin.

When she looked a question at him, he said, "Pray recall that just an instant before you inquired about my former betrothed, I had urged you to unburden yourself of a personal anxiety. I told you that one may share things with friends. Do you remember?"

"Yes, my lord," said Sarah in a low voice. She was no longer looking at him, but instead glanced out at the couples whirling about on the dance floor.

"You trusted me, Miss Sommers. But I did not reciprocate," said Lord Eustace. "I therefore must reject your apology."

Sarah looked around at him, again startled. "What?"

Lord Eustace picked up her hand and briefly squeezed it. "My dear Miss Sommers, I know that you were not asking me about Miss Leander because you had an inordinate interest in my affairs. No, you were concerned for your sister. When I finally realized what your motive was, I became ashamed that I have treated you so callously. Miss Sommers, you were not out of line to inquire what my thoughts about Miss Margaret might be. I understand and appreciate your loyalty toward her."

Sarah said nothing. She did not know how to reply because she was suddenly feeling incredibly guilty. She was not so disinterested nor as loyal as Lord Eustace was assuming. His next question took her completely by surprise.

"Do you recall that you promised to reserve a waltz for me, Miss Sommers?"

Sarah looked up quickly. She searched his face. "Yes, I do, my lord."

"Could I persuade you to honor me with this set?" asked Lord Eustace.

Sarah hesitated only the fraction of a second. "Of course, my lord." She accepted his hand and rose from her chair.

Lord Eustace led her out onto the dance floor. Sarah felt a tingling go through her body. Anticipation heightened her senses. The bright candlelight, the myriad colors of the ladies' gowns, all reflected in the long mirrors, now seemed twice as dazzling and twice as bright.

Lord Eustace clasped her hand warmly in his own. His arm circled her waist and they whirled away. Sarah knew at once that they moved together remarkably well on the floor. It was as though they were made to be with one another.

Sarah's pulses fluttered. She felt light as air. She was acutely aware of Lord Eustace's embrace and of the pleasant sandalwood scent that he used.

She glanced up into his face. Her head just brushed his chin. When he glanced down and met her gaze, she blushed faintly even as she smiled. "It is a lovely dance, is it not, my lord?"

"Indeed, Miss Sommers. And you perform it exceptionally well," said Lord Eustace quietly.

Sarah glanced away, full of confusion. There was such conflict between her heart and her head. Her heart was soaring with happiness, even as her head whispered a warning.

Despite Lady Frobisher's freely worded opinion about the danger in being attracted to her brother, Sarah did not want to thrust aside the deep attraction that she felt toward Lord Eustace. She was a fool, of course. She knew it, but she didn't want to heed what her head was telling her.

Was Lord Eustace still in love with Miss Leander? Was he in love with Margaret? Or anyone?

Sarah didn't want to believe any of it. If Lord Eustace was still in love with his former betrothed, Miss Leander, then there could be only unhappiness in store for any lady unlucky enough to fall in love with him.

There you are, Sarah! Draw back before it's too late! Sarah ignored her reason, rationalizing that it was already too late.

If Lord Eustace had simply been influenced by his memories to fall in love with her sister, Margaret, then she was still caught hopelessly in the same snare. Lord Eustace was as far away from being hers as the moon. She could never betray her sister's interests and go after Lord Eustace for herself. *Fool, fool! It was better when he wasn't speaking to you! Now look where you are!*

Sarah knew the insurmountable barriers. But she didn't care. Her heart beat strongly, drowning out the cries of her head. The strains of the waltz carried her into a peculiar reality where everything was possible, even the improbability that Lord Eustace was falling in love with her.

Lady Alverley desired to leave the Frobishers' ball at an earlier hour than was her usual wont. She complained that her new headdress was pressing into her head. "I should never have purchased it. I shall not listen to Constance Philby again, I assure you," she said irritably as she entered Alverley House, followed by Sarah.

Their entrance was heard, and Miss Hanson and Margaret emerged from the drawing room. Lady Alverley greeted them and repeated her complaint about her headdress, adding, "It is giving me the headache."

"Perhaps a glass of ratafia would be in order, my lady?" inquired Miss Hanson.

"Yes, that would be nice," said Lady Alverley, nodding. She gave her cloak to the butler. "See to it, Herbert. You may bring it into the drawing room."

"Yes, my lady."

Lady Alverley preceded the rest of the ladies into the drawing room. Immediately she pulled off the offending, heavily jeweled headdress and dropped it onto an occasional table. "Detestable thing. I would toss it into the garbage, but it came too dear."

"Perhaps you might take it back, my lady?" asked Miss Hanson.

"I shall certainly do so." With a sigh, Lady Alverley sat down on a silk-striped settee. "Come sit down beside me, Margaret. You appear completely hagged this evening. Didn't you have a good time?"

Margaret nodded. Her smile did not quite reach her eyes. "Of course, I did, Grandmama. I always do."

Lady Alverley patted her youngest granddaughter's hand. "Never mind being civil, Margaret. You did not miss a thing. It was a surprisingly insipid affair, I thought. We shall all feel better for some ratafia."

"I enjoyed myself, at least," remarked Sarah. She was still savoring the sweet memory of her waltz with Lord Eustace and the mending of the breach between them. She had been reluctant to leave when Lady Alverley declared it to be time to do so. It had been the best function she had attended in some time.

"I am glad, Sarah. By the by, I have been meaning to tell you. Earlier this week I sustained a visit from Lord Tottenham. He made an offer for your hand," said Lady Alverley.

Sarah abruptly came out of the clouds. She stared at her grandmother. "Oh! And what did you tell him, ma'am?"

"I told him, quite civilly, that since he has a nursery of hopeful children, he would do better to solicit the hand of a maiden lady already grown stable in her character, rather than that of a flighty young miss," said Lady Alverley with a thin smile.

"Really, my lady! Sarah is not in the least flighty," said Miss Hanson, shocked.

"At least, I hope that I am not," said Sarah with a laugh.

"Of course you aren't. However, it was a simple, effective way of discouraging his lordship without giving offense," said Lady Alverley.

"Quite masterly," said Miss Hanson admiringly.

"I thought so," nodded Lady Alverley.

"Have-have you had any offers for me?" asked Margaret with a studied indifference. She did not look up, but was seemingly more interested in making pleats in her skirt than in the answer to her question.

"As a matter of fact, Margaret, I have."

Margaret looked up quickly. Sarah was astonished by the intensity of the expression in her blue eyes. "Who from, Grandmama?"

At that moment, the door opened, preventing Lady Alverley from answering. The butler entered with a decanter and glasses on a tray. He served each of the ladies and exited.

Lady Alverley and Miss Hanson tasted the ratafia with every appearance of gratification. Sarah set hers aside, untasted. She didn't need a glass of wine to enhance her sense of well-being that evening.

Margaret took a small sip and wrinkled her nose. "Ugh! How disgusting." She put down the wineglass. "Grandmama, were any of the offers from gentlemen that we know?"

"Why, yes, of course. I have had to turn away Mr. Lawrence and Captain Jeffries, as well as a score of gentlemen whom I can most kindly describe as hanger's-on and witless puppies," said Lady Alverley.

At Margaret's downcast face, Lady Alverley patted her hand. "Never mind, my dear. I know that you are disappointed. But there will be an acceptable *parti* come forward before the end of the season. I am sure of it."

Her ladyship's reassurance did not appear to elevate Margaret's deflated spirits. Margaret got up from the settee. "If you do not mind, Grandmama, I shall go up to my room. I have a bit of the headache."

"Do just as you like, Margaret. Now kiss me and go on," said Lady Alverley in a kind tone. When her granddaughter had kissed her cheek and exited the drawing room, she said irritably, "What ails the girl? She is bluer than I have ever seen her."

"I am sure that Margaret is simply overtired, ma'am. She will be better for an early night," said Sarah quickly.

Lady Alverley nodded. Her frown did not lighten, however, as she reflected for a few moments. "Do you know, I quite thought that Lord Mittenger was going to come up to scratch. But all of a sudden he simply stopped calling. We scarcely see his lordship any more."

"I can explain that, Grandmama. Lord Mittenger did make me an offer. But I refused him," said Sarah quietly.

"What?" Lady Alverley glanced swiftly at her companion. "Why did I not know of this, Marie?"

Miss Hanson looked alarmed. "My lady! I had no notion! That is, I wondered but—"

"Lord Mittenger broached the subject to me in a private moment, Grandmama," said Sarah quickly. She did not want her grandmother's wrath to fall upon Miss Hanson's helpless head. "His lordship quite took me by surprise. I had no inkling of his intent."

"I find it difficult to believe that Lord Mittenger so lost his head that he forgot all convention! His lordship's manners are generally so correct," snapped Lady Alverley.

"Nevertheless, that is what happened," said Sarah with a steady look.

"One may never predict what a gentleman might do under the inspiration of the moment," said Lady Alverley, obviously much put out. "And you refused him, Sarah! Lord Mittenger! What, pray, were you thinking?"

"I was thinking that I did not love him," said Sarah quietly.

"Love! Nonsense! This is naught but caprice! You have whistled down the wind the most obliging offer that you are now likely to receive," said Lady Alverley angrily.

"I know it, ma'am." A smile suddenly hovered about Sarah's mouth. "I have thought about it any number of times since, believe me."

"Regretted your mistake, have you? Well, and so I should hope! Oh, go away! I cannot bear to look at you just now."

As Sarah obediently left the drawing room, she overheard Lady Alverley's complaint to Miss Hanson.

"What am I to do, Marie? Margaret has fallen into the megrims and Sarah insists upon holding fast to this ridiculous romantic nonsense!"

"I'm sure I don't know, my lady."

"Oh, must you always be such a witless parrot, Marie!"

Chapter Eighteen

The great actress, Mrs. Sarah Siddons, was on the bill at the Theatre Royal in Covent Garden. She was a commanding figure with dark locks and eagle eyes, perfectly cast in Shakespeare's tragedy *Macbeth*. It was a magnificent performance.

Between acts, the torches came on. Those seated in their private boxes overlooking the stage and the pits were soon visiting and being visited. Several gentlemen seated in the pits took advantage of the brighter lighting to openly ogle the ladies in the boxes through their quizzing glasses.

Sarah saw Margaret look over the edge of the box and smile suddenly. Her sister waved her fan, acknowledging one of the bold gentlemen. Margaret realized that Sarah was watching and instantly she stepped to the back of the box.

Sarah glanced out over the pits below to discover who had won her sister's notice. She had no difficulty in picking out Captain Jeffries. The cavalry officer was a half-head taller than anyone around him and he was still looking toward the box. When Captain Jeffries saw that he was under observation, he smiled and raised a gloved hand to Sarah, before he turned away.

Various admirers came into the box to pay their respects to Lady Alverley and her party and to offer to fetch refreshments. Lord and Lady Frobisher were among the stream of visitors. Lady Frobisher requested the favor of their company at a dinner that she was planning for a fortnight hence. Lady Alverley accepted for them all. She inquired about Lord Eustace. "We have not yet seen him this evening."

"Eustace will probably be along later. He ran into an old friend who begged his company at supper," said Lord Frobisher.

As the Frobishers left, Lord Darton arrived with his sister, Miss Barbara Darton, and another young lady, who was introduced as Miss Emma Jennings. Sarah liked Miss Jennings, thinking that she was a quiet, shy girl. She wondered why she had not met Miss Jennings earlier in the Season.

Lady Alverley and Miss Hanson engaged Miss Jennings in conversation. Margaret and Miss Darton at once put their heads together and exchanged whispering confidences.

Lord Darton continued to exchange pleasantries with Sarah, but his lordship seemed increasingly distracted. Sarah glanced consideringly at him. He was sitting at his ease beside her, but his gaze kept straying to Miss Jennings. His expression was oddly anxious.

"Lord Darton, is there anything wrong?" asked Sarah quietly.

His lordship started. He glanced at her, seeming to hesitate. Then he cleared his throat. "Not at all, Miss Sommers. Er-I wish to make known to you that I will shortly be entering an announcement into the newspapers. Miss Jennings has honored me by accepting my suit."

Sarah was surprised, but she greeted his pronouncement politely. "I wish you and Miss Jennings very well, my lord."

Lord Darton glumly nodded. In a burst of candor, he confessed, "Miss Jennings is the daughter of a respectable, very well-to-do cloth merchant."

"I thought that I had not met Miss Jennings before. She has lived very quietly up to now, of course," said Sarah. "I like her, Lord Darton. She is quiet and shy and I thought her prettily behaved. It is a wonder that she is not overawed by her exalted company, but I think she is handling my grandmother and Miss Hanson very well."

Lord Darton threw another glance toward his betrothed. With a surprised inflection in his voice, he said, "Yes, I suppose that she is." He suddenly smiled and there was a grateful expression on his face. He caught up Sarah's hand and briefly pressed her fingers. "Thank you, Miss Sommers. Your opinion means much to me."

Sarah turned off his compliment. Lord Darton's voice and expression were almost embarrassingly grateful. His lordship had obviously been suffering from agonies of uncertainty over the way his betrothed would be received. Sarah was glad that she had been able to reassure him, at least about her own views.

As Lord Darton retrieved his betrothed and his sister in order to say good-bye, his eyes again met Sarah's. He bowed over her hand. "Good-bye, Miss Sommers."

Sarah realized that not only would Lord Darton no longer form part of their court, but hereafter when they met, it would be as distant acquaintances. He had chosen another path and the lady who was on his arm would trod it with him.

After the Dartons and Miss Jennings had left, Margaret said, "Barbara was telling me the most extraordinary thing. Lord Darton and Miss Jennings are to be wed in a few weeks."

"I own, I am astonished that the wedding is to be so soon, but I suppose that Lord Darton's affairs are rather more urgent than I had heard," said Lady Alverley.

"Miss Jennings is the daughter of a cloth merchant," said Margaret.

"Apparently Lord Darton did not feel that his chances were good in winning an heiress from his own social order," said Miss Hanson in a regretful voice.

Sarah thought it was time to offer her own opinion. "For my part, I thought that Miss Jennings was quite nice. Her manners were unexceptional and she presented a very neat appearance."

"Indeed, I was pleasantly surprised. I learned from Miss Jennings that she attended a rather exclusive school for girls. No doubt that explains her outward gentility," said Lady Alverley.

"How is it that it is acceptable for Lord Darton to marry a lady whose birth is so far beneath him? Yet it is not acceptable for me or Sarah to consider anyone who is of our own social order, but who is not blessed with all the advantages of position?" asked Margaret intensely.

Sarah leveled a long thoughtful glance at her sister. She had not forgotten whom Margaret had stolen out of the town house to attend a masquerade with, nor had she missed Margaret's acknowledgment of Captain Jeffries's bow from the pits. Decidedly, Margaret seemed to be forming a marked partiality for Captain Jeffries and that was what had precipitated her sister's question now.

Sarah understood her sister's confusion. Their grandmother had made very plain her views on what she considered to be an eligible *parti* and Captain Jeffries had been firmly barred from that group. Of course, Sarah thought it only fair to remind herself that Margaret had also formed a strong friendship with the Lawrences. Mr. Lawrence had also been pronounced by Lady Alverley to be an ineligible. It must seem to be an injustice, indeed, that Lord Darton had done what she and Margaret were forbidden to do. Not that it was in the least likely that either of them would marry to disoblige themselves, but nevertheless it was a hard lesson for Margaret's tender, kind heart.

"Wealth counts for something in this world, Margaret," said Lady Alverley bluntly. "A gentleman can have every advantage of birth and position, like Lord Darton, and not have a feather to fly with. His lordship has bowed to necessity and he has made a wise choice. Though Miss Jennings is beneath him in birth, she brings a fresh infusion of much needed financial stability to an old and distinguished family. In short, it is a very respectable match," said Lady Alverley.

"Then an acceptable match is one in which at least one of the parties profits?" asked Margaret.

"Vulgarly put, but accurate enough, Margaret," said Lady Alverley repressively.

"I detest it! Such hypocrisy. We are all like prime bits of blood held up at auction," exclaimed Margaret.

"Margaret, I will not tolerate such vulgar parlance. Prime bits of blood, indeed! I suppose that I need not inquire too far in where you have culled that phrase. It is the fault of that rakish set that you are so fond of," said Lady Alverley. "I almost wish that I had never introduced you to Mrs. Jeffries."

Margaret jumped up, spots of color coming into her cheeks. "I know what I am to make of that! You object to my dearest friends!"

Lady Alverley stared at her youngest granddaughter in astonishment and disapproval. "What means this sudden heat of yours, my dear?"

"The air has gotten close, Grandmama. I feel it myself," said Sarah hastily. "I shall go with my sister for a walk in the hall. Do you wish to accompany us, Miss Hanson?"

"Of course, if her ladyship permits," said Miss Hanson, glancing at Lady Alverley.

Lady Alverley waved her hand, her expression irritated. "Yes, do go with them, Marie. Perhaps a few minutes of walking will soothe Margaret's megrims. That is what comes of attending these tragedies. One's emotions tend to run higher than the usual."

As Sarah and Margaret left the box, Miss Hanson dawdled behind to adjust her shawl. Margaret seized the moment of privacy to whisper fiercely, "Whyever did you invite Miss Hanson? I don't want her around me!"

"Our grandmother would not have given us permission to leave the box without a chaperone," said Sarah. She had linked her arm with her sister's and she urged Margaret down the hall. Miss Hanson was left behind, but Sarah saw in a swift glance cast over her shoulder that she seemed content merely to have them within sight. She put her head close to Margaret's as they walked. It was an awkward place for a private conversation, but there was little choice. "What is wrong with you, Margaret?"

"Nothing! Everything! Oh, Sarah, I don't know what to do!" said Margaret in an anguished voice.

Sarah glanced up into her face in alarm. "My dear! You must tell me, so I can help."

"No one can help me," said Margaret, biting her lip. There were tears sparkling in her eyes and a bleakness in her expression that Sarah had never seen before.

"Margaret—"

"Hush! Here is Miss Hanson," said Margaret quickly. She blinked back the tears and put on a credible smile. "Yes, Miss Hanson? Did you want something?"

"I believe it is time that we turn around and return to our box, Margaret, Sarah. You will not wish to miss the beginning of the next act," said Miss Hanson, anxiously consulting a watch she had hanging on a ribbon at her waist.

Sarah did not care a single snap of her fingers about the play. She was far more concerned about her sister. She knew that Margaret had no interest in the performance, either, for there remained a shadowed expression in her eyes which had nothing to do with Shakespeare's *Macbeth*. It was only Miss Hanson who was so desirous of returning to the box.

"Pray allow us five minutes more, Miss Hanson. It cannot matter that greatly, for the torches must still go down and the curtain be raised," said Sarah.

"I am afraid that I must insist, Sarah," said Miss Hanson with a prim expression. "I would be behind in my duties if I sanctioned this loitering in the public hall."

Margaret turned aside sharply, as though she could not bear the constraints that Miss Hanson represented. Sarah felt for her and rounded on their chaperone. "You must see that Margaret has not fully recovered from the closeness of the box, Miss Hanson. If you do not care to wait, then I shall be happy to remain behind with her while you return to the box."

"You must know that I cannot do that, Sarah! Lady Alverley would have my head if I were to abandon you two here," said Miss Hanson with an appalled expression.

"Then what is to be done, Miss Hanson?" asked Sarah. "For I shall not return to the box just now and so I tell you!"

"Oh, do stop your wrangling! Just stop it!" exclaimed Margaret. "I can't take any more." She started to flee, then stopped. "Lord Eustace!"

At Margaret's exclamation, Sarah and Miss Hanson both turned.

"My lord, what a pleasure to see you here," said Sarah, extending her gloved hand to him. She had stepped forward to meet him, so that her sister would have a moment to gather herself together.

Lord Eustace took her hand and bowed. "Well met, Miss Sommers. I was just going to step into your box to pay my regards to Lady Alverley and all of you."

"Margaret and I wished to take a few minutes of exercise before the play began again," said Sarah. "But my grandmother remained in her seat. Will you walk back with us, my lord?"

"I wish I didn't have to return!" murmured Margaret with a defiant glance.

Sarah was embarrassed. She hoped that Lord Eustace had not overheard her sister's impassioned aside, but apparently he had.

"These performances can seem rather long at times," said Lord Eustace, glancing at Margaret. He smiled down at Sarah. "You appear enchanting this evening, Miss Sommers."

"Thank you, my lord," said Sarah, pleased and surprised. He had not ever ignored Margaret in order to compliment her.

Lord Eustace acknowledged Miss Hanson's slight curtsy. At last he turned to address Margaret. "I see that you are also in beauty, Miss Margaret. May I offer my escort?"

Margaret smiled into his face. The distraught look in her eyes had disappeared. "Thank you, my lord. That is very kind of you."

Lord Eustace and Margaret led the way back to the box. Margaret responded to his lordship's light and friendly talk and by the time that they reached Lady Alverley's box, she was laughing as gaily as she always had.

Sarah was glad to see that her sister had thrown off her odd distress. She was grateful, too, that Lord Eustace had been able to aid Margaret's recovery of spirits. At the same time, however, she could not quite banish the wistful thought that she would like it very much if he would pay such assiduous attentions to her.

Sarah felt a touch on her elbow and she glanced around to meet Miss Hanson's gaze. Miss Hanson nodded significantly at the couple who was going ahead of them into the box. "Perhaps we see a match forming up," she murmured.

Sarah did not reply as she walked into the box.

Chapter Nineteen

A week later, Sarah looked around the mingling company in the ballroom. She was seated in her chair on the edge of the dance floor and was momentarily by herself. It had been a wonderful evening. She had danced the waltz twice with Lord Eustace and only discretion had kept her from doing so again. She had remembered Miss Hanson's early warning that a young lady must never dance three times with the same gentleman in an evening or she risked having it said that they were an engaged couple.

She was smiling as she fanned herself. Lord Eustace would never urge her to flout the conventions, of course, but it was nice to think it was only that which had stopped him from asking her for another set. At that moment, she was waiting for Lord Eustace's return. He had offered to bring an ice to her after their last waltz.

Sarah suddenly caught sight of her sister. Margaret was being escorted from the dance floor by Mr. Matthews. She was laughing up at her admirer. Sarah was glad to see that Margaret was enjoying the ball, too. She had not paid much attention to Margaret that evening after satisfying herself that Margaret was in fair spirits.

Margaret had refused to confide anything more to her since their hurried exchange at the theater. Sarah felt that she had done as much as she could to help her sister by offering to listen. Short of browbeating Margaret, or threatening to bring Lady Alverley in on her, Sarah did not know what else she could do.

Sarah's feeling of well-being was wiped out at the altering of expression on her sister's face. Mr. Matthews had left Margaret, and Captain Jeffries had immediately walked up to her.

He was saying something. Margaret's expression had become tense.

Sarah watched as Margaret gave a quick shake of her head and made a movement as if to turn away. But the cavalry officer caught hold of her hand and held her by him. He spoke with intensity until Margaret reluctantly nodded.

Sarah left her chair and started making her way toward them. She had noticed that since the night when they had been to see *Macbeth*, Margaret had been avoiding Captain Jeffries. She had even denied herself to the cavalry officer whenever he had come to call and she had made excuses not to go riding with Mrs. Jeffries.

Sarah had guessed that Captain Jeffries was at the root of Margaret's uncharacteristic unhappiness. She had tried to talk to Margaret about it, but had not gotten very far. "Margaret, are you angered with Captain Jeffries?" she had asked.

"No, of course not! What a very odd thing to say!" said Margaret, looking up from a copy of *The Lady's Magazine*.

"Then why have you begun to avoid him?" Sarah had asked.

Margaret had gotten up hurriedly. "I don't wish to discuss Captain Jeffries."

Before her sister had reached the door, Sarah had in desperation asked, "Margaret, are you in love with him?"

Margaret did not turn around. She stood quite still with her hand on the doorknob. In a strangled voice, Margaret had said, "Captain Jeffries made an offer for me, which Grandmama has rejected. He will shortly be returning to duty. It is best that I do not see him."

"Oh, my dear!" exclaimed Sarah, starting forward in compassion. But her sister's next words stopped her.

"Mind your own business, Sarah!" exclaimed Margaret fiercely, and she had fled the sitting room.

As Sarah recalled the misery encompassed in that impassioned plea, she wanted only to protect Margaret from any further hurt. Margaret had chosen to distance herself from Captain Jeffries and Sarah honored her sister's decision. She therefore made her way as quickly as she could to her sister's side, in order to help Margaret detach herself from the cavalry officer's now unwelcome attentions.

Just as Sarah came up, Margaret and Captain Jeffries started away in the opposite direction. They were headed straight for a doorway that led out of the ballroom into an anteroom.

Sarah hesitated, then followed. She did not like the feeling that she was spying on her sister, but she felt that she could not leave Margaret on her own. Her sister's face had been white and as she and Captain Jeffries left the ballroom, she had cast an almost desperate glance over her shoulder which had stirred Sarah's heart.

Sarah also left the ballroom and entered the anteroom, hesitating when she no longer saw her quarry. Then she heard voices from a half-open door set behind a supporting column. Sarah swiftly crossed the marbled floor to the doorway. There she stopped again, assailed by guilt and distaste for what she was doing.

Then Captain Jeffries's voice rang out, almost ragged in intensity. "I must see you! I am going mad."

"I'm sorry! I cannot!"

Suddenly the door was thrown open and Margaret rushed out. Blinded by tears, she did not see Sarah standing beside the door.

Sarah watched her go, then turned and entered the room. It proved to be a small salon, informally furnished and lit only by the fire in the grate. Sarah shut the door.

Captain Jeffries turned his head from contemplation of the fire. He was frowning heavily and there was an unfriendly light in his hooded gaze. Not by a flicker of his eyelids did his expression lighten when he recognized the lady who returned his regard. "Miss Sommers."

"Forgive me." Sarah gestured with her fan. "I could not help overhearing just a little."

"Then you know that I am hopelessly in love with your sister," said Captain Jeffries harshly.

"And Margaret?" inquired Sarah quietly, coming farther into the room.

He stared at her, before sighing heavily. "I believe that she loves me, also. But she will not see me. Nor will she allow me to proffer my suit again to Lady Alverley."

"I had wondered what was bothering Margaret, and now I pity her with all of my heart. Margaret knows quite well that our grandmother will not hear of a match between you," said Sarah. "She is torn in two, I think. And she is afraid."

"Why am I not acceptable? I am as good as any man, and better than some. I possess a decent living and my birth is equal with hers," said Captain Jeffries angrily. His frustration was evident in the hard line of his jaw. "Can you explain to me why Lady Alverley would reject an offer from me, Miss Sommers?"

"Yes, I can. May I sit down, Captain Jeffries?" Sarah calmly seated herself. She could see that her assertion had both startled him and captured his attention. "Do you know anything about our background, Captain Jeffries? About our parents?"

"No, I do not," said Captain Jeffries with a narrowed look. "What has it to do with Margaret and myself?"

"It has everything to do with it," said Sarah. "Our mother was Annabelle Alverley, her ladyship's only daughter. She came out when she was seventeen and, from what I have heard, she took the town by storm. She was pretty and lively and could have had any gentleman in the land."

"Like Margaret," said Captain Jeffries, still frowning. His eyes were fixed exceedingly sharp and keen on her face.

"Much like Margaret," agreed Sarah. She played with her fan for a moment. "Annabelle Alverley fell in love with a younger son of few prospects, my father, Sir Francis Sommers. Lady Alverley vehemently refused her consent for their betrothal and denied the house to my father. Her ladyship had ambitious dreams for her daughter, and a younger son of modest means had no place in those plans."

"I begin to understand you, Miss Sommers," said Captain Jeffries grimly. "Go on."

Sarah looked up. Quite flatly, she said, "Annabelle Alverley and Sir Francis Sommers eloped. It was a blow from which our grandmother has never recovered. It haunts her to this day."

"You are telling me that my suit is hopeless," snapped Captain Jeffries, very white about the mouth.

"Lady Alverley is blinded by an old grief, Captain Jeffries. It would be difficult indeed to persuade her that your suit is in any way acceptable," said Sarah with gentle regret.

"As Margaret's guardian, Lady Alverley can deny Margaret permission to consider my suit and have me barred from approaching Margaret either in private or in public," said Captain Jeffries in realization. He smashed his fist down on the mantel. "It is a hellish situation!"

"Lady Alverley is not Margaret's guardian, Captain Jeffries."

He turned swiftly, his gaze once more riveted to Sarah's face. "What are you saying, Miss Sommers?"

"Only this, Captain Jeffries. Our father is still very much alive, and though he adjured us to follow Lady Alverley's advice this Season, I don't believe that he would wish either of us to do so to our ultimate unhappiness. Sir Francis is a forgetful father, which is perhaps why it does not often occur to either Margaret or myself to apply to him for advice. Perhaps in this instance it would be wise," said Sarah. She had risen from the chair. Now she smiled up at the tall mustached gentleman who stood staring down at her. "Margaret can give you his direction, Captain Jeffries."

The cavalry officer seized her hands. There was a blaze in his eyes. "You have given me hope, Miss Sommers. Thank you! I am eternally grateful." He raised her hands to his lips.

At that instant the door opened and Lord Eustace entered. He stopped short at sight of the intimate gesture. "Pardon me for intruding, Miss Sommers," he said in a neutral voice.

Sarah colored hotly and snatched her hands from Captain Jeffries's grasp. "Lord Eustace! You have surprised me."

"Obviously," said Lord Eustace in a dry voice.

Captain Jeffries glanced swiftly from one to the other. A gleam of amusement lit his eyes. He smiled warmly at Sarah and in a low voice, he said, "I shall leave you now, Miss Sommers. You may imagine on what errand I go." He went toward the door, nodded to Lord Eustace as he passed him, and exited.

Lord Eustace closed the door after the cavalry officer with a snap. Then he looked across at Sarah.

"It is not what you think, my lord," said Sarah quickly. She read condemnation in his steady regard.

Lord Eustace walked forward. "And what is it that I think, Miss Sommers?"

"An assignation, a-a clandestine meeting," said Sarah, stammering on the words. There was an expression in his eyes that she did not like.

Lord Eustace reached out and took hold of her hands. "How uncanny. You have read my thoughts precisely, Miss Sommers."

"But you are wrong, very wrong!" exclaimed Sarah. "Captain Jeffries and I—"

"If it is stolen moments and kisses that you desire, Sarah, why not mine?"

Before Sarah could react or say a word, Lord Eustace had pulled her into his arms. He crushed her to him and proceeded to kiss her thoroughly.

Sarah's senses swam. She did not know how long it was that he kissed her before he raised his head. She heard him murmur something, before he took her mouth again.

She clung to his lapel, swaying against him. She had dreamed for a very long time of this very moment. Time seemed to stand still.

When he forcibly set her aside, Sarah nearly stumbled. Her eyes wide and dazed, Sarah slowly raised her fingers to her lips.

Lord Eustace was breathing heavily. There was a tight, white look about his eyes and mouth. He said hoarsely, "Very satisfactory, Miss Sommers. I congratulate you on your natural talents."

Sarah's world reeled and crashed. She felt her heart break in two. "Dastard!" she breathed. Hands covering her face, she brushed past him and ran to the door, jerking it open.

Lord Eustace took a hasty step after her. Something snapped under his foot. He bent down and slowly straightened, the shattered ivory sticks of Sarah's fan in his hand.

Sarah went at once in search of her grandmother. She petitioned Lady Alverley to be allowed to leave for the evening. "I have the beginning of the headache," she said, not far from speaking the truth.

Lady Alverley frowned in irritation. "But I do not wish to bring an early end to my own enjoyment, Sarah."

"I would not think of asking you to, ma'am. Perhaps Miss Hanson could chaperone me?" asked Sarah. She was desperate to be gone, afraid that Lord Eustace would again seek her out. She did not think that she could stand that. Her emotions were so near the surface that she felt as though she was going to burst into tears at any instant.

"Very well! Marie can have no objection, after all," said Lady Alverley.

When Miss Hanson was informed that she was to cut her own evening short in order to escort Sarah home, she sighed regretfully. "A pity, for I have truly enjoyed myself. Lord Tottenham has been so friendly toward me this evening. I have not known where to look."

Sarah did not care. All she wanted to do was to leave. As she and Miss Hanson said good night to their hostess, she caught sight of Lord Eustace. He was standing some distance away, regarding her with a peculiar expression. Sarah turned away swiftly and hurried out.

Sarah spent the minutes in the carriage going over and over in her head what had happened. She felt despair and anger and humiliation. She could not bear the thought of seeing Lord Eustace again, knowing that he held her in such contempt.

Sarah spent a restless night. By morning, her feelings had not undergone any transformation. She thought if Lord Eustace called that day, she would deny herself to him. His lordship could very well make do visiting with her sister. Sarah did not want to see him. Every time she recalled how he had kissed her, and the words he had spoken, she felt mortified all over again.

But Lord Eustace did not call. Instead, he sent a billet along with a slender package. Sarah accepted the billet and package reluctantly from the butler. "Thank you, Herbert." She waited until the butler had exited and she was alone before she read the note. It was a short apology, and inside the package she discovered a pretty fan, which was almost a duplicate of her own.

Sarah recalled that she had dropped her fan. It must have broken since Lord Eustace had not sent her the original. Sarah debated for some hours whether or not to accept Lord Eustace's apology. There was more at stake than a mere broken fan, as surely his lordship must realize.

Sarah finally came to a realization of her own. She knew how much he had hurt her, but that did not necessarily mean that Lord Eustace was aware of it. She had hidden away her feelings for him, after all, by carefully cultivating a friendly manner toward him. She had never indicated that she was fonder of him than she was of any of her other acquaintances.

Sarah decided that she was being stupid. Her best course was to accept Lord Eustace's apology in the spirit in which it had been offered. He had insulted her unbearably, which he had owned in his billet. It would be uncharitable to hold it against him when he had no inkling how much he had hurt her.

Sarah decided when she next saw Lord Eustace, she would treat his lordship just as she had always done. She chose to forget the cruel thing he had said. It was a difficult thing to do, but Sarah thought that if she was not to run scared like a rabbit for the rest of the Season it was necessary. Otherwise, she would not be able to meet Lord Eustace without forever being reminded of that unpleasant incident.

Sarah was mildly surprised that night when Margaret came into her bedroom to say good night. She and her sister had been on such wary terms of late that Margaret's small olive branch brought tears to Sarah's eyes. "I do love you, dear Margaret," she whispered.

"Oh, Sarah! You are such a goose!" said Margaret, hugging her. "Now let Bordon put you to bed. You have looked perfectly hagged today."

Sarah gave a watery laugh. "Have I? Then I shall be certain to get a good night's rest so that I shall be fresh in the morning."

"I think that you should have a glass of warm milk to help you sleep," said Margaret. "Bordon, see that my sister has one before she goes to sleep."

"Yes, miss."

When Sarah lay down in her bed, she felt much more at peace than she had in some weeks. She had missed the intimacy that she had shared with her sister. At last Margaret was no longer holding her at arm's-length. She sighed, allowing sleep to overtake her as the world and its troubles faded away.

Chapter Twenty

Sarah slept late the next morning. When she finally arose and dressed, it was already after luncheon. She was horrified that she had stayed in bed so long. It was something that she never did. But Lady Alverley was not at all distressed, for she also had just come downstairs.

"Pray do not be so anxious, Sarah. You have not missed anything but your morning ride and going out with Margaret shopping," said Lady Alverley. "Why don't you accompany me this afternoon on my calls? You have not gone with me in several days and I do not like going out alone. I have given Marie today to herself and she has quite deserted me."

"Very well, ma'am. I will be delighted," said Sarah with a smile. Her hazel eyes gleamed as she took in the significance of Lady Alverley's invitation. She was obviously a poor choice behind Miss Hanson.

Thus it was that Sarah spent the day with Lady Alverley. They returned to the town house an hour before dinner, separating at the foot of the stairs. The butler had stopped Sarah, saying that he had a message for her.

"No doubt from one of your friends, Sarah," said Lady Alverley dismissively. "I shall go on up to my room, for I am in need of a rest."

"Allow me to show you into the drawing room, miss," said the butler. "You will wish to read Miss Margaret's note in private."

"Oh, is it from my sister?" asked Sarah in surprise. She passed through the doorway into the drawing room. "Thank you, Herbert." She scarcely noticed that the door was closed behind her as she unsealed the sheet.

Sarah recognized her sister's childish rounded scrawl and a

smile touched her face. Margaret had never been an apt pupil with her copperplate. She started to read the note. Shock suddenly widened her eyes.

Sarah read the note again, so stunned that she could scarcely comprehend the lines. She sat down again, rather abruptly, the note dangling from her numbed fingers. She shook her head. It could not be true. But there was the proof in her hand.

Margaret had eloped. Margaret had eloped with Henry Jeffries. That very morning, while Sarah had still slept, her sister had driven out of London to be married by special license.

"I must do something," said Sarah aloud. But still she just sat there. There was a queer helplessness inside her. She did not know what to do. There was no one to turn to, no one to confide in. Her father was far away, too far to help her. As for Lady Alverley!

Sarah shuddered when she considered what would be that lady's likely reaction. Lady Alverley had never gotten over her daughter's elopement. She still refused to talk about it. It would be a harsh blow to her ladyship to be told that her granddaughter had committed the same social solecism.

Margaret was her ladyship's favorite. Sarah had accepted that and had not begrudged Lady Alverley's affection for her sister. She understood well enough that Margaret reminded Lady Alverley of her own younger self.

Sarah's first impulse was to go after Margaret herself, but she as swiftly discarded it, for she knew nothing more than what Margaret had written. She did not know the direction the runaways had taken, nor what their destination was to have been.

"Dear God! Not Gretna Greene!" breathed Sarah. As unworldly as she was, Sarah knew that was a likelihood, for Margaret was underage. Where else could they have gone and found a clergyman willing to wed them?

Sarah stood up, too agitated to sit still any longer. The scandal! There would be one, of course, especially since there were still those in society, like Lady Cromes and Mrs. Plummer, who could recall how Miss Annabelle Alverley had eloped with the Honorable Francis Sommers. Like mother, like daughter. She could almost hear the whispers and the laughter. Horrible, horrible. Oh, how could Margaret do such a thing?

How could Margaret expose them all to such torment? Sarah put her hands up to her cheeks, disregarding the note as it fell from her fingers.

The door opened and the butler stepped inside. "Miss Sommers, his lordship, Lord Eustace."

Sarah turned swiftly. "No, no! Not now—"

But it was too late. Lord Eustace had already stepped past the butler. He stood looking at her with mild surprise on his face. "Miss Sommers?"

Sarah took one wild look at him and then turned away so that he could not see her face. Her mind was all in turmoil. It was the greatest misfortune that he should come in just then. She did not know what to say to him. He had naturally come to call on Margaret, but not finding her at home, he had requested to see her as was his invariable custom. Sarah practically wrung her hands. She had to compose herself, to say something, anything—

His hand touched her elbow and Sarah nearly started out of her skin. She whirled, looking up at him as though at bay.

Lord Eustace stayed where he was. "I am sorry, Miss Sommers. I did not mean to startle you. I saw that you were distressed and hoped that I might—"

Sarah gave almost an hysterical laugh. She dashed her hand across her eyes. "Oh, my lord! Indeed, indeed, I do not know what to say! Forgive me, I-I am not myself just now."

Lord Eustace noticed a small sheet on the carpet and he bent to pick it up. "Did you drop this, Miss Sommers?" He started to hand it to her, but then his gaze fell carelessly to the sheet. A few words leaped off of the page. He looked up swiftly, meeting her horrified expression.

"Give it to me at once, sir!" exclaimed Sarah, snatching it away from him. She crumpled the sheet into a ball and stuffed it into her pocket.

Lord Eustace watched her frantic action, his own expression frozen. "Miss Sommers, is what I just read true? Has your sister eloped with Henry Jeffries?"

"I-I don't know," stammered Sarah. She glanced swiftly at his face, then away. "That is to say, I know nothing more than what you have gathered, my lord. The note was just given to me only a few moments before you came in."

"Then there may be a chance that they have not gotten far," said Lord Eustace. "Have you consulted with Lady Alverley?"

Sarah stared at him, appalled by the suggestion. "My grandmother? No, of course not!"

"Miss Sommers, do you not think that Lady Alverley should be informed?" asked Lord Eustace. His dark brows had jerked together at her unfathomable reaction. "She will be able to send someone after your sister!"

"You do not perfectly understand. I cannot say anything to my grandmother. Her pride is such that—oh, she will be angry, so very angry! In short, I was trying to think how best to handle this myself," said Sarah in a rush.

Lord Eustace shook his head impatiently. "It will not do, Miss Sommers! You cannot go careering off alone."

"I know! I know! I don't know where to go or where to look," said Sarah, almost beside herself. "Margaret is underage. I greatly fear—" She stopped, appalled by her indiscretion.

"Gretna, you mean?" Lord Eustace's lips thinned. "You would never catch them. I shall go after them myself."

"You!" exclaimed Sarah, staring at him in astonishment.

"Yes, I!" said Lord Eustace. He went to the bell pull and yanked on it, glancing over at her. "It cannot have escaped you that I have shown a marked interest in your sister, Miss Sommers!"

"No, no, it did not escape me," said Sarah, avoiding his eyes.

"I am sending for your sister's maid. She ought to be able to tell us something," said Lord Eustace, turning toward the door as it opened. "You there, send down Miss Margaret's maid. Miss Sommers requires a word with her."

The footman looked from Lord Eustace to Sarah and back again. "But, my lord, Miss Holby is not here. She left early this morning, saying that her brother was ill and that she did not know when she would return."

It was a blow. Sarah straightened, trying to preserve her countenance. "Oh, I did not know. I just came in a few minutes ago and have not been upstairs. Undoubtedly Holby left me a note, which I have not yet seen. Thank you, that will be all."

The footman bowed and exited, closing the door behind him. Sarah and Lord Eustace looked at one another. "I think it plain enough that the maid was included in the conspiracy," said Lord Eustace shortly.

"I cannot believe that Holby would agree to such a wild scheme," said Sarah, shaking her head. She pressed her fingers to her temples. She knew it was inevitable that she had to tell her grandmother. The thought almost made her feel faint. "There must be some mistake. It is a nightmare. I cannot believe that this is happening."

"Unfortunately, it appears to be all too true," said Lord Eustace sharply. He took a couple of turns around the room, various emotions chasing across his grim countenance.

Sarah watched him. She knew that he was angered and affronted. She believed that she could guess his thoughts. He had favored Margaret with his admiration and condescension. He had the reputation of holding himself aloof. He did not dangle after every new debutante. And Margaret had repaid him by preferring an unknown cavalry officer to him. It was outrageous, unpardonable! In short, Lord Eustace was obviously suffering from lacerated pride.

Lord Eustace turned abruptly to Sarah. "Miss Sommers, will you do me the honor of marrying me?"

The words that left his lips apparently surprised him almost as much as they surprised Sarah. Sarah turned white. Shock widened her eyes. She grasped for the support of a chair back. "What?" she whispered.

Lord Eustace's expression smoothed so that it was unreadable. "I am asking you to marry me, Miss Sommers."

One of Sarah's hands crept up to her throat. The dazed feeling inside her began to dissipate. "Why have you asked this of me?"

Lord Eustace seemed momentarily bereft of speech. He frowned. "I admire you greatly, Miss Sommers. I have given some thought to marriage lately and I think that we would suit very well."

Sarah smiled sadly. She shook her head. She was completely mistress of herself again. "My lord, when you thought of marriage, it was not I who was in your thoughts. Indeed, I doubt that you have thought about me at all in that way."

"Of course I have, Miss Sommers," he said explosively. "I have always enjoyed your company. You are handsome and of a good understanding. Your cool self-possession, especially under such trying circumstances as these, is a trait that I much admire." He halted, apparently becoming aware that his reference to the circumstances had been incredibly inept. He cleared his throat. "I would consider it to be an honor to call you my wife."

Sarah was pale. "My dear sir, you credit me with a good understanding, and it is true. I understand perfectly well that my sister's defection has come as a terrible blow to you. Your pride has been wounded and you are angered."

"No such thing!" exclaimed Lord Eustace, reddening under his tan.

Sarah shook her head. "Pray do not deny it, my lord. We have become friends and so I make bold to state my opinion. You have offered for me from the impulse of the moment, an action that you will no doubt heartily regret once you have taken a moment to reflect."

Lord Eustace stepped forward to take her hand. There was a stubborn set to his expression. "Miss Sommers, I protest! I have much warmer feelings for you than you know."

Gently, Sarah withdrew her hand. Drawing a shaky breath, she said slowly, "You have done me honor, Lord Eustace. I recognize that. However, you will understand when I ask you to give me time to think over what you have said today. It-it comes as such a shock, you see."

Lord Eustace stepped back again. Without expression, he said, "Of course, Miss Sommers. It was not my intention to push you into a decision with which you do not feel comfortable. Forgive me for speaking out so precipitously. Perhaps given time we shall come to a better understanding."

"Perhaps." Sarah managed to smile. She held out her hand to him. "I do not wish to be impolite by rushing you off, my lord. But you will naturally understand that this is a difficult time for me—for all of us."

Lord Eustace picked up his hat and gloves quickly. "No, of course I understand. I shall leave you now. No doubt you will prefer to be alone just now. I promise you that I will do my utmost to retrieve the runaways. I will send you word."

Sarah waited only long enough to allow Lord Eustace time to leave the town house before she exited the sitting room. She ran swiftly upstairs to her bedroom, her chest tight with pent-up emotion. Closing the door, she threw herself across the bed and burst into tears.

Chapter Twenty-one

Margaret had not left it to her sister to break the news to Lady Alverley. She had thoughtfully left a note for her ladyship as well. Lady Alverley's reaction was explosive and was heard nearly all over the town house.

About the time that Lady Alverley was indulging in one of the most spectacular rages of her lifetime, Sarah had dried her eyes and washed her hot face. The bitterest bout of tears that she had ever experienced had left her drained, but determined. She had made up her mind what she was going to do.

Sarah changed into a fresh dress with the help of her maid. Then she prepared herself to meet with her grandmother. Sarah knew her own heart very well. She had known for quite some time that she was in love with Lord Eustace. It had been a hopeless passion from the beginning, of course. Lord Eustace had been attracted from the first to her sister, Margaret, rather than to her.

Sarah had struggled against depression and despair all Season, while she watched Lord Eustace's attentions toward Margaret grow more marked. She had had a front-row seat to the courtship, for she and Margaret had attended the same entertainments and had shared many of the same beaus.

When Lord Eustace came to call, he always asked after them both as a matter of form. However, if Lord Eustace had chanced to find himself with Sarah, he had inevitably talked to her about Margaret. Sarah had listened when he had extolled Margaret's virtues and sung his praises of her beauty. All the while, she had carefully cultivated and maintained a cheerful manner.

For Margaret's sake, Sarah had disciplined herself to show only friendliness toward Lord Eustace. It was not for him to guess that she had cherished their short minutes together and stored up memories of his expressions and his smiles. She had nothing to complain of, really, for Lord Eustace had been unfailingly polite and considerate toward her.

Only once had his lordship's innate courtesy deserted him, and that had been when he had kissed her in such an insulting way. The following day he had sent a note of apology, but without explanation. After some soul searching, Sarah had accepted it and nothing more was ever said between them about the incident.

In every other instance, Lord Eustace had always behaved circumspectly. He had always included her in his conversations with Margaret and in the plans that he had made for her sister's enjoyment. Lord Eustace had never let it be seen that he would have preferred Margaret's company over her own. However, Sarah had rarely allowed herself to be blinded to the fact that Lord Eustace's kindness toward her was of an indifferent nature.

Sarah had envied her sister for having the good fortune to attach Lord Eustace's interest, but she could not dislike her. Margaret was vivacious, pretty, kind, and sweet. Never once had Margaret lorded it over Sarah by preening about her most distinguished beau. There was a genuine bond of affection between the sisters. Sarah had reflected more than once that it might have been easier if she and Margaret had detested one another. As it was, Sarah had been generous enough to want her sister to be happy. If Margaret had chosen Lord Eustace, (and Sarah had been satisfied that he was actually in love with her sister instead of his memories of Vivian Leander), she would have pinned a smile to her lips and wished them every blessing.

But now Margaret was gone. She had chosen someone else over Lord Eustace. Sarah still could scarcely believe it. But it was true.

When she had first read Margaret's note announcing her elopement, Sarah had been stunned but she had been strangely happy, too. That emotion had swiftly led to a feeling of guilt. What kind of monster was she to be glad that her sister had thrown away all of her chances and plunged headlong into scandal?

However, now Sarah recognized that she had not actually taken pleasure in her sister's downfall. Instead she had felt a conflicting and giddy relief that she need not pretend any longer that she cared nothing for Lord Eustace.

However, his lordship's proposal had plunged her into the cold water of reality. Her situation had changed, but his had not. Lord Eustace was still in love with Margaret. He had not proposed to her because he had suddenly suffered a violent reversal of feeling. No, he had wanted to exact a sort of revenge upon her sister. Lord Eustace had wanted to punish Margaret and at the same time assuage his wounded pride, by proving that he could marry anyone whenever he wished. Sarah had simply been the only available lady at hand. Sarah was quite convinced that he would have thrown down the handkerchief to any unwed woman who might have happened to be present at that moment.

Sarah had seen all of this in an instant of blinding, painful clarity. In that light, Lord Eustace's offer for her had been a slapping insult. Despite everything, however, she could have accepted his suit. Oh yes, she had been tempted to do just that. She could have settled for a marriage of convenience to the man whom she loved, hoping to ignite in him a similar love for her.

Her head had overruled her heart, however, telling her that it would have been more likely that she would have become the object of resentment and hatred. Eventually, the last rejection would have been worse than the first.

And so Sarah, sensible, clever Sarah, had resisted temptation and thrown away her one chance of happiness. Or so she had thought when she had thrown herself across her bed and given way to despair.

It was a queer thing about weeping until one could weep no more. Emotion was spent and there was just the mind left. When Sarah stopped crying, she had started thinking. It was true that she was no longer bound by sisterly devotion. It was also true that more than anything else she desired Lord Eustace to offer for her because he loved her and only her. But there was only one way that she would ever know whether Lord Eustace could ever love her.

Sarah made up her mind to try to win Lord Eustace's affection for herself. Whether he was ensnared by love for her sister or by memories of his former betrothed, Sarah thought that she would surely regret it if she did not make a push to discover if his heart could be changed.

Sarah was worldly enough to realize that she could not launch a campaign for the gentleman's heart without advice. She went at once to find her grandmother. Of course, the first hurdle to get over was to inform Lady Alverley of Margaret's flight. Sarah did not relish that task at all, but she knew that it had to be done.

Lady Alverley was in her own apartments. The dresser opened the door to Sarah's knock, but the tiring woman was reluctant to let her come in. Sarah could hear the unmistakable sounds of breaking glass. She almost felt relief. Obviously Lady Alverley had already heard the news. She would not have to be the one to break it to her grandmother. She quietly insisted to be allowed in. "I shall try to calm her ladyship," she said.

The dresser widened the door and stepped aside. "If you can do that, miss, I am sure I'd be most grateful," said the woman in a low voice.

When Sarah entered the dressing room, another fragile object was being hurled against the wall. It splintered, a thousand crystal pieces tinkling to the floor. Overpowering scent filled the air. Obviously Lady Alverley had sacrificed a glass scent jar.

Sarah saw that her entrance had not been noticed by her grandmother. "Grandmama, I wish to talk to you."

Lady Alverley whirled. The sight of her eldest granddaughter did not appear to gratify her ladyship. Instead, Lady Alverley's mottled face grew darker. She waved a parchment crushed between her bony fingers. "Did you know anything of this? Did you? Speak! No! So she pulled the wool over your eyes, as well! Ungrateful girl! Viper in my bosom!"

Lady Alverley ranted on about Margaret. It was difficult for Sarah to listen to the diatribe against her sister, but she was shrewd enough to understand that it would be impossible for her to stem the flow. A deep well of bitterness and hurt had been torn open in Lady Alverley that had never been addressed. Now the dam had burst and old, ugly emotions roiled out. Sarah thought that all she could do was to wait until her grandmother's tantrum had tired her. Then she might be able to speak what was on her mind and be assured at least of a hearing.

Suddenly Lady Alverley collapsed into a chair. Her hands worked on the chair arms. She stared at Sarah. Her eyes were cold and hard. "I suppose that you, too, will go the same way! So be it! I wash my hands of the pair of you, just as I did your mother!"

It was not the most opportune moment, but Sarah chose it. "Grandmama, I have decided that I want to wed Lord Eustace!"

Lady Alverley was stunned to speechlessness. She stared at Sarah with almost a blank expression. Recovering, she said, "What did you say?"

"I said that I wish to wed Lord Eustace," said Sarah, more quietly. Though she was quivering inside from the magnitude of her temerity, she said firmly, "I have come to ask your advice and help in animating his interest in me."

"My dear Sarah!" Lady Alverley's high color faded and her enraged expression was replaced by a wreath of smile. She seated herself on a settee and held out her hand. "Dearest girl, pray come sit down with me. I want to hear all about you and Lord Eustace."

Sarah obediently joined her grandmother on the settee. "There is nothing between myself and Lord Eustace but friendship. I have not previously put myself forward because of his obvious infatuation for my sister. But Margaret has made her choice in quite another direction. I feel myself to be entirely freed of all constraint against following my own inclinations."

"Quite right, too," said Lady Alverley, nodding. "You need think only of yourself, my dear."

Sarah ignored her grandmother's interjection. She didn't want to think about the selfishness of her motives. "However, at this point in time Lord Eustace is, I think, completely indifferent toward me. I have wondered, too, whether he is not still harboring fond memories of Miss Vivian Leander. Can you advise me, ma'am?"

"Dearest Sarah." Lady Alverley reached over to give a quick squeeze to her hand. "I could not hope for better news than this. Lord Eustace is perfect for you. You have made a delightful choice. Of course, I will help you."

"Then what must I do?" asked Sarah. She felt that she was plunging into a heavy current.

"Leave everything to me. I shall see to it that Lord Eustace sees you constantly. He will be invited to all of our entertainments, of course, and I will make certain that you are invited anywhere he might conceivably be. I would not worry overmuch about Vivian Leander. She is long dead. The man would be a fool to prefer fading memories to a flesh-and-blood woman. You have only to display yourself to good effect and encourage him a little. You are already friends, so that should not be too difficult. Do not be anxious, my dear! We shall have his lordship making an offer in a trice," said Lady Alverley.

Sarah had not meant to reveal to her grandmother what had transpired belowstairs earlier between herself and Lord Eustace. However, now she thought it wise that Lady Alverley should be told. Her ladyship needed to know precisely in what case the matter stood.

Sarah took a deep breath, wondering if she was about to trigger another show of temper. "Grandmama, I have something to tell you that you will not like."

Lady Alverley's face tightened. "Yes, my dear?"

"Lord Eustace is aware of Margaret's elopement. He was shown into the sitting room just as I finished reading her note. I had dropped it to the carpet and he picked it up. He-he was terribly upset," said Sarah.

"So I should imagine! It was a blow to him, naturally," said Lady Alverley, nodding. "It was an indiscretion on your part, certainly, Sarah, but it could not be helped. Pray rest easy, my dear. I am not angry with you." She patted Sarah's hand reassuringly. Her lips twisted suddenly. "It does not matter greatly, in any event. Everyone will know of it soon enough! News such as this does not long remain in the dark."

"Grandmama, that is not all. Lord Eustace made me an offer. I refused him because I could see that he had only done so out of bruised pride," said Sarah. She looked at her grandmother. "I hope that you are not too angry with me, ma'am."

Lady Alverley stared at her for a long moment, several emotions chasing across her face. She made a swift recovery.

"Naturally I would have liked you to have accepted his lordship's offer at once, for I do not believe Lord Eustace made it without some underlying feeling for you. However, I understand your reasoning, Sarah. You are a sensible girl. A gentleman who makes an offer so rashly will have second thoughts later."

"That's what I thought," said Sarah. She was relieved that her grandmother was taking things so well. "I could see that he was already regretting what he had said even as he said it."

"Then you did quite right. Lord Eustace might not have followed through with it, since the offer was made in private directly to you. He could very well have drawn back before ever a proper announcement could be made," said Lady Alverley.

"That did not occur to me," said Sarah. She wondered if Lord Eustace would have abandoned his declaration once he had had time for reflection. She decided that he would not have. He was a gentleman of honor. No matter how much he felt himself to be at a disadvantage later, he would have stood by his word. Unfortunately, he would probably have come to resent the fact that he had trapped himself.

"What we want from his lordship is a formal offer, one well thought out and firm of purpose. And it should be made to me since I am responsible for you," said Lady Alverley. She frowned a little. "Indeed, I am rather surprised that Lord Eustace forgot that tenet. He knows very well that he should have applied to me first before he addressed himself to you."

"I believe that Lord Eustace was so overset he did not know what he was saying," said Sarah.

"No doubt," said Lady Alverley, accepting it. "Regardless, a gentleman who harbors resentment and feels that he has been trapped, even if it is by his own words, is very resistant to making agreeable bridal settlements. I trust that Lord Eustace will be in a more amenable frame of mind when he repeats his offer for your hand, Sarah."

"I hope so, ma'am," said Sarah quietly. Her grandmother had merely confirmed her own instincts. She hoped that Lady Alverley was as knowledgeable in her assumption that Lord Eustace would indeed repeat his offer.

Lady Alverley looked at her granddaughter with the faintest lift of her brows. "It occurs to me that you once stated you would wed only where you felt affection. Have you changed fronts, my dear, or do you nourish feelings for Lord Eustace?"

Sarah felt her face grow warm. "I have not changed my views, Grandmama."

"How sensible of you to feel a regard for an eligible *parti*, Sarah," said Lady Alverley. "I could wish that Margaret had as much wit! But I will say no more on that head. I have washed my hands of that affair."

"But will you not try to send after Margaret?" asked Sarah, startled.

Lady Alverley leaned back against the cushions. There was again a cold look in her eyes and a thin smile played about her mouth. "My dear, you forget that I have been this road before. Like her mother before her, Margaret has made her bed. Perhaps she will be as happy as you say that your mother was. I do not know. Nor do I care overmuch. It will suit me not to see Margaret again, for I do not intend to embroil myself in her affairs any longer. Instead, I shall turn all of my resources to bringing about a favorable outcome to your own worthy endeavor."

"Grandmama, I think that you should know. Lord Eustace said that he was going after Margaret. You may have to deal with the situation whether you wish it or not," said Sarah. She was angered. Her grandmother's callousness dismayed and disgusted her. Apparently there was little depth of love or loyalty to be found in her ladyship. It occurred to Sarah that it would be wise to remember that for her own sake.

"Pray, what do you mean?" asked Lady Alverley sharply. "I'll not have that young woman back here after this! What could you be thinking of, Sarah, to send Lord Eustace off after her? Of all people, too! It is absurd! He has no obligation to our family."

"I could hardly stop him, my lady. He, at least, feels some responsibility toward my sister!" exclaimed Sarah. "He thinks enough of her to wish that nothing evil befalls her!"

"Be careful, miss! I'll not tolerate impertinence, even from you!"

"I am sorry, ma'am, if I displease you. However, I shall speak my feelings plainly," said Sarah hastily. "Margaret is my sister. She has made a grave error in judgment and it is your responsibility as her guardian to make a push to save her from the consequences of her actions!"

"I have already told you! I wash my hands of her! She has made her choice, as her mother did before her. I'll have nothing more to do with it!" said Lady Alverley.

"What will you write to my father, ma'am? That you made not the least push to bring Margaret back? That you deliberately allowed scandal to break over her head?" demanded Sarah. "I know nothing of your objectives, ma'am, but I do know it will not suit me to have my sister's name bandied about by every malicious tongue!"

For a long moment, Lady Alverley regarded Sarah with narrowed eyes. Abruptly, she nodded. "Very well! I shall do what I can. You are quite right. We must see to it that any scandal is hushed up, for it will not reflect well on your own reputation. If Lord Eustace cannot be brought up to scratch, we do not want to scuttle any other chances you might have at a decent offer."

"That was not my motive, ma'am," said Sarah shortly.

"I know it was not. You are a good, sensible girl, Sarah. I have always said so," said Lady Alverley. She patted her granddaughter's arm. "Now go call Marie to me. I must make plans and I need her."

Sarah rose obediently. On impulse, she bent down and kissed Lady Alverley's wrinkled cheek.

Lady Alverley did not look up. "Thank you, my dear."

Sarah crossed the floor. Just before she left the dressing room, she looked back. Lady Alverley had walked over to her vanity glass. But she did not seem to be looking at her reflection. There was a queer blindness in her ladyship's eyes. Slow tears trickled down Lady Alverley's cheeks. Quite distinctly, Sarah overheard her ladyship murmur to herself. "Drat the girl. Drat her."

Without a word, Sarah exited.

Chapter Twenty-two

Several hours later Lord Eustace returned to inform Sarah and Lady Alverley that he had been unsuccessful in locating any clue to the whereabouts of the runaways. "If they fled to Gretna Greene, they were amazingly adept at escaping attention on the North Road," he said, frowning.

Lady Alverley stiffly thanked him for his efforts. "I appreciate the trouble that you have taken on our behalf, my lord, especially when we have no claim on you."

Lord Eustace bowed. "Pray disregard it, my lady. I was glad to be of service. It is my regret that I have not been able to bring you better tidings."

Lady Alverley held her hand out to him. "You have done your best, my lord. Now it is time for me to do my best. I know that you will understand."

"I do, perfectly. And you may rest assured that I will not speak about this matter to anyone," said Lord Eustace.

He was turning to take his leave of Sarah when the door to the drawing room opened. The butler showed in Mrs. Jeffries, who came in with a rush. The lady was pale and she clutched a smelling salt in her hand. "My lady! You must believe me! I came at once when I discovered—" She saw suddenly that Lady Alverley was not alone and swift color rose into her face.

Lord Eustace exchanged glances with Sarah. He addressed Lady Alverley. "I shall take my leave now, my lady."

"Yes, no doubt that will be best." Lady Alverley nodded. She waited until Lord Eustace had exited and the door had been closed behind him before she turned her gaze on Mrs. Jeffries. Her voice was cold. "Well, Elizabeth?"

Sarah rose hastily and went over to Mrs. Jeffries. She put a friendly arm around the distraught lady's waist and urged her toward a wingback. "Come sit down, Elizabeth. I can see that you are operating under grave distress."

Mrs. Jeffries threw a grateful look up at Sarah as she sank into the chair. "Thank you, Sarah!" She turned again to meet Lady Alverley's hard stare and her smile fled. "My lady, I came to you at once when I discovered a note from my brother-in-law. You may guess at its contents."

"Indeed?" Lady Alverley's demeanor was not at all encouraging.

Mrs. Jeffries's countenance whitened even more. In a suffocated voice, she cried, "Lady Alverley! I did not know! I swear I did not know!" She dissolved into tears and searched wildly for her handkerchief. "I didn't know that Henry and Margaret— Oh, it is too terrible!"

"Had you no clue that your brother-in-law was making himself indispensible to my granddaughter?"

"None, my lady! None!" gasped Mrs. Jeffries. She looked up suddenly. "Oh, my lady, pray do not lay this at my door! I could not bear it if you did so!"

Sarah was moved to compassion. "Elizabeth! Of course it was not your fault, which my grandmother very well knows. Isn't that right, ma'am?"

Mrs. Jeffries was unheeding as her gaze remained riveted upon Lady Alverley's stiff countenance. "My lady, I beg of you. Do not blame me. Do not bring grief down upon my head. You know of my circumstances. If you were to say anything—! In short, my position would be blasted beyond recovery. Lady Alverley, pray say that you do not blame me!"

It dawned on Sarah that Mrs. Jeffries's distress was not for the runaways, but was being exercised for herself. Sarah realized that Mrs. Jeffries feared losing Lady Alverley's favorable patronage. She was sparing little or no thought for the plight of her brother and Margaret Sommers and the scandal they must face.

Sarah was disappointed and disillusioned in one whom she had thought to be a close friend to both herself and to her sister. She had considered Mrs. Jeffries to be one of her best friends in London, but the lady's fear of social ostracism had revealed a shallowness of character that Sarah found to be sorrowing. "Oh, Elizabeth. I thought you actually cared for Margaret," she murmured.

Mrs. Jeffries's green eyes flashed. "I do! She was like a younger sister to me. And as for Henry, why, we were always close. I don't know how I shall bear the humiliation and betrayal. But such it was! He never breathed a word to me. Not one suspicion crossed my mind, I assure you! Dear Lady Alverley, you must believe me. I had nothing to do with this horrible elopement."

Lady Alverley nodded. "Of course, I must believe you if that is what you tell me, Elizabeth."

"Oh, I am telling you the truth!" cried Mrs. Jeffries passionately.

"I am glad of it. Or otherwise I would have to be very angry with you. Very angry, indeed!" said Lady Alverley harshly. "I hope that I may count on you now, Elizabeth."

Mrs. Jeffries shuddered. "I shall do anything, my lady."

"Good. Then this is what I wish you to do," said Lady Alverley. "You must tell everyone that your brother-in-law received a sudden termination of his leave. He was required to return to duty at once. He did not even delay to fulfill the remainder of his obligations because of the urgency of his orders. You may be as overset as you please, but do not say another word about your brother's movements than what I have told you to say. Do you understand, Elizabeth?"

Mrs. Jeffries stared at her, wide-eyed and bewildered. "Yes, my lady. I understand. At least—but I shall do it, of course."

"Be sure that you do. I shall hear otherwise if you fail me. And you will not like the consequences of that, I am quite certain," said Lady Alverley warningly. "Now you may take your leave. I am an old woman and this situation has profoundly overtaxed me."

Mrs. Jeffries rose at once, profusely apologizing for impinging upon her ladyship. Seconds later, she had exited. Her manner at leave-taking was almost that of a prisoner who had received a stay of execution.

Sarah looked at her grandmother, a faint frown pulling together her brows. "What are you trying to accomplish, Grandmama? You have practically bullied Mrs. Jeffries into compliance with your wishes."

"I wanted to stop that woman's mouth, Sarah. Elizabeth Jeffries has panicked. She would have taken her lamentations and protestations to every ear that she could have gotten to listen," said Lady Alverley. She gave a sudden, bitter laugh. "And those ears would have been plentiful, I assure you! This is just the sort of *on dit* that this town thrives on. There will still be questions, but now, hopefully, there will also be a reasonable explanation for Captain Jeffries's sudden removal from town that might be halfway believed."

"But what of Margaret, ma'am?" asked Sarah quietly.

"I have consulted with Marie. We have decided that our best course is to put it about that Margaret has been coming on for a bad bout of the measles. More than one acquaintance has made comment to me that Margaret has not been herself lately. It will be believed that she has been hard hit by the disease. There have been a few scattered cases, and fortunately Marie recalled that Margaret had actually spent the afternoon recently with Lady Frobisher and her children, who are now known to be suffering from the disease. Naturally, it has been my judgment to remove Margaret from the putridness of the town air. She will have been taken down to your father for nursing and proper recovery," said Lady Alverley.

"But what of me? How can I be expected to continue to go about in society if I have supposedly been exposed to measles?" objected Sarah.

Lady Alverley smiled triumphantly. "My dear Sarah, you had the measles when you were quite small! I recall it distinctly. I was preparing to make one of my rare visits to your parents, when your mother wrote to me, warning me that you had come all over with spots."

Sarah thought about it very carefully. She could see how the story, flimsy as it was, might possibly work. Then she shook her head. "This is all very well, Grandmama. But it is only a delaying tactic, when all is said and done. It will still come out that Margaret eloped with Captain Jeffries."

"We must hope that it does not do so, however, until the Season is over and you are established. Then let the gossips talk to their hearts' content. The summer is long enough to wear out even the most titillating of tales," said Lady Alverley dismissively.

"What of the servants, ma'am? Have you given thought to them?" asked Sarah. "Holby went with Margaret, I am sure of it. There must already be rumors flying around, for you were quite overset when I came up to visit you in your dressing room, while Herbert knows full well that my sister's note to me contained bad news."

Lady Alverley frowned. "Yes, Marie pointed out the same difficulties. But I do not think that they are insurmountable. My dresser will attest to anyone who has the impertinence to inquire that I was vastly put out over a gown which I ordered and which was found to be atrociously cut. I shall have to send a stiff note to my modiste to give greater credence to the story, of course, but I drop such sums in the woman's shop that she will swallow whatever outrageous blame I may accuse her of."

"That is perfectly horrid," said Sarah.

"Perhaps, but it is also convenient. As for Herbert, I shall speak to him myself." Lady Alverley smiled. The cold expression had returned to her eyes. "Believe me, if he wishes to remain as my butler, he will do his utmost to put a stop to any speculation that the servants under his sway may have the audacity to utter."

Sarah left her grandmother soon after to get ready for the first public appearance that she was to make without her sister. It was a picnic to which both she and Margaret had been invited, and it was a harrowing hour and a half for Sarah as she began putting into place the story that Lady Alverley had concocted. Fortunately, Miss Hanson accompanied her and bolstered her report with little details of her own. By the time that the picnic was over, Sarah had accepted several sincere wishes for her sister's speedy recovery. She was profoundly relieved to be able to take her leave at last and return to the town house.

In the carriage, Miss Hanson commended Sarah for her performance. "I was very pleased with your display of *sangfroid*, Sarah. I shall inform Lady Alverley of the consummate way that you handled even the most difficult of questions."

Sarah accepted the compliment with mixed emotions. She was not used to uttering falsehoods and it had gone hard against the grain for her to do it. "I wish that we were not forced to this subterfuge," she said.

"Quite! But we have no other choice. Remember that, Sarah," said Miss Hanson firmly.

Upon their return, the ladies found out that the plot had thickened.

A second housemaid was found who was of a similar height to Margaret. She was dressed in Margaret's clothes, a bonnet and a veil drawn closely about her face, and another maid was attired in traveling clothes. The two were handed up into one of Lady Alverley's traveling chaises and bid farewell by Lady Alverley herself. The two maid servants were to be let off at a remote inn, where they could catch a mailcoach and go on an extended holiday to their respective relatives.

Lady Alverley told Sarah with satisfaction that as far as anyone was concerned, it had been Margaret who had been sent off in the chaise.

"This is all very well, ma'am, but what of Margaret? I am concerned for her," said Sarah.

"I have no doubt that your sister is faring well or we would have heard otherwise," said Lady Alverley. "This little performance was just to still any rattles who might be inclined to believe that it was no coincidence that Captain Jeffries and Margaret should disappear from town at the same time. In fact, I made certain to wave to two personages passing by so that they stopped to talk with me as the carriage carrying our false Margaret was bowling out of town."

"You amaze me, ma'am," said Sarah, shaking her head. "I never thought of taking the subterfuge to such elaborate lengths."

"People believe what they want to believe, facts to the contrary. Margaret was well liked, and we now have witnesses who will sincerely declare that they themselves saw her leaving town. There are malicious tongues, of course, but the majority will accept that Margaret was in that carriage and that everything has happened just as we have said," said Lady Alverley.

The next few days were uncomfortable for Sarah. She fielded several questions over her sister's welfare, laughingly disclaimed her own risk of infection since she had had measles as a child, and altogether upheld Lady Alverley's fiction.

"But surely your sister had the measles at the same time, Miss Sommers? That is usually how it happens. One child

contracts the disease and then the whole nursery has them!"
said one lady.

"I had the measles before my sister's birth, my lady," said
Sarah with a smile. "Margaret had always considered herself
to be fortunate that she had missed taking the childish complaint, at least until now!"

The lady laughed. "Yes, I can well imagine! Well, it is to be
hoped that she is not left with horrid scars on her face. Margaret was such a lovely girl!"

Sarah wrote to her father, breaking the news of Margaret's
elopement as gently as possible. She did not really expect to
receive a reply and so when a letter came for her from her father's hand, she was greatly astonished. She broke it open and
spread out the single sheet. After she read it, she went immediately to her grandmother's dressing room where Lady Alverley was getting ready for the evening. "Grandmama, I should
like a private word with you."

Lady Alverley took one look at her face and dismissed her
dresser. When the woman had exited, she turned to her granddaughter. "What is it, Sarah?" she demanded. "You look rather
pale."

"Perhaps you should read it for yourself. It is a letter from
my father," said Sarah, giving the sheet over to her ladyship.

Lady Alverley quickly made herself mistress of the letter's
contents. She folded it thoughtfully and returned it to Sarah.
"Make certain that you put that in a safe place. I would not
wish its contents to become common knowledge among the
household."

"No, indeed," agreed Sarah. "I shall lock it in my jewel box.
It appears that Margaret was not completely lost to all convention after all."

Lady Alverley managed to smile. "That is the only beam of
light that I have had in this whole business. At least she did
not run off to Gretna."

"No, she went home," said Sarah quietly.

"It occurs to me that Margaret is a very strong-willed young
woman," remarked Lady Alverley.

Sarah laughed. "Yes, she is! Captain Jeffries had not appeared to me to be easily persuadable to anything, and yet
Margaret managed to persuade him to go down to meet Papa."

"Your father's reservations over the marriage are plainly stated. I would have thought that he would have refused his consent when Margaret appeared on the doorstep with Captain Jeffries in train," said Lady Alverley, her lips tightening a little.

"And what would have been the result, ma'am? A flight to Gretna, after all?" asked Sarah. She shook her head. "I know Margaret well enough to realize that she would not have been balked at that point."

"Nor would have Captain Jeffries," said Lady Alverley thoughtfully. "He is said to be a brave man, having already distinguished himself on the field of battle. In all honor, he would not have relinquished Margaret and left her to utter ruin. I imagine that he stated the matter rather forcibly to your father."

"Poor Papa! Dragged away from his books by high drama to attend a hastily contrived candlelit marriage ceremony," said Sarah, laughing again.

"Did he not say that after they were wed, Captain Jeffries and Margaret had formed the intention of leaving England for the Peninsula?" asked Lady Alverley.

"Yes, I believe so. Captain Jeffries was shortly due to return to duty in any event."

"That is very good," approved Lady Alverley. "In a few weeks' time, we shall be able to announce their marriage in all good conscience and that will be the end of it."

"I shall be glad of it, ma'am. These half-truths and lies come unhandily to my tongue," said Sarah honestly.

"A little while longer, Sarah, for Margaret's sake as well as your own."

Chapter Twenty-three

Throughout the trying period, Lord Eustace proved himself to be a strong co-conspirator. He called frequently at Alverley House to offer himself as an escort for Lady Alverley and her granddaughter whenever one was required. His attentions toward Sarah began to be remarked upon by a few mutual acquaintances. It was agreed that Miss Margaret's removal from town had given the elder Miss Sommers the opportunity to shine in his lordship's estimation.

Lord Eustace referred to the elopement only once, as he was driving Sarah back home from the park, and then only to compliment Sarah on Lady Alverley's masterly handling of a difficult situation. "There has not been a whisper of scandal. Your sister should thank God on her knees that she has Lady Alverley in her corner," he commented.

"She is Mrs. Jeffries now," corrected Sarah.

"Indeed!" Lord Eustace glanced quickly at her. "Have you had word from her, then?"

"I have had a letter from my father. My sister and Captain Jeffries threw themselves upon his mercy. They were married from our home under the auspices of a minister, a special license, and with my father's permission," said Sarah.

"A respectable ending for all concerned," said Lord Eustace. "Does the happy couple return to town?"

Sarah shook her head. "Captain Jeffries was due shortly to return to duty. My sister accompanied him to his post."

"I am certain that must come as a relief to Lady Alverley, and to you, of course. It is now all neatly buttoned up," said Lord Eustace.

"Yes," agreed Sarah.

Lord Eustace was silent for a moment. His hands expertly

guided his horses through the busy street toward Alverley House. "My mother mentioned that Lady Alverley called on her a day or two ago. Lady Alverley let drop the interesting information that you have had at least two respectable offers this Season, which you have rejected."

Sarah flushed. She wondered what her grandmother's motive could have been for revealing that personal fact to Lord Eustace's parent. It also amazed her that his lordship had repeated it to her. That was certainly a breach of convention. "That is quite true, my lord."

"May I know why you turned away those gentlemen?" asked Lord Eustace quietly.

Sarah turned right around to stare at him, amazed at his boldness. A touch of anger entered her eyes. "Is this to be a sharing between friends, my lord?"

Lord Eustace opened his mouth, as though he meant to say something. Then he appeared to change his mind, and he said nothing.

Sarah was disappointed that he had not taken up her challenging statement. She shook her head. "I am sorry, my lord! In this instance, I prefer to preserve my privacy!"

"I quite understand," said Lord Eustace unemotionally. He guided his team to the curb and snubbed the reins.

"Do you, indeed!" Sarah stared at him. "I wonder whether you do, my lord!" She swiftly turned on the seat and, catching up her skirts, jumped down to the pavement.

Without glancing back, Sarah started quickly up the steps of the town house. She was startled when Lord Eustace caught her elbow and firmly escorted her inside. She would have turned in the entry hall to say good-bye, but he did not give her the opportunity.

Lord Eustace nodded a greeting to the butler. "Miss Sommers and I shall be in the drawing room, Herbert. Pray see that we are not disturbed."

"What are you doing?" exclaimed Sarah furiously.

Lord Eustace did not reply, but only directed her unwilling steps into the drawing room. Releasing her, he turned the key in the plate, locking the door. "There! Now we will be assured of privacy."

While Sarah was still staring at him in speechless consternation, Lord Eustace pulled her into his arms. "No!" she exclaimed, pushing at him.

"Yes!" Lord Eustace kissed her lingeringly. Sarah's resistance abruptly melted. His palms came up to cup her face. When he drew back, he said, "I've wanted to do that properly for a long time."

"Why didn't you?" whispered Sarah.

Lord Eustace sighed and dropped his hands to her shoulders. "I held back because I did not know what you would think. I had made it so plain that I was infatuated with your sister. On top of it all, I behaved like a fool the first time that I kissed you. I was afraid that you would reject me, turn away from me in disgust."

Sarah shook her head. "I would never have turned away."

His hands tightened on her shoulders almost painfully. "Sarah! How can you forgive me? I thought that I was in love with your sister. When I lost her, I offered for you out of pique and wounded pride. How can you forgive such an insult?"

"Insult? Yes, I was insulted. But the hurt was worse. It was so difficult for me." Sarah looked up into his eyes and a smile trembled on her lips. "I already loved you, you see. I had done so almost from the first. When I realized that it was Margaret that you had eyes for, I thought that I could not bear it. But I had to, for she is my sister and I wanted only her happiness. I thought—I thought that your friendship was all that I could ever hope for. And a half loaf is better than none, is it not?"

"I was a rank fool!" exclaimed Lord Eustace, turning away from her and running his fingers through his hair. "I thought that I had fallen in love with Margaret, but it was only an illusion born out of the strange miasma of my soul."

Sarah clasped her hands together. "It was Miss Leander, wasn't it?"

Lord Eustace turned quickly. "Why did you ask me about her that evening? How did you know?"

"It wasn't really difficult. I began to suspect—there were certain things that you said. It wasn't really Margaret you were in love with, but Vivian Leander," said Sarah. She drew in a steadying breath. "And it is Miss Leander whom you are still in love with."

"No!" The word was ejected forcefully.

Sarah started at his vehemence and stood staring at him with questioning eyes.

Lord Eustace faced her, his whole frame tense. "Pray listen to me, Sarah. I am not in love with Vivian Leander. I know now that I never was. I was infatuated with her, yes, enough to have contracted her hand."

He gave a bark of appalled laughter. "My God! When I recall what I went through when I realized the mistake that I had made! She was beautiful, spoiled, completely self-absorbed. She cared nothing for me. Once we were formally engaged, she told me that she wanted nothing from me but my name and my fortune. She suggested that after we wed I should acquire a mistress, for she had no intention of sharing my bed. She hinted that she might produce an heir, but it would not be my child. I repulsed her, you see. She wanted someone else, someone ineligible, but she had to settle for position and fortune."

Lord Eustace had spoken swiftly, a hard edge to his voice, But Sarah could see the shadows of hurt in his eyes and expression. She put out a hand to him. "My lord!"

He threw up his hand. "Wait! There is more. I must tell you of the rot in my own soul, so that you will understand. I was trapped by convention. I could no more draw back from the betrothal than I could have flown across the Channel. The nuptial agreements were signed and the bride-price delivered. The announcement had been published. The invitations to the wedding had been sent out. Then Vivian was killed in the carriage accident. And I was glad! Sarah, I was glad! For just that short moment when I was told, all I felt was an immense wave of relief. The nightmare was over. So I thought!"

"What—what do you mean?" Sarah faltered. She was almost frightened by the intense passion in his voice. She was torn by pity and appallment. His confessions were almost beyond her comprehension. The young woman had certainly been a monster of cruelty. But the look in his lordship's eyes promised further revelations and she did not know that she wished to hear more.

Lord Eustace ran his fingers through his hair again. He sighed. Dropping his hand to the back of the chair, he grasped it tightly. "Sarah, when Vivian Leander was killed, I was at once freed from what had become an intolerable situation. But the shackles that I have worn since then have been almost as heavy. All of society assumed that I must be enduring a passion of grief. There were pitying glances and stilted condolences and wordless thumps on the shoulder. I was told how stoic I was, how strong, even heroic! I became an object of pity and compassion. No one mentioned Vivian's name to me. No one asked my thoughts. It occurred to no one to wonder what I wanted to do with my life, now that it had been given back to me. I became burdened by guilt and shame. Sarah, I came to hate myself. What kind of monster was I that I had rejoiced in that young woman's death? The woman that I—I had chosen to share my life with. It was unpardonable! It was depraved."

"Oh, no, no!" exclaimed Sarah, distressed for him.

Lord Eustace gave a short bark of laughter. "Oh, yes, my dear Sarah. Those were the reflections that haunted me. I thought that if I had managed things differently—if I had insisted upon a conventional marriage—" He broke off, shrugging. "If I had simply used an iron fist with her, she might be alive today."

"But that is not the kind of relationship that you wanted," said Sarah gently.

"No, I did not. I did not want a marriage where I would be forced to browbeat my wife into submission," said Lord Eustace. "With Vivian, it would have been a constant battle of wills. And yet, I wished that I had had the opportunity to do things differently."

"And when you met Margaret?" said Sarah.

Lord Eustace smiled painfully. "When I saw Margaret, I saw fleeting shadows of Vivian Leander. Margaret's vivaciousness, her charm, a certain turn of phrase—all were poignant reminders."

"But Margaret is nothing like Vivian Leander in character. She is sweet and kind and compassionate," said Sarah, confused.

"That is the crux of this madness, Sarah. Your sister bears no resemblance to Vivian at all. But she is the picture of what I had desperately wanted Vivian to be. Can you understand that?" said Lord Eustace.

"Yes, I think that I can," said Sarah slowly. "And so you found yourself drawn to Margaret. It was as though you had been granted a second chance with Vivian Leander."

"All an incredible fantasy! The strangest part was that I knew that it was unreal, but it didn't seem to matter," said Lord Eustace. "It was as though I was standing outside myself, observing my actions, listening to my words. I was literally acting out a courtship which had never occurred. I was unraveling some of the deepest longings of my imagination. My blighted hopes—the guilt and self-hatred that I had endured— all were being purged through my relationship with Margaret. In short, Sarah, I used your sister in an infamous manner. More than once I tried to draw back, for even in the midst of it I knew that what I was doing was completely unethical. I struggled to maintain some sense of balance. I made an effort not to make Margaret the sole object of my attentions. It would have been disastrous if I had excited expectations that I actually had no intention of fulfilling. But more than that, I could have wounded Margaret immeasurably. Dear God! If she had fallen in love with me—!"

"But she did not." Sarah pointed out the irrefutable fact. She looked up at him with just a touch of a smile on her face.

For the first time in several minutes, Lord Eustace's expression lightened and he laughed. "No, she did not, thank God! Once I had gotten over my initial outrage that she had preferred young Jeffries to me, I realized how fortunately things had turned out. But then I had a new problem. I had offered for you in the confusion that was left in the wake of my coming out of my fantasy. And I thought that I had made another mistake."

"Yes, I realized at once that you were already regretting your impulsive offer," agreed Sarah. "That is one reason why I did not accept you that day."

"Was there another reason?" asked Lord Eustace with a penetrating glance.

Sarah's color rose. She gave a small nod. "I did not want a marriage of convenience, you see. I thought that you were still halfway in love with my sister, or thought that you felt you were. At the very least, I supposed that you were still entangled by memories of Vivian Leander. I didn't want to wed a gentleman whose heart had already been claimed. And so I turned you down."

"How very close you were to the truth, dear Sarah," he said, going over to her again. He took her hands and held them, compelling her by his very proximity to look up into his face. "I was in a state of confusion. My emotions were in chaos. I did not know then what I wanted. Or who I wanted! But that is all changed."

"Is it?" asked Sarah quietly. Her heart bumped in her breast. There was a smiling, tender expression in his eyes and his mouth was curled in an attractive grin.

"Yes, it is. I have finally exorcised the demons that have beset me for these last two years. My painful memories of Vivian Leander have been laid permanently to rest. Your sister, though I hold her in great affection, has no power over my heart." Lord Eustace raised her hands and placed them firmly against his chest. Very quietly, he said, "You are the one who has that power, Sarah."

High color flamed in her face. She could feel the strong beat of his heart under her fingers and her hands trembled in his clasp. Tears stung her eyes, half blinding her. "Oh, Gilbert. How I have longed to hear you say just those words. Or something to that effect, in any event!"

Lord Eustace laughed. "My darling, are you still so willing to settle for half a loaf? I will not hear of it. Listen to me. Sarah, I love you. I love only you and only you forever. There is no one else whom I could possibly desire more to make my wife. Will you marry me?"

For answer, Sarah gave a happy gurgle of laughter and threw herself into his arms. "Oh, yes! Yes, I will, Gilbert! With my whole heart and being, I will wed you."

Lord Eustace caught her close and kissed her. At last, they were both where they had wanted to be all along.